Praise for the works of V

The Lines of Happiness

The Lines of Happiness is a beautiful but poignant tale that speaks of loss, bravery in the arduous seasons of healing and a lasting encounter with love when it's least unexpected.

-Nutmeg, *NetGalley*

Lush and poignant are the two words which come immediately to mind to describe this debut novel. The writing itself is lush, luxurious, and brimming with wonderful, exquisite language, images, rural landscapes and rural life, horses and emotional depth. A real little gem of a book lovingly edited and polished. The story is poignant with loss, trauma, grief and coming to terms with it...The author doesn't succumb to the quick and easy "solutions" and stays away from the temptation of "love heals all."

-Henrietta, *NetGalley*

The characters make this tale something special. Both the main and secondary characters are well-developed. I became quite invested in Lo and Gloria especially. They made the novel a must read for me. If you are into deeply serious, thought-provoking love stories, then pick up this book. You won't be disappointed.

-Betty H., *NetGalley*

I sank down into *The Lines of Happiness* and allowed myself to wallow in the fullness of the language. The story of grief, loss and discovering love in an unlikely place is exquisitely written. It reminds me of the elegance of Jane Rule's writing in her novel *Desert of the Heart*. Di Pierro must be blessed with a third eye as her novel speaks of life, grief and love in meaningful poignancy and perception.

Underneath it all, *The Lines of Happiness* is a haunting love story slowly evolving from the devastation bequeathed one family. It is not a typical romance novel encompassing endless activities and interactions between the main characters. *The Lines of Happiness* is a deep dive into our motivations and self-awareness as we fall in love. Something I am sure most of us have forgotten over time. This is an essential reminder.

-Della B., *NetGalley*

Venetia Di Pierro wrote a beautiful story about loss, grief and finding love and hope when you're close to giving up.

-Anna S., *NetGalley*

HAPPINESS
IS A
SHADE
OF
BLUE

Other Bella Books by Venetia Di Pierro

The Lines of Happiness

About the Author

Venetia Di Pierro is the author of *The Lines of Happiness* and *Happiness is a Shade of Blue*. You can find her on Facebook at Venetia Di Pierro Author or on Instagram at VenetiaDiPierro_ Author.

HAPPINESS
IS A
SHADE
OF
BLUE

VENETIA DI PIERRO

BELLA
BOOKS
2023

Bella Books, Inc.
P.O. Box 10543
Tallahassee, FL 32302

First Edition - 2023

Editor: Heather Flournoy
Cover Designer: Kayla Mancuso
Photo credit: Nick Walters

ISBN: 978-1-64247-388-9

PUBLISHER'S NOTE

Acknowledgments

Thank you to the team at Bella Books who help bring wonderful stories to life and give a voice to so many. Grateful to be among a group of hardworking professionals and creatives.

A huge thank you to Heather Flournoy, not only for her editorial skills and light touch, but for being an ever uplifting person.

And Richard Conron. You give me the kind of quiet hype in life that the Quality team gives an audit on the Fruit Bowl. Thank you.

Dedication

For Sue

CHAPTER ONE

Gloria coaxed along the baggage cart with its turned-in front wheel, trying to keep its halting, jerking metal form away from the slow-moving crowd around her. Travelers in their crumpled clothes, carting suitcases and bags of duty free, emerging from customs looking for fresh air and familiar faces, and she was one of them. She ran her tongue across her teeth, hastily brushed in the aircraft bathroom before landing, but still feeling less than best. She had been much too excited to sleep for more than half-hour stints on the flight from Melbourne and with each stopover, another block of excitement had been added to the tower building inside her, until she felt full of hollow blocks that might topple at any minute. The Jackson Hole airport was small compared to the international airports she had claimed residency at for stretches of hours, but it still carried the buzz of emotions. Now that the moment was nearing, her mouth felt dry and her eyes stung, as though all the moisture was being sucked out through her pupils. She blinked and raised an arm to wipe her eyes with the sleeve of her denim jacket. That face;

she was searching for it, that copper hair and those hazel eyes. There were people but they weren't her people, not her person.

"Oh, sorry." She swung the cart away from the foot it had met and looked up. It was the smile she saw first, and her eyes welled and she swallowed against her dry throat.

Lo didn't move, but watched her approach with an indulgent focus, held in the pleasure of the moment. Gloria sniffed and abandoned the cart a step too soon and she was in Lo's arms, her ear being squashed by the side of Lo's jaw, but the smell of Lo's woolen coat was in her nose and the feel of Lo's cold hands under her jacket, and Gloria knew this was close to heaven. A moment, any moment, in Lo's company after months apart, feeling her in her arms, just like she'd rehearsed so many times in the theater of her mind. Letting go seemed like something that was near impossible, and they stood, not letting go, while the quick crush of people dispersed and the arrival/departure board flicked out a new schedule overhead.

"Let me look at you," Lo said, pulling back, her hands gripping Gloria's upper arms. Her eyebrows drew together like she might cry. "You're so tan, and what happened to your chin?"

Gloria reached to touch the cut on her chin. "I ate the dirt in front of a fence, of course."

"Chester?" Lo asked.

"Yup." They both laughed because Gloria had kept Lo as up to date as she could about her life as she packed it up in Melbourne, especially the antics of the stubborn gelding Chester, who, when he was in a mood, was either brilliant over fences or refused to partake at all. "And you..." Gloria shook her head, then was unable to form words for the swell of emotion she was feeling, and said instead, "Let's go."

"Your bags, silly."

Gloria laughed again and turned to drag the cart back around in a stuttering arc. It occurred to her how much laughing they did when they spoke, and after a spell among a humorless crowd, she realized how blessed they were.

Lola, Lola, Lola, her heart beat its steady drum in time to the cart's squeaking wheel.

Everything felt new and magical: the icy black air hitting her face as they left the stark lights of the airport interior, the smell of snow overwritten with the chemical tones of jet fuel. The white pickup truck was like a metal farm dog, waiting joyfully for her. She felt like hugging it because it represented everything happy. Unlocked, it seemed to wag its bumper bar as she climbed in.

"Let me turn the heat right up. It'll probably warm up by the time we get home!" Lo said as the truck growled to life.

"Home," Gloria said, trying the taste of the word in her mouth. "Home." It had a new flavor; thrilling and nerve-racking.

"Tell me everything!" Lo said, the lights of passing cars flashing across her face.

And as the temperature in the car thawed and became less affronting, the words flowed from Gloria, and she loved to say them, watching the changing expressions on Lo's face—the closing in, the softening, the quick flick of surprise, the expansive roar of laughter. It was what she'd been waiting for, and she glowed with it, the heat generated from the energy between them.

Oh, I love you, she thought, but she didn't say it, instead keeping it as a warm coal, burning a hole in her pocket.

Despite Lo's warnings, arriving via air mail in envelopes bordered with blue and red stripes, the ground was slushier than Gloria expected and the cold more bitter than she was prepared for. Those letters, scribbled in Lo's slanting scrawl—a blue ink embodiment of Lo's essence—had kept Gloria afloat as she bobbed along on a sea of uncertainty, winding up her life, properly this time, to walk across the bridge of their relationship into the unknown. And now, here, in the unfamiliar landscape of late-November Wyoming, where angels lived and breathed and Hamlet was waiting for her in his layers of quilted rugs, a veteran to the cold more than Gloria, she was home. The windows of the old house glowed yellow against the midnight gloom and the pine trees bowed beneath the stars under the weight of the recent snow. Gloria's breath spilled from her mouth in great plumes as she met the night with her warm body.

Lo hurried ahead, her form tipped sideways with the baggage, but Gloria walked slowly, taking in the fresh palette of sights and scents, the smoke from the chimney curling up to meet the sky. Lo's silhouette, backlit against the doorway, shrugging out of her jacket, disappearing for a moment, but Gloria's memory followed her movements, picturing Lo throwing her keys into the bowl on the sideboard. She appeared again to hold the door open wider for Gloria and Gloria abandoned her panoramic postcard and loped up the path to meet her.

Gloria stopped again in the kitchen doorway to look around. Everything was the same except on the kitchen table there was a bunch of pink roses wrapped in white tissue paper and cellophane, and on the counter was a large, frosted cake. Lo was already setting the kettle to boil.

"Are you coming in, or are you just going to stand there and admire the cobwebs?"

Gloria smiled. "I'm looking for them, but I think Sue-Anne's duster has created an unnatural disaster across the local spider community."

"Those flowers are yours, so is the cake."

Gloria went to pick up the flowers. "Who are these from?"

"Your number one fan."

"Who could that be?" Gloria ran a finger over one of the pale pink petals and held the roses close to breathe in their fragrance. "They're beautiful, I love them."

"I'll pass that on to your fan."

Gloria wandered over to the counter to peer at the cake. "Did they make this too? I'd have a kiss for them if they were here. Maybe next time."

"That was Sue-Anne's effort. You can save your kisses for her. Well, maybe I'll take one on her behalf."

"Just one?"

Lo's eyes were teasing. "How many can I have?"

"I thought it was for Sue-Anne."

Lo smiled, but she was looking at Gloria's lips and it felt like time had slowed and then they were kissing and Gloria dropped the roses on the counter and her hands were in Lo's hair and close wasn't close enough and kissing only made her want to kiss deeper until their faces were pressed together and she realized she'd grabbed a fistful of Lo's hair. She let it go and they pulled apart. "Best not pass that one on to Sue-Anne. I don't think she'd sign for it."

"She doesn't know what she's missing."

Gloria looked down at the roses dumped beside the chocolate cake and felt suddenly shy. It was just the two of them now, alone. Sue-Anne, the housekeeper, was at her own place; the guest houses were empty; Kip, the farmhand, was probably raising the roof of his cottage with his snoring. This was new territory, and they didn't have a map yet. She glanced down at her hands with their short nails and callouses from holding a pair of reins all day, and Lo turned to take two mugs from the cupboard. The kettle started to whistle, and with Lo otherwise occupied, Gloria looked back up.

"Is there a vase?"

"Sure, too many of them. After Terrence passed my mother had to keep going and buying vases for all the flowers people were sending. Unless Sue-Anne has taken all of them to Goodwill or something." Lo poured hot water into the two mismatched mugs. "Come to think of it, those are the first roses that have been in this house in a long time. Sorry, I shouldn't have said that." Lo replaced the kettle and looked ruefully at Gloria.

Gloria left the roses where they were and went to take Lo into her arms. "Don't be sorry."

"Take it as a measure of my affection that I didn't give it a thought. Until now." Lo hugged Gloria and gave her a brisk pat on the back. "Come, sit down."

"What about this jug...can I put the flowers in here?"

"You do what you like, my love. This is your home now too." Lo took the cups to the table and set them on top of cork coasters, then returned for the cake.

Gloria filled the glass jug with water from the sink and freed the roses from their wrapping. It didn't feel like her home yet, even though it had come to in the months she had lived there over spring and summer. Now autumn had all but passed and she was about to experience the idiosyncrasies of the ranch in winter. A summer rose, landed in the winter frost.

Lo looked for the best spot to stab into the cake with its pale brown frosting and lopsided white writing that read WELCOME HOME GLORIA, and Gloria was reminded of another time when she and Lo had cake in the kitchen. There had been an electricity between them that day of a different kind.

"Should we wait until everyone's here tomorrow to serve the cake?"

Lo gave her a withering look. "Do you think Sue-Anne hasn't drilled me on what to do? *Heat up the leftovers from supper, make sure she gets some cake, make sure she's not hungry!*" Lo recited in Sue-Anne's anxious tones. "You know culinary pursuits aren't my forte."

Lo eased a fat slice of gooey cake onto a yellow plate and put it in front of Gloria who dug her fork in, hopeful that her appetite would be piqued by the first taste, but weariness had set in and she put the fork back down.

"Too tired?"

Gloria nodded. "Can we save it for tomorrow?"

"You must be exhausted. I don't know why I let Sue-Anne boss me into force-feeding you cake at one in the morning."

Lo removed the cake and Gloria's head leaned gratefully into her arms folded on the table. She couldn't tell if she was hot or cold or maybe both. She listened to the muted sounds of Lo packing away the cake. She wanted a shower. Hot water running over her cold skin, washing away the journey still clinging to her like a film. She felt Lo's fingers on the back of her neck.

"Come on, Ms. Grant."

Lo's voice came from far away, but Gloria stood and followed her obediently from the room. Her bags were waiting at the foot of the stairs that led to the bedrooms. Gloria looked up at the closed door of Terrence's bedroom and wondered if it was still kept as it had been the day he died, or more to the point, the day he lived. She dragged her eyes away. Now was not the time.

"I didn't know where you'd want to sleep. I thought it would be presumptuous..." Lo trailed off.

"You decide. I'm having a shower."

"Let me take these. There's new everything in the bathroom." Lo stifled a yawn.

It seemed they were both too tired for anything more than stunted communication.

There was a reason rituals of birth and rebirth involved water. Like passing from one realm to another. Gloria brushed her teeth properly, grateful for Lo's careful forethought: toothbrush, towels, even a new pale blue robe hanging on the back of the door. Gloria felt a strange sense of being younger than her years, a freshly bathed child, scrubbed clean, without agency. After all the enormous decisions she had been making, it was a relieving feeling to fall backward into a routine that someone had cared enough to set out for her. There was another decision, though, but really it was no decision at all. Clutching her towel around her, braced against the cold, she tramped up the stairs and dragged her suitcase from where it sat indecisively on the landing into Lo's room—their room—where Lo was sitting in bed, propped up on pillows, holding a finger in between the pages of the book she was reading. She took her glasses off, looking barefaced and tired and beautiful. She picked up a bookmark from the bedside table and Gloria noticed a little pinecone sitting beside the lamp. She smiled.

"You still have it, the pinecone."

Lo slotted the bookmark in between the pages of her book and carefully placed it on the bedside table where her gaze stopped to regard the pinecone. "To me, that's you." She looked back at Gloria to see if Gloria had understood, and Gloria had understood perfectly. To Gloria, that pinecone was the moment she fell for Lo, or the moment she recognized something within herself, a question that suddenly begged to be answered.

Lo shook her head. "I can't believe you're actually here." She peeled back the corner of the sheet on the empty side of the bed.

Gloria thought Lo would look away while she slid her clothes on beneath the towel, but she didn't. Instead, she watched with feathery eyes that carried more vulnerability than Gloria felt. To look plainly and honestly was to lay yourself more bare than to shyly change in front of someone to whom, more than anyone in the world, Gloria wished to be beautiful. Even her sweatpants and T-shirt, were they right? Was she right?

"Just throw the towel over the door and come to bed, it's freezing."

Gloria's skin was rough with goose bumps and she wasn't even confident she was completely dry. She climbed into the big bed with its white sheets and Lo flipped the covers back over her and Gloria trembled, nerves fighting the cold. Her head sank gratefully against the pillow, and she could feel she was shaking the bed with her trembling.

"Are you okay?" Lo asked, reaching to take Gloria's hands in hers.

"Are you sure this is what you want?"

Lo squeezed her hands. "This is what I want. And you?"

"This is what I want. You are what I want."

Lo's warm legs entwined with Gloria's tremoring cold ones and Gloria did what she'd been dreaming of doing for months on end—touched her fingers to Lo's cheek and kissed her perfect mouth. Kissing Lo was absolute magic. Gloria had been fantasizing about her soft lips and cool tongue for weeks, and finally having Lo pressed against her was a blissful sensory explosion. In Gloria's mind, Lo was still a miracle. Slow kissing felt like it was lighting up her neural pathways and sending electricity zinging through her veins. Gloria made herself stop and, they held each other close, and that was enough to feel safe and content and they rolled slightly away, their feet still touching, and fell asleep.

CHAPTER TWO

There was a lightness to the morning. Neither Gloria nor Lo had slept much but this new feeling had coated everything in a pearly sheen. Gloria stood at the kitchen window with Lo's chin resting on her shoulder, watching snow sift down, her hands wrapped around a hot coffee.

"Not long until we can go find our tree," Lo said.

"Our tree?"

"Our Christmas tree. You pick it and Kip will cut it."

"Oh, how beautiful. Can we cut it?" Gloria looked through the white toward the stables.

"Sure we can, we can do whatever we like."

Gloria felt her chest expand to accommodate her heart and her breath grew swift and shallow. She repeated it inside her mind: *we can do whatever we like*. She was here, with Lo, and when Lo spoke of her plans, they were plans with Gloria. It was such a wonderful feeling that it scared her slightly. She touched her fingertips to the balling cotton of Lo's blue flannel sleeve so gently that only she could feel it. Happiness was a shade of blue, the buried blue of the sky, the blue of a worn-in shirt, the flecks of blue reaching toward the limbal ring of an eye. The blue shadow leaning into the edges of a happy glow. Gloria's fingers found the pocket of warmth inside Lo's cuff. "The weather looks so picturesque, but how do you get the horses worked?"

"That's what the barn is for. Every winter the boys clear it and we have our own indoor space. All of Peter's toys are gone, which freed up a whole corner. I'd love to build a proper indoor arena, though."

"I can't wait to see Kip."

"He'll be in soon, no doubt. I'm surprised Sue-Anne isn't here yet. I keep telling her to stay home in this weather, but you know what she's like."

"Wait." Gloria turned toward a sound in the corridor and Lo moved a step away as though she'd been caught doing something she shouldn't.

"Gloria!" Sue-Anne's voice announced her imminent entry.

Gloria and Lo looked at one another, suppressing giggles, then Sue-Anne rounded the corner with her granddaughter clutched to her bosom with one hand and a bag of groceries in her other. Little Hayley looked out with round eyes from beneath her gray beanie with its white pom-pom.

"Oh, my goodness!" Lo held out her arms for Sue-Anne to pass the baby over. "Hello, honey-pie, you've grown."

Sue-Anne let the bag of groceries fall to the table with a thud. "Gloria!" She swallowed Gloria up into a warm embrace. "When Dolores said you were coming back, I just about cried tears of joy. We missed you when you left, even Clarence was quiet." She released Gloria.

"Probably because he had no target to spit at. I missed you all, Sue-Anne. Well, not Clarence."

"I'm sure you haven't been eating properly. You girls mind the baby and I'll get to fixing some breakfast. This weather makes everyone hungry as wolves, just you watch, Gloria. Those men will come in and start growling if there's not something hot. Beth's been called in to work so I said I'd bring the baby with me. Now, Gloria, tell me everything. What's been going on?"

Lo was jiggling Hayley up and down and kissing her tiny hand. "We've missed you too," she said to the baby, and Gloria was dragged back through time to what she was sure must have been a similar scene in this very kitchen several years ago: Lo happily bouncing her own baby, unaware of just how cruel fate could be. It reminded Gloria what Christmas must be like for Lo without her child. As if reading her mind, Lo looked over at Gloria. She was smiling, but there were tears in her eyes. Gloria winked at her before going to foist her assistance on Sue-Anne, who was most unwilling.

If Dolores liked cuddling the baby, she had nothing on Kip, who soared Hayley around like an airplane and made funny faces to make her laugh and smelled her head and held her on his lap as he ate, not minding her hand squishing through his food. When he saw Gloria, it had been a rapturous reunion, with Kip swinging Gloria around much like he'd done to Hayley, kissing her cheek and telling her she was all theirs now. Even Samuel the junior ranch hand had kissed her shyly on the cheek and told her he was glad to see her. His voice had stopped cracking, but he still blushed at every second word. Sue-Anne was none too pleased that the cake had been cut and not eaten, but she said it would do for morning tea, which Gloria thought was ludicrous as breakfast was so gigantic. Despite her skepticism, she couldn't stop eating: eggs, hashed browns, corn cakes, pancakes, Sue-Anne's fruit preserves, yogurt, muesli. It was more generous than a hotel buffet.

"So, tell me, Kip, how's the big boy?" Gloria meant Hamlet, Lo's dressage gelding, who Gloria had been competing on while Hamlet was in training in Melbourne.

Kip finished chewing a mouthful of bacon and swallowed. "He was a bit aloof when he got home, wasn't he, Lo? Didn't want to do anything."

"Oh, poor Hamlet." Gloria had missed the big horse when he'd flown back home from Melbourne with Lo, even though Lo had kept her updated about his antics, but she felt bad that he'd been caught up in things, packed off to Australia for a few months then sent home to Wyoming again. His passport had more stamps on it than most people's.

Lo leaned over and moved a coffee cup from Hayley's reach. "He moped for days and pretended he didn't know who we were. He didn't even come to the gate at feed time, he'd just wait until we walked away before coming over."

Kip shook his head. "I said to him, 'Buddy, why the long face?' But he just gave me the cold shoulder."

Gloria smiled. "Better not stirrup trouble."

Lo joined in. "Get off your high horse and leave Hamlet alone."

Sue-Anne looked at them all in astonishment and was about to say something before Samuel said, "Quit horsing around and eat your food."

"Thank you," Sue-Anne said. "I couldn't have said it better myself."

They all laughed and Kip stood up and went to squeeze Sue-Anne's shoulder before handing her the baby. "This weather ain't too inviting but I'd better get back to it."

"Wait, I'm coming!" Gloria drained her coffee cup and took her dishes to the sink.

"Gloria, take my jacket and hat hanging out the back," Lo said.

"And put on gloves!" Sue-Anne called.

As Gloria followed Kip out, she could hear Sue-Anne fretting about newcomers not understanding the cold weather.

Outside there was a cruel wind that hit Gloria harder than she was expecting. It sliced at her exposed cheeks and bit into her legs. The walk to the stables was a battle against the elements, and she would have taken her hat off to Kip and Samuel for their daily struggle were she able to do so. In the stables, Hamlet was trussed up like a Christmas turkey with his navy-blue rugs. In usual fashion, he was leaning against his stall door, watching out for food, a piece of sawdust stuck to his whiskers.

"Hello, my Christmas Ham!" Gloria called as she approached.

Hamlet looked over, his bright eyes curious. When he saw her, he let out a low, rumbling whicker. Gloria went to rub his face under the hood.

"You have food on your face, as usual." She wiped his muzzle with her gloved palm. "Oh, and you're next door." She peered over and saw Sonnet, Lo's gray mare, looking slightly resentful in the next stable. It was only due to the training Sonnet had received in Melbourne that she was able to stand calmly in a loosebox at all. Previously she would have kicked the walls in and injured herself in the process.

Hamlet swung his head around to look at Sonnet as though he had understood exactly what she'd said. Sometimes she felt that he did understand her. He was a comforting presence, a living, breathing teddy bear.

Gloria made a little fuss over Sonnet, who tolerated it for a few seconds then decided she'd had enough, then Gloria went to get Hamlet's saddle and bridle and brushes from the tack room. As she combed his bushy tail, she reflected on what her new life was going to be like. She and Lo had spent hours on the phone and via letters, planning how things would work. It seemed they had made plans to paint the broad brushstrokes of life—the division of labor, the living arrangements, the horses, the ranch—but had yet to fill in the detail. The detail, she supposed, would be filled in via day-to-day experience. It was the omission of detail in some cases that said as much as any conversation could. They hadn't discussed how they would handle their relationship in front of the ranch staff. Kip, who was generally easygoing and an advocate for love, was canny and hard to faze, but their relationship was still in its tender, formative stages. How could they articulate what it was when they didn't yet know themselves? It was love and it was a force that neither of them questioned, but it was a place that needed no plaque on the door to announce its existence. She supposed that would come naturally as they grew into the world around them. It felt so natural from the inside out, but to stand outside, looking in…she knew some people would struggle to interpret what they saw.

Hamlet was happy to be out of his box and doing some work. He trotted merrily along, his vast rump swinging. Gloria could barely feel her hands as the wind howled over the sidings and the snow on the roof had dimmed the barn so that the lights above swung shadows over everything. Aboard a horse, forming shapes and patterns across the floor, Gloria felt at peace, her mind relieved of deep thinking. As she cantered up around the tight space that had been created, she saw Lo standing inside the doorway, her arms folded across her chest, jiggling her legs against the cold. There were snowflakes across the shoulders of her ski jacket and in her hair. Her nose was pink and her eyes alive. Gloria slowed Hamlet to a walk and went to meet her.

"I love watching him go with you on top. He never works that hard for me."

As if to prove his allegiance, Hamlet snuffled at Lo's sleeve.

"See, you're his first love."

"He just knows that's where I keep the treats! Keep moving, I'm here for the show." She pushed Hamlet's face away. "Go do some work, Bozo."

Gloria urged Hamlet on again. "You heard the woman, it's showtime. What have you got in your bag of tricks, Hammy?" There wasn't enough room to really turn the motor up, but Gloria took him through some canter pirouettes and piaffe, then some simple canter-walk transitions. She was conscious of how cold it must be standing still to watch, so she rode over and took her foot out of the stirrup. "Hop up."

Lo looked up at her, a slow smile spreading across her face. "Up there with you?"

"Yeah, here." Gloria moved forward to allow Lo room. "He won't mind." She reached down, and Lo put her foot up in the stirrup and Gloria helped to haul her up.

"Very elegantly done," Lo said, laughing. She wrapped her arms around Gloria's waist.

"Okay," Gloria said. "You be legs and I'll be hands."

"Walk on, Hamlet."

Hamlet walked forward slowly, his ears swiveling around. He was too well-mannered to object to this new way of moving. They walked a lap, then Gloria said Lo should ask for a walk to canter transition and Hamlet leapt forward. They were both slightly uncomfortable, Gloria half sitting on Lo, feeling like she might slip sideways as his big stride made short work of the ground.

"If we were bareback this would be a whole lot more fun!" Lo said as they zoomed along. "Oh, trotting's hard!" She pressed Hamlet back into a canter.

"Oh, crap, I'm about to fall." Gloria slowed Hamlet to a walk, and they saw Kip come in.

"What in the world are you doing to that poor horse? I heard shrieking and thought someone was being murdered in here."

"Just my butt," Lo said.

Hamlet stood with an alarmed look on his face as Lo slid to the ground.

Kip held out a hand to steady Lo. "I think this snow ain't getting any easier. I'm going to run Sue-Anne and the little one home in the truck before it gets worse. I told her not to bring her here when it's like this."

"Tell her not to come in tomorrow. The roads are dangerous and we're all big enough to take care of ourselves. Tell her it's an order. I'll come with you when it eases to run her car back if need be."

Kip nodded grimly and Gloria let Hamlet stretch his neck and cool off while Lo went to sit on a stack of hay bales to watch. When Gloria decided he was cool enough to not get cold, they took him back to the stables and rugged him up again then left him chomping on a near-frozen carrot as they joined hands and ran through the snow, all the way up the path along the white fields, through the ghostly garden, to the back door.

"Oh my god, I had no idea it would be this cold!" Gloria said, shaking the snow from her jacket before she went in to hang it up.

"It's still November, you ain't seen nothing. Lucky your flight didn't get delayed. I can't wait for a hot drink. I feel like that's all I do in this weather."

Gloria's pink hands slowly regained their feeling as they sat in front of the fireplace in the living room. Outside was whitewashed, the mountains barely visible in the distance.

"You know, I've been thinking, I'd like to return to law, maybe just from home. Not the crazy hours I used to do, but just dip my toes in the water and see how I go. I can't go into town without people asking me for advice, so I'm sure I'd get work."

Gloria felt pride well up inside her and could tell it was written on her face. "If you feel up to it, then I think it's wonderful." She knew Lo's mind was too sharp to be idle. "But financially we'll be okay either way. I've never had trouble finding clients, they just seem to come."

"I don't doubt it for a second. Klaus is like an international PR machine. Soon you'll be busier than I am."

Gloria smiled. She was looking forward to getting started again. "We really do need an indoor arena, though."

"See, I knew there was a reason I needed to start earning real money again. Most girls want diamonds, but you want an arena."

"Can't work a horse on a diamond."

"Well, we could claim an arena on our taxes."

Gloria laughed, but she was thinking of the hard work it had taken by both her and Lo to apply for her green card and how final it all felt. She was entering a new tax system now. Her life as she knew it was all but turned upside down. She hadn't said it to Lo, but her dressage trainer, Klaus, had been grooming her as an Olympic hopeful, trying to get her to stay with offers of his best horses. Even if she ended up as a citizen in the States, Olympic competition might be out of reach, or at best she would be competing against Australia, which was an odd thought. She had always dreamt of representing her country, even though Klaus was the only person she'd ever told. He treated it as a serious goal, not as a ridiculous fancy, and had her entered in all the right competitions. Despite his rigidness and disdain for most things that didn't directly relate to him, Gloria would miss his work ethic and drive that had equally motivated and enraged her. She had told him she was moving back for a job, but he knew she wouldn't get better mentoring than with him, and in one of his rare softer moments he'd said,

"Don't sell your dreams for a man." She'd assured him that she wasn't, but he'd told her to hang on to the key to the bedsit in case she changed her mind. Gloria had almost welled up at the unexpected display of emotion, but then he'd told her that her seat looked sloppy and unless she fixed her hands she wouldn't be fit to ride a donkey, and she got over it. She pictured Klaus back at his yard, preparing for summer, the evening sun stretching the days long, the paddocks getting drier and the workload sweatier. She loved the productive bustle of summer, where the yard was full of people and horses moving about their business and there was a cheer in the air of the approaching holiday period. The summer dressage day Klaus always hosted where the grooms dressed up as Christmas elves and gave candy canes out with the trophies and people stayed to drink beer and jump in the pool.

"Why don't we have people around for Christmas drinks?" Gloria asked. "I mean, I don't know anyone in Diamond Rock outside of this household."

Lo had been watching the fire, deep in thoughts of her own. "Like networking?"

Gloria grinned into her hot chocolate. "I meant making friends, getting to know the locals, but in professional parlance, yes 'networking.'"

Lo looked alarmed. "But I don't speak to anyone. I mean, no one's been in here apart from transient ranch guests, not since… and you and me, I'm not sure…" She put her cup down on the coffee table and dropped her forehead into her hand as though the answers to her problems might be found within her palm.

And perhaps they were. Gloria took Lo's other palm in her own and laughed softly. Lo looked at Gloria sharply for daring to create levity from gravity.

"Would it be so bad to see people in your home? The same people to whom you say hello on the street? If you want to work with people in the community, you will have to speak to them, you know."

Lo's mouth opened slightly. "Must I?"

"Yes," Gloria said firmly.

Lo looked into Gloria's eyes intently and Gloria knew she was rapidly ticking through possible scenarios and outcomes. After a moment her expression softened, and she entwined her fingers through Gloria's. "You know, with the pleasure of having you here is the fear of ripping apart coping mechanisms. I'm worried I'll crash."

This time Gloria's face fell. She loved the way they constantly cut to the soft place of vulnerability and shocked one another into learning, but it ruined her for small moments when Lo wore her grief so plainly. "I know, but sheltering away from life in that safe place will ensure you never leave it."

"I'm trying. I've been trying. I knew I couldn't ask you to come if I didn't." She sighed and looked away. "Things don't come easily anymore. I have to brace myself against any type of resistance."

"And you're worried what people will think of you and me?"

Lo shrugged. "Yeah, I am."

"Why?"

"Gloria, you didn't grow up around here. You're so damn accepting of people as they are, but not everyone is like you!"

"Okay." Gloria shrugged. "Well, what can we do? Pretend we are just friends?"

"I don't know. Yes, I guess so."

Gloria felt the familiar sensation of having to conceal hurt from Lo. Practical Lo and romantic Gloria; both knew their own minds in strong but opposing stances, and they softened and hardened one another in painful but necessary ways. Now was not the time for Gloria to wrap herself around Lo's concern and warm it into a malleable thing. She would let Lo put a structure in place to confine the situation.

"Okay," Gloria said. "If you think that's the best, I'm here to run the stables for you and that's that, but I think we have to get used to opening the professional part of our lives to others."

Lo seemed to relax, and she leaned forward to kiss Gloria. "Thank you."

But to Gloria it felt like a wall had been erected between them in Lo's safe house. Gloria was familiar with balancing along that wall, keeping Lo safe within herself.

Lo looked outside to where the sun was illuminating the back of the clouds. "Do you want to come with Kip and I to drop Sue-Anne's car home?"

"Lola, I want to go wherever you're going," Gloria said. To be beside Dolores; the sweetest place, where roses bloomed and butterflies roamed and all was golden. Where shadows lurked and spiders spun their silvery webs. At the ever-changing center of Gloria's earth at the bottom of Dolores's pulsating heart. There by the grace of god and a roll of the dice.

The town of Diamond Rock River was decked out in her winter gown. Tourists tramped purposely around and cars with snow chains on their tires lined the street. In the center of the square, a giant pine tree blinked its merry lights, and two oversized wooden blocks counted down the days until Christmas.

"That wasn't here the other day," Lo said, slowing the truck so they could get a look at the tree as they drove past. "The nativity goes up on the first, but it seems the shops get competitive with their displays earlier and earlier each year. Soon Santa will be sitting in the toy shop ready to hear all those Christmas wishes. The line goes down the street right before Christmas."

The lampposts were covered in spirals of green fir and all the shop fronts glittered red and gold. Gloria watched the passing scenery with childlike wonder. Even the plastic horse outside the saddlers had a wreath around its neck.

"I've never had a white Christmas before."

Lo smiled and squeezed Gloria's thigh. "I want this to be wonderful for you." Her hand returned to the wheel, guiding the truck slowly out of the main street, checking to see Kip was still behind them in Sue-Anne's little blue car. She started to speak, then stopped.

Gloria turned her attention from a couple lugging skis over their shoulders to Lo. "What?"

"Oh, nothing."

Gloria stared at Lo's profile, trying to divine what secrets it held. The straight nose and upturned lip gave nothing away. Gloria looked out ahead through the windscreen, her view the same as Lo's—the sludgy tire tracks and bumper of the car in front—but her conscience none the wiser.

"Oh, okay," Lo said then let out a puff of air. "I'm trying to be more...open." She stared at the road hard, as though it was all the road's fault.

Gloria knew it must be difficult for Lo to speak plainly after so many months of locking herself away from the world. She waited for her to continue.

"There's a lot riding on this, isn't there? And it's going to take some work to make it a success."

The breath left Gloria's chest. "You having regrets?"

Lo looked over and smiled softly. "Not for a second. I'm just feeling the pressure of the situation. I want this to work for you. You've given up everything to come here, you won't see your family over the holiday period, you've left your trainer and job behind, your friends...for me." She shrugged. "And every day I'm worried that you'll realize it's a mistake."

Gloria remembered having awkward conversations with her mother in the car during her teenage years. The conversations no one wanted to have, where they could both stare elsewhere and her mother was occupied by the task of driving. The feeling of unease returned to her now.

"You're right, it's a big step, but you of all people know how I looked at it from all angles."

Lo got too close to the car in front and slammed the brakes. "Sorry. Shit, this weather isn't for cars without brake lights. Yeah, I know you did, we both did, but theory and practice are very different." She indicated to turn into Sue-Anne's street and checked to see that Kip was behind her.

Gloria turned in her seat to better look at Lo. "Is this going to disintegrate immediately?"

Lo pulled over to the curb to let Kip park in Sue-Anne's driveway. The car's indicator blinked slowly and the low rumble of the engine kept them from silence. Lo pulled the handbrake and turned toward Gloria. Her eyes were moist. "That's not what I'm saying at all. Shit." She shook her head once and looked into her lap as a tear escaped and plopped onto her jeans in a dark blue spot. "I'm clearly not very good at this." She swiped at her cheek with the back of her hand. "I'm not telling you to go. I'm trying to tell you that I'm scared that you'll go."

"But I'm not going. I just got here!" Gloria tried to keep the exasperation from her voice. She had known it wouldn't be calm sailing with Lo, who was trying to recover from her own trauma. Over Lo's shoulder, she watched Kip's smudged form through the foggy glass, skipping down the front steps of Sue-Anne's porch and checking before he crossed the road toward them. There was still so much to say. "Kip's coming, but we can talk later."

"No, that's okay," Lo said, turning back to the front and wiping her nose with the sleeve of her coat.

Gloria knew they had just hit Lo's emotional wall again and wished she had reacted more gently, but Kip was opening the door and she knew it wasn't the time.

"Well, how was that? I think I almost ran up your behind three times." Kip brought a blast of cold air and warm cheer as he swung up into the truck.

"Sorry, Kip. The car in front of me had no brake lights. I should be more careful in this weather. I guess I was chitchatting." Lo's voice was light, but there was a thinning over the vowels and her lower lashes were damp. Kip rubbed his hands together, none the wiser.

Gloria's nerves were frayed. Her eyes were stinging with tiredness and her pulse beat insistently in her temples. It was strange to think that not so long ago she had been at Klaus's yard, hosing down horses in the heat, traipsing through dry paddocks, lying on the banana lounge by the pool. It was like viewing a far-off island through a telescope. She knew Lo was trying to break through the habitual silence, even if she was making a mess of it. They both were. Gloria wanted to put her hand on Lo's denimed thigh, run her fingers along the seam of her jeans, press her palm along the rough stitching, do as she pleased with those legs, that body. Things they hadn't done yet, things Gloria had thought about, but it wasn't just Kip's presence in the truck, it was the unsaid things between them.

They each had their own intentions, conceptual mysteries to one another until they became concrete actions, but there was a translation that happened along the way from intention to action, the baring of desire which offered the threat of rejection. It was exhilarating and terrifying. Gloria closed her eyes and her temples beat louder. Kip was leaning across toward Lo, saying something about hunting deer. Lo, who loved hunting too, was agreeing. She heard Lo say her name, but she kept her eyes shut. She didn't want to go hunting and she didn't want to hide her feelings and she didn't want to be the cause of Lo's concern. Lo's voice dropped to a whisper and Gloria didn't care if they thought she was asleep. Surely the long journey owed her that much. Her body pulsed with the thrumming of her veins. After a while she opened her eyes and let the watery scenery move them for her.

When they pulled up outside the house, Lo squeezed the middle of her thigh. "You okay?"

Gloria nodded. "Yeah, thanks."

"You tired there?" Kip asked as they traipsed through the slush up to the front door.

Gloria smiled. It was tempting to retreat into herself, but she couldn't for her own sake and for Lo's. It would be checkmate if they began that game. She hoped they had become wiser in the intervening months. Lo dropped her keys into the bowl where they lived and Kip said he was going to check on the horses in long meadow.

"What will we have for dinner? What do you eat apart from vegetables? You're just like the horses, maybe I can put carrot in your oats." Lo wriggled free of her jacket and hung it on a peg by the door.

"We could make soup? I think it's soup weather."

"Come here, my honey." Lo put her arm around Gloria and pulled her close. "I've forgotten how to make soup and I've forgotten how to love." Her cheek was soft against Gloria's brow.

"Don't be scared to talk to me, will you? When you're silent it feels like you're light-years away. Don't go where I can't find you again." Gloria felt tears sting her eyes, the journey getting its revenge for her feigned sleep.

"I'm sorry."

They rocked gently together as the wind picked up again outside and the sun began its descent into the mountains.

CHAPTER THREE

Dinner was a quiet affair without Sue-Anne officiating the ceremony. Samuel and Clarence had gone home, and even Kip washed the dishes and made himself scarce. Soup had been a success with Lo cobbling together something with white beans that she said resembled what her grandfather used to make. When the dark was thick outside the windows, Lo and Gloria lay on the cream rug in front of the fireplace, the Scrabble board between them.

"What's that?" Gloria asked, reaching her foot across to touch Lo's big toe, poking through a hole in her orange woolen socks.

Lo looked along the length of her body and wriggled her toe. "Pure elegance. I've dressed for the evening-gown portion of the evening."

"I'm scoring you a two. You're showing way too much flesh."

Lo was lying on her side, propped up on an elbow. "I regret to inform you that my swimsuit shows my legs."

"We can't have that. You'd better take it off, then, or risk a low score."

Lo's brows disappeared beneath the rusty wisps of hair across her forehead. "Could be my lucky day. I think I forgot to put it on at all." Her foot traveled up Gloria's shin.

"Look at that, 'Quiz.' What's that? Twenty-two points?" Gloria grinned and Lo gave her shin a little kick. Gloria winced. "You're such a sore loser."

Lo squinted at Gloria and screwed up her nose. "I don't want to show you my lack of swimsuit anymore."

"Yes, you do," Gloria said. "Come here."

"You're bossy."

Gloria could feel her heart beating its wings against the inside of her chest. Her face was hot and she was suddenly aware of her own skin, a pride rising for her own body, viewed through Lo's eyes. A feeling like a bell chiming where the forces of desire swung straight and true, colliding with the same intensity, producing the correct note. She had wondered what it would feel like, to have her arms full of Lo, to have her warm naked body pressed against her own. Lo lay down beside her and Gloria moved back so she could share the cushion she was lying against. That smell, vanilla and orange blossom and milky skin that was Lo. Gloria's hand shook as she pushed the fringe from Lo's eyes.

"How did you get to be so perfect?"

Lo's eyes dropped and she shook her head slightly. "Hardly."

"You are, to me and to all the world." Gloria's hand slid to Lo's neck and she kissed those pillowy lips.

Lo's lips parted and she made a little noise that made Gloria's gut twist with desire. Lo's fingers crept up into Gloria's hair and she drew her close and Gloria was on top of Lo and they were pressing into each other, and Gloria was tasting whiskey and burnt vanilla and longing and Lo's arms were surprisingly strong.

"I have waited so long to do this," Lo mumbled into Gloria's mouth, and Gloria made her own intelligible noise as her hands climbed the ivory keys of Lo's ribs and her thumbs found the underside of Lo's breasts. She had been nervous about doing the right thing, touching the right places, but the way their bodies moved together was as easy as a leaf dropped into a river finding the direction of the water's flow.

The fire crackled beside them as their clothes decorated the floor and Gloria couldn't believe the way Lo's body leapt beneath her fingers like a marble statue coming to life. She kissed the hollow of her throat and the taut knot of her belly button, ran her fingers along her sculpted arms, and pressed her thumbs into the dips of her hip bones. They laughed and squirmed and yelped and Gloria banged her ankle on the coffee table.

Lo lay alongside Gloria, twined around her like a vine. "Oh my god, I just discovered a magical land. Luckily I didn't know of its existence until now or I would have been impatient all my life." Her eyes were large and clear, the light from the fading flames flickering across her face.

Gloria drank her in through her own large pupils in the half light, her fingers caressing the banks of her spine, feeling the pebbles along its sinewy stream. She couldn't imagine hiding this feeling from anyone. It was a natural drawing together, a light easy floating, as though it had always been. "My Christmas angel." It always seemed to her that Lo, aloof and slightly preoccupied with higher things, was not of this earth. By comparison, Gloria felt all the more human, aware of her coarse reactions. Now, though, she felt swept up into the clouds as though she belonged.

"You know you taste like the ocean. Like clear water and sun and salt," Lo said, idly running her fingers along Gloria's upper arm. She reached up to touch the healing cut on Gloria's chin, then leaned forward to kiss it gently. Of all the blossoms in Lo's garden, the petals of those pale rose lips were Gloria's favorite. "A treasure island. My treasure island, hidden out at sea, all mine to explore." Lo's eyes traveled all over Gloria's face as though reading a map. "My dark-haired pirate princess. We need to get you a gold earring."

Gloria's lips curled up into a smile. Goose bumps prickled along Lo's back and Gloria pulled her in closer, speaking into her hair. "Should we get dressed? Finish our drinks and go to bed?"

"Mmm." Lo's voice vibrated against Gloria's jaw. "I'm not sure where I put my swimsuit."

"You weren't wearing one, remember? Don't tell me this was about getting a good score."

Lo rolled back and reached for her underwear. "Oh, it was a good score all right."

Gloria pulled her back in, kissed her once, then let her go. "Come on, Miss Wyoming, it's the talent portion of the evening. Those good looks will only get you so far, I need to see you put your heart in."

"I do play the harmonica like nobody's business."

Gloria pulled her jeans back on. "Nope, that's not it."

"Those bucking bulls at the bar, I can stick on real good."

"Nope." Gloria put the screen across the fireplace.

"Rub my belly and pat my head?" Lo asked as they traipsed upstairs.

"Clever, but that won't set you apart."

"I can blow big bubbles with gum. Bigger than my friend Jessie in junior high." Lo flicked the lamp on beside the bed.

"Got no gum."

"I think I'm licked," Lo said, and then they both burst out laughing as they flopped onto the cold sheets of the mattress.

"This is the best slumber party of my life."

That night, after the moon had risen milky in the sky and the air had grown cold and still in the room, Gloria lay, watching Lo's sleeping form. Before this week, she had never lain before in this snow-banked room with the sleeping form of a woman, Lo—her Lo—whom she had just made love to. It was with wonder, a detached distance, that she drank in the scene. She had crossed a mysterious pond to a new land—how, she wasn't sure—but here she was on the other side, a new self that felt at once both foreign and inevitably familiar. The midnight veil of a new world. She reached out a finger to lightly touch Lo's hair, like a mother reaching out to touch her newborn, *who are you?* Someone who had come from within, a fully formed mystery. Gloria lay back on the pillow and smiled up into the ceiling. Behind her the boat she had crossed on drifted silently away.

When Gloria woke, the room was still dim. Despite her jet-lagged body clock, her senses tingled with morning. She turned her head to see the empty spot beside her. A long pale red hair lay curled in an indent on the white pillow. Gloria reached to touch the spot where Lo had lain, like checking for a pulse, but it was cold. It scared her more than it should, and she sat up and threw her legs over the side of the bed before she had even thought about what she might do or where Lo could be. The digital clock on the bedside table said 7:03 a.m. It was still early then. What she hadn't been prepared for was the silence winter afforded. The ranch in summer had been replete with the morning voices of animals and machines and Sue-Anne's homely bustling, but devoid of wind, there was just the creaking of the house. It filled Gloria with an urgency nearing on panic as though she was the last person on earth. She pulled on a navy-blue cable-knit jumper of Lo's over her sweats and went to peer over the landing to see if Lo was in the living room.

She found Lo leaning against the counter in the kitchen, her long fingers wrapped around a cup of steaming coffee. She was looking out across the monochrome scenery of white fields and black pines. Only the red barn and the deepening blue sky, clashing brilliantly against the white snow, provided any indication that they were viewing the world in color. She turned slowly and held out an arm for Gloria to step into. She was still in her green-and-white-striped pajamas, a fluffy blue robe over the top. Gloria melted into Lo's side, desperate to leave the lonely feeling behind.

"Are you okay?" Lo asked, wrapping her arm around Gloria's ribcage.

"I'm okay. Are you?"

Lo smiled. "I'm good."

Gloria accepted Lo's coffee and took a sip. "You didn't wake me."

"No, I didn't like to. I know how precious sleep is. And really, I don't know what to do yet. This is all so new." Her eyes fell to the rug on the floor by the sink and a blush crept across her pale cheeks.

A sympathetic blush crept to Gloria's own cheeks. "Having second thoughts?"

Lo shook her head, eyes still on the mat. "Not second thoughts, no, just a rearranging of thoughts." Her eyes shifted to Gloria's empty hand, and she took it and sighed. "What am I going to do with you?"

"Love me?"

"How could I not? But practically speaking, Sue-Anne, Kip, the whole township. We need a plan."

"A plan?" Gloria echoed, the unmoored drifting feeling she had known so well in previous months rising up to take her.

"You know how I need a plan."

Gloria passed Lo the coffee cup and turned to face her. She wasn't a planner, but she had enough sense to realize Lo's requirement for a plan wasn't a slight against her but rather an assurance that she was part of the future. Still, she felt the emotional sting of love being shelved in favor of practicality. "I do."

"You're not going to fight me on that one?" Lo arched an eyebrow.

Gloria smiled. The distance between them concertinaed back into the range of comfort. "No, it's too early in the morning. Isn't there a law that states coffee before conversation?"

"Sure, you've probably heard it in the cop movies. The right to remain silent until caffeinated." Lo turned to reach for a mug and tipped some black coffee into it.

Gloria chuckled but she was not to be deterred. "So, when the snow has vanished and the holidays have finished and Sue-Anne is here before we wake up and there are guests swarming all over the ranch, who am I?"

Lo handed her the cheerful yellow mug. Her expression was pensive. "I want you to be you."

"Well, I will be me, but am I your friend? Your employee?"

"Gloria Grant, come to bring dressage to the Wild West."

"Do I start sleeping in the other room?"

Lo chewed her bottom lip. "No. Yes…I don't know. What do you think?"

It was Gloria's turn to sigh. "I don't know either. I guess we could try being friends again. Maybe we'll sleep better if we're in separate beds anyway."

"But I don't want to sleep better, I want to feel your frozen feet against my shins."

"What about the plan?"

"I don't know. It's too early in the morning to hatch plans. We have at least another day before Sue-Anne can no longer control herself and busts in here to cook breakfast."

Gloria held out her hand for Lo's. "You wanted the plan."

"I do want a plan, but I don't like what it means. I don't want to just be your friend." Her voice dipped and cracked a little. "This is serious for me."

Gloria's nose tingled with a small crush of emotion. "Serious enough that I moved here."

Lo nodded. "I know. I don't want to mess it up." She squeezed Gloria's fingers before letting go. "We can't plan on an empty stomach anyway."

"Right now, I'd keep my distance if it meant Sue-Anne's pancakes."

"You would not," Lo said, bumping her shoulder against Gloria's.

"I might." Despite her words, she took Lo into her arms and caressed her neck, feeling the lump of her vertebrae. "It was really those pancakes I traveled all this way for."

Lo hugged her back, her lips on Gloria's neck. "I'd better tell Sue-Anne to get back here."

"Not yet," Gloria said, wanting to hold the moment forever.

By the time breakfast was finished, the only plan that had been hatched was to go out for a ride with Kip.

Gloria crunched out into the white patchy fields in Lo's huge blue parka and long johns under her jeans, to collect her faithful comrade, Dodger, the buckskin with as much mane as he had juicy neck. Dodger greeted her with an affable indifference, accepting her offer of oats and trudging after her like a little woolly mammoth. Gloria had to admit she was outclassed by Kip on his appaloosa, Bugsy, with her gleaming conker coat and bright amber eyes, and Lo on Hamlet, who picked up his hooves as though the aim was to have as little contact with the ground as possible. Great clouds of white preceded them as the horses puffed and jogged. The air was sharp in Gloria's lungs and on her gloved hands, but the magic of the glittering day was alive in her like a song. Kip rode like he walked—with a swagger. Hamlet trotted dutifully along as Bugsy and Dodger cantered, flicking up sludge. Lo still managed to look elegant in her blue jeans and green jacket with a cream beanie, her cheeks and nose a merry pink.

"What do you say we teach Gloria to barrel race?" Kip asked.

Lo squinted at her against the sun hitting the snow, appraising Gloria on Dodger, then she laughed. "Lord help us, Kip. Can't you just picture her in chaps and a hat? She'd be all cowgirl languor until she hit the arena, then it'd be a massacre."

"Oh, it would not," Gloria said, but she was grinning.

"Trust me, I've seen her during a dressage test. She departed this world for the land of win or die."

Gloria burst out laughing. "Can we put that on the ranch banner? It can be your coat of arms, 'win or die.'"

Kip shook his head. "I like that, Miss Gloria. In fact, the next fiery foal we get I'm going to name 'Win Or Die' in your honor."

Gloria glanced back at Lo and her smile faded from her lips. Lo squeezed Hamlet on into his expansive trot and Gloria heard Kip's laughter close off.

"What say we send it up a gear? Dolores?" Kip called.

Lo didn't respond, but she gave Hamlet an unwarranted kick and they took off up the hill, sending up a flurry of dirty snow behind them.

The wall of pines blurred by as Gloria let the wind tear at her and the exhilaration of giving herself to the whim of an animal at high speed fill her senses, leaving no room for thoughts of frosty little ghost boys, patiently waiting on the mountainside for their mothers. As the track opened up to the swollen river, they slowed and the horses came to a puffing walk even though they jangled at their bits and saw monsters in the shadows. Across the river the mountains rose black and white, as patchy as Bugsy's rump.

"The river just sort of merges with the ground. The banks are so flat," Gloria observed.

"That's why the animals use it as a watering hole and crossing point. Oh, look, Gloria!" Kip's voice grew hushed and he pointed across the river. "Elk!"

Gloria sat up a little straighter in the saddle and watched as two elk across the river stopped to look at them then passed on through a clearing and disappeared again. "Reindeer!" Her eyes shone at Lo, but Lo only smiled sadly before turning Hamlet for home.

"We should keep these horses moving."

Gloria looked to Kip, her lips pressed into a line, and Kip gave her a slow blink of understanding. Gloria silently thanked the heavens for Kip as a comforting presence who knew and understood Lo and the situation at the ranch.

Back at the barn, Gloria and Lo looked after the horses while Kip disappeared with a trailer load of hay to distribute to the livestock. Wilbur, the rangy mongrel, padded up and down the stable aisle between Hamlet's stall where Lo was and the tack room where Gloria was putting saddlery away. Gloria rubbed his neck as she walked by with a bucket of feed. Hamlet thrust his face over the stall door at the thud of the feed bin lid and let out a rumbling whicker. Gloria could sympathize; the cold weather was making her hungry all the time. Lo pushed Hamlet gently aside and took the bucket from Gloria to tip into his feed tub.

"Gloria." Lo hesitated, then plowed on. "My mother called yesterday. She wants to meet in town for lunch."

Gloria leaned on the stall door with her forearms and Lo put the empty bucket down and brushed the chaff from her palms.

"That's good isn't it?" Gloria asked. "Or you don't want to see her?"

"You wouldn't be offended?"

Gloria understood then. "Oh! No, you go ahead. I want to work Sonnet and some of the others."

Lo reached to take Gloria's hand in her cold fingers. "Not today, another day when the weather's clear. It's not that I don't want you to come, it's just that, well…she's old-school and she bangs on about Peter all the time. She'll probably bring her frightful suitor. She'd only interrogate you about why you'd want to work with horses and how they are a financial drain."

"She'd probably be right." Gloria attempted a grin which fell short of convincing. "Lo, I understand. Your mum doesn't know me, and I don't expect you to send out a family announcement or anything."

"Okay." Lo's smile was watery like the half-frozen molasses in the feed room. She squeezed Gloria's fingers and Gloria squeezed back.

"I'm going to sort out the mess in the tack room before I come in. This walkway could use sweeping too." Gloria disengaged her fingers.

"Yeah, it's pretty messy. I'll grab the broom."

In the tack room, folded rugs had fallen from their pile, bridles were dumped in a heap to be cleaned, bits were still soaking, and saddles sat on pegs waiting to be oiled. Gloria set about sorting out whose gear was whose and putting things back in their right spots. Lo came and swept the floor, working around Gloria and back out into the walkway. Gloria could hear Lo negotiating the vocal gymnastics of a country song as she worked, her voice dropping from husky lows to soaring peaks, punctuated by taps of the broom to get rid of dust.

As they walked back to the house, Gloria felt off-kilter, like the world was sliding away from her. Had she done the wrong thing in coming? She was just starting to get back on her feet with Klaus and building up a base of clients. Now she was back to square one, and what was the incentive for coming was also the obstacle to overcome. The thought of living a secret life sat like a lump of dread in her stomach.

Inside, the phone was ringing from the living room and Lo went to answer it. Gloria put the kettle to boil and stood contemplating the naked fruit trees in the garden, damp, rough figures writhing up toward an equally bare sky. She could hear the cadence of Lo's voice but not her words. She reflected that she wouldn't be getting any phone calls herself. She had told her friends or family that she would call them, not wanting to burden them with overseas call rates. She had an urge to be sitting at her favorite café with June, drinking a cappuccino in the fragrant blue summer air, listening to the trials of June's latest love interest. She wanted to tell June how it was being here with Lo. Through the bare tree branches, she could see a gray smudge of smoke rising up from the chimney of Kip's cottage. She turned the burner off.

Kip was pleasantly surprised to see her at his door. He stepped aside to allow her entry. "My favorite Australian. Come in before the heat runs out. It's like a cat—you have to block its exit."

"This is worse than trying to get through customs. They tried to confiscate my Tic Tacs." Gloria sidled past Kip.

"Now, that is a crime. Come, sit." Kip swept his arm in a welcoming gesture toward the table and chairs of his cozy kitchen. "I just made a coffee and I'm about to do a cheese melt. It's about the only thing I cook."

"A toastie, right."

Kip turned to give her a funny look on his way to the kitchen counter. "You Aussies are weird, do you just stick an 'ie' on the end of everything?"

"Yes, Kippie, we do."

"I earned that, didn't I?"

"Kippie the Bush Kangaroo." Gloria fell about laughing and Kip gave her a troubled look before disappearing behind the fridge door.

The room smelled of wood smoke from the fireplace and grilling cheese. Along the windowsill were little plants in pots, an exotic pop of green against the landscape outside. Everything was neat and tidy. After the vastness of Lo's house, Kip's place was comforting. Gloria picked up a paper from the pile on the table. It was a letter of registration for one of the youngstock.

"I've been doing admin when the weather's bad outside. You're going to have to stay on top of Lo with the finances. Peter had his faults, but he was organized with all of that. Lo's bright but she gets tunnel vision, and I'm worried that when the money from the sale of assets dries up, we'll be back to sticking our hands down the back of the couch for pennies. Well, not quite, but you know what I mean. It's been a tough year and we may not be set up as well for the winter. We just didn't have the staff." Kip placed a bowl of sugar on the table and went to retrieve Gloria's coffee.

"It's hard, I know. I have some clients lined up, but we don't have a proper arena to accommodate training. We need an indoor. I can travel to them for now, but we can't host clinics or set up jumps until the weather improves, which will be months. Plus, it's hard to work the horses properly." Gloria stirred her coffee thoughtfully. "Are there any local indoor arenas?"

Kip put a pile of toasted cheese sandwiches on the table and sat down on the white painted chair opposite Gloria. "Let me see. Well, the only one I can think of is Caroline Bandiana's. She lives a few miles west, but she and Lo don't see eye to eye no more."

Gloria nodded. "Yes, Lo told me that Peter threatened to sue her over Terrence's death and as a consequence they no longer speak."

"Could be her beef is with Peter, not Dolores. Caroline is a lovely lady, one of those tough but fair types. Why don't you see if you can help Dolores mend that bridge? I don't know much about dressage and the like, but you'll need a trainer yourself, won't you?"

"Yes. I've heard good things about her, and Hamlet certainly goes well. I've been thinking, too, if we can get a good breeding program happening. I mean, Sonnet has good bloodlines. I'd like to get her out and about, see if we can make something of her after all."

Kip smoothed a callused hand over the checkered tablecloth. "You know how I feel about that idiotic animal. Don't you think it'll be a slap in the face to Lo if you're flaunting her about the competition scene?"

Gloria shrugged. "I don't see it like that. Sonnet is a horse and you, of all people, should know that animals react the only way they know how. It wasn't her fault and there's no use having her hanging around eating her head off and getting laminitis. She may not be up to it anyway."

"I'd be careful with her in a crowd."

Gloria sighed. "I don't like seeing talent go to waste. She's a good horse and Klaus was good for her. You know he offered me his favorite mare to stay."

Kip took a bite of toast, the cheese oozing out the side. "You must be good at what you do."

"Some people think so." Gloria chose her own cheesy triangle and took a bite. "Oh, yum."

"Like Dolores?" Kip's eyes were steady on Gloria's, but Gloria dropped her gaze first.

"I guess so."

Kip nodded slowly and turned his concentration to his food. "She must be pretty keen to fly you all this way to train her horses, considering she seems to have lost her nerve."

Gloria chewed and swallowed. "Dolores is a tough person, she'll never truly lose her nerve."

"Might be you're right. And what about you, Miss Gloria? What made you turn down offers of superstar mares and sunny weather?"

Gloria could feel the heat rise to her face. "Time for a change, I guess. Plus, you guys made me feel at home."

"I'm your friend, you know, Gloria."

Gloria picked at a hardened blob of melted cheese on her plate. A friend was exactly what she needed but the words wouldn't form in her mouth. She'd barely told a soul about her feelings for Lo, only June back home. She'd pushed them down for so long that now they were buried deep. It was up to Lo to tell Kip if she chose. She nodded. "I know."

"Good. What do you say we grab Lo and drag her into town for a beer on Friday?"

"I'd like that. Back to our old hangout, Rock's?"

Kip toasted his coffee cup. "No finer establishment."

"You bringing a date?"

Kip shrugged. "Don't want to be the third wheel. I guess I could ask Mallory."

Gloria slammed her coffee cup down and leaned forward, grinning. "Who's Mallory?"

"Oh, never you worry. Now, the feed store is coming to pick up a load of hay, so if you don't mind, I am going to eat and run. Stay as long as you want."

Gloria laughed. "It's okay, I'm not some kind of serial over-stayer. I'll come give you a hand."

By the time she got back to the house, the sun was melting into the earth like a huge ball of fire. She was covered in hay seeds and her hands were sore from pulling bales up by the hay twine, but she was warm and happy. Lo was wrestling a tray of potatoes and onion into the oven. The sleeves of her oversized black sweatshirt were pushed up and Gloria could see she had odd socks on below the cuffs of her gray sweatpants. She remained endearing in her scruffiness, half of her hair out of its low bun. She didn't care, and Gloria loved her all the more for it.

"Nice socks," Gloria said on her way through to shower.

"I know what you like." Lo grinned at her, and Gloria shook her head as she walked off. Despite the jest, she did like it.

At night, Gloria and Lo slept wrapped together for warmth and for the joy of feeling each other close, but in the early hours of the morning, Gloria crept to the spare room, to the desolation of crisp sheets.

It was lucky she did, because Sue-Anne arrived, heralding the sunrise with the clanging of pots and pans. Gloria couldn't sleep anyway. She'd been curled in a ball, thinking about Lo's mother and Peter and all the other reasons Lo had to fear going into town together. Kip was nobody's fool, and Gloria was grateful later that morning over breakfast when he brought up the idea of going to Rock's on Friday.

Sue-Anne's mouth puckered in disapproval but Samuel's eyes lit up.

"I don't know…" Lo said, looking at Gloria. "What do you think?"

"I'd like to go."

"Two single girls like you," Sue-Anne said. "Just be careful of the men down there, but in saying that, you should be meeting boys."

"Boys?" Lo's eyebrows shot up. "Sue-Anne, I'm almost forty years old, and to be honest, meeting men is far from my mind. Very far!"

"Oh, for Gloria then. She's come all this way, it'd be nice for her to find a beau. She's still young and new in town."

Lo didn't look like she found the idea so nice, but she was rescued from comment by Kip offering to bring Mallory, and Sue-Anne was distracted into mining Kip for information on the subject. Kip took it good-naturedly and Gloria felt grateful for his presence once again.

Lo pushed her eggs around on her plate, then interrupted Sue-Anne's monologue about the virtues of marriage to announce that Rock's was a great idea. Gloria and Kip eyed her warily and Sue-Anne changed tack and said that perhaps they should give Rock's a miss and wait for the Christmas barn dance.

"Barn dance?" Gloria perked up.

"If there's a dance this year, I'm asking Amy," Samuel said, blushing with pride. "She's a real good dancer."

"She'd better wear steel-capped boots if she's going with you," Kip said, helping himself to more bacon.

"There's no way I'm hosting the barn dance. All those people here, no thanks." Lo stood up and began to clear her dishes. "I'm meeting Peter in town to discuss some work he might have for me."

A silence descended on the table, and even Sue-Anne stopped chewing.

"Well, I think that's great," Kip offered. "The town has missed your counsel."

Sue-Anne put her knife and fork together primly and turned toward Lo. "Does that mean you and Peter—"

"No!"

Sue-Anne turned back around and made a face into her plate. "A union that is made in the eyes of the Lord."

"Sue-Anne, not now," Kip said quietly and stood to clear his plate.

No sooner had breakfast finished than Lo pulled Gloria out into the corridor to vent.

"What is it with that woman? She is always meddling in my life. What I do is none of her business, and don't you say she means well!"

Gloria took Lo by the elbow to move her farther from the doorway. "I understand, but she is the way she is."

"Ugh!" Lo rolled her eyes.

"And, sorry, but that's what I've been saying to you. Who cares what people think? It's your own life. Do what you want."

"Gloria, don't. Not everyone sees the world the way you do. Case in point!"

"That's true, so I prefer not to think about it. And also, what was that? I didn't know that you were going to take on some work with Peter."

"Oh, believe me, it's not a friendly negotiation. More like, 'You're well enough to cope, so come do your share.' Sorry, I should have told you that he called yesterday, I just needed time to think about what I want to do, and I don't want to stay out of the game too long. As it is, I'll need to brush up on current changes to law. I'm lucky that Peter kept my paperwork up to date, I'll give him that, and we did discuss his cases, but I feel slightly panicked at the thought of going out on my own. Anyway, it certainly isn't an opportunity to reconcile."

Gloria reeled back slightly. "You want me to book a flight home?"

Lo crossed her arms. "You can't keep saying that. I just said I have no intention of reconciling with Peter and somehow you got the opposite?"

They both turned to the sound of Sue-Anne's footsteps and her head poked around the doorframe. "Everything okay, girls?"

Lo turned on her heel and stormed off toward the living room. Gloria wanted to cry, but instead she said, "This time of

year must be stressful for Lo, and now having to face Peter…
She's probably feeling anxious."

"Well, don't let her get high-handed with you. She tries to
do that to me, but just because she pays you doesn't mean she
can treat you like that."

Gloria's mouth popped open in amazement, then she hastily
shut it again. "I'll keep that in mind, thank you, Sue-Anne."

Sue-Anne nodded once and disappeared around the door
again. Gloria stood in the corridor and stared at the space Sue-
Anne had just vacated, wondering whether to let Lo be or to go
after her. She blinked back a tear that threatened to escape and
decided to go find Lo. Before she had made it across the living
room, Lo was walking back toward her.

"I'm sorry. Forgive me?" Lo's face was strained.

"Nothing to forgive."

"I think I know what we need."

"What's that?"

Lo held out her hand. "Come with me."

Lo led her into the study to the tall walnut and glass cabinet
that contained medals and ornaments and old photos. "Hello,
Uncle," she said, tapping the photo of a bearded man with a
generous belly, fly-fishing in the river. Inside the cabinet was
a safe. "This is where I keep the guns." She grinned at Gloria
before turning her attention to the safe code.

Gloria looked on in alarm, unsure if Lo was joking or not.
When the door swung open, she was not. Lo took a rifle down
from its rack and admired it.

"Here, have a hold."

Gloria recoiled. "No thanks."

Lo laughed. "Don't be such a scaredy-cat, it's not even
loaded. Here, just hold it like this."

Gloria tested the weight of it in her two hands. "It's heavier
than I thought it'd be. Are you going to send me to the firing
squad?"

"No, we're taking this with us in case of wild animals and
we are going to get our Christmas tree." Lo unclipped another
locked drawer with deft movements and pulled bullets out of a

case. "There was a time, not so long ago, I sat out, night after night, in the forest, hoping to get that cat." She took the gun from Gloria and slipped the bullets into the magazine, her face a calm mask. "An eye for an eye."

"Do we need that?" Gloria knew her distaste was plain. Part of the chain of events that led to Terrence's death had involved a mountain lion, but unlike Lo, Gloria didn't hold the lion personally responsible.

"I ain't got him yet. There's no way I'm taking you out there on foot without it." Lo stood up straight. "If I see him, he's toast."

Gloria could see Lo was resolute, but guns made her more nervous than the idea of big cats. She didn't even want to hear a bang, let alone see a majestic creature fall like a warm sack of flesh.

The stony weather suited Gloria's mood as they went to the shed to select a saw. Brutal weapons that added discomfort to Gloria's uncertainty. As Gloria blundered alongside Lo through the snow, she was reminded of the blundering of their relationship. Every now and then, Lo stopped to pull a half-submerged twig from the snowy trail and cast it aside. Gloria's muscles ached, and she felt bewitched and silenced by the solemness of the tall snow-laden trees and the formidable sky through the branches. Perhaps Lo was right; it would be better to approach the relationship with the cool precision of separation than the warm blundering and heart-treading of romance. Twice Lo halted Gloria by throwing a firm hand to her chest, the sight of something moving in her peripheral vision or the sound of a snapping twig. Lo seemed another person, a masculine energy coursing through her, tightening her jaw and shoulders. Even though they hadn't been walking long, Gloria had no idea where she was, disoriented by the monochrome sameness, and when Lo stopped and asked, "This one?" Gloria had no idea what she was talking about. "Our tree?"

"Sure." Gloria felt no joy in the moment.

"You want to cut it?" Lo pointed to a spot down near the base.

Without responding, Gloria squatted down, took hold of a tree branch, and, as she was about to cut, looked up at Lo. "And what if you shot the cat, what then?"

Lo gazed down, a pulse jumping at her throat. "Even."

"You really believe that?"

Lo shrugged, the gun relaxed beside her, pointing toward the ground. Gloria looked at that set face a moment longer before gritting her teeth and biting into the trunk of the small tree with the serrated blade. Lo pushed the tree away from her, giving one final shove as the tree cried out and fell to the ground.

The walk back, dragging the tree along the trail, was not easy. Gloria didn't complain and Lo didn't remind her that it had been her idea to take it on rather than let Kip sort it out. By the time they dragged it up onto the veranda, they were needled in more ways than just the physical. Sue-Anne stood in the doorway, admonishing them for bringing snow and dirt in, and Kip paused at the fence he was mending, pliers in hand, to openly laugh at them. Lo ignored Sue-Anne and hoisted the tree the rest of the way into the kitchen, as determined as a retriever puppy with a heavy stick. Sue-Anne slid the door closed behind her and Gloria peeled off her gloves to examine her already hay-stung hands, which were now even redder and sorer. Her hair clung damply to her forehead with perspiration.

Lo wiped her own forehead with the back of her wrist and addressed Sue-Anne. "Did I throw the ornaments out?"

"Heavens, Dolores, why would you have thrown them out? I never would have allowed that."

"I thought about it, I can't remember if I did."

"Go and put that dang rifle away, Dolores. You know how I get."

Gloria felt herself unclench as Lo dropped the top of the tree and left the room. "I'm not sure I can get used to it, Sue-Anne."

But Sue-Anne had returned her focus to Lo's statement about the ornaments. "What a relief to be able to celebrate Christmas again. The black gloom that descends upon this house at Christmastime. I have a special ornament on my tree at home for Terrence. A little boy angel. Dolores doesn't want to know, but I pray for them both."

Gloria pictured Lo's face as she spoke about killing the mountain lion and wondered how she had ever felt joy, it seemed so remote from the feeling she had right now.

The decorations were found in a box in the attic along with the stand for the tree. They dragged everything into the living room beside the dry bar where Lo said they used to put the tree. The first ornament Lo pulled from the box was a white china dove carrying red berries in its mouth. Lo looked at it for a moment, hung it on tree near where she was kneeling, then began trimming the tree with brisk, businesslike movements. Gloria sat and worked on untangling a string of colorful lights. When they were done, they stood back to admire it. Gloria had to admit, it did look beautiful despite the eclectic adornments, obviously collected over time. She slipped her hand into Lo's and Lo's whole body seemed to sigh.

"That felt like war."

Gloria knew exactly what she meant.

"You know," Lo said, turning to look at Gloria. "I might have something in mind for you already."

"A present?" Gloria smiled in spite of herself, the idea such a novelty. A present chosen by Lo.

"Yes, but you don't have to get me anything." She saw Gloria's expression. "No, I mean it. I don't want anything. You, well, you're here." She dropped her eyes. "I'm not sure why, but you're here."

The angel on top of the tree in her blue and cream robes and golden halo gazed down with serene eyes. Gloria smoothed her thumb over the fleshy part of Lo's palm. "This is a special Christmas."

"I think you'll like your present."

"What is it?" Gloria still felt touched that Lo had bought her something. She began racking her brains for what she could get Lo.

"I'm not telling you!"

"It's not a gun, is it?"

Lo laughed. "Got plenty of them. That's it, though, I'm not telling you anything else. Go get ready and come into town with me while I meet with Peter. We can have lunch."

CHAPTER FOUR

Gloria was not prepared for the Lo that emerged from the bedroom ready for her meeting, black heels in her hand, smelling of perfume.

"Do I look okay?" Lo asked, bending forward to slip her feet into the shoes. "I feel a bit nervous."

Gloria ran her eyes over Lo's navy suit with the tailored pants and sharply cut blazer. "Come here." Lo stood up straight and Gloria adjusted the collar of her cream silk shirt underneath. "You look like you run the world," she said, quite truthfully.

"Exactly what I am going for. I'm starting from the outside in." She brought Gloria's chin up to kiss her lips.

To Gloria, who had never had an office job, Lo looked so adult and sophisticated. To her, the age difference of ten years meant nothing, but perhaps Lo saw her as unformed and uninteresting. The feeling that she wasn't good enough returned to hover at the periphery like an uninvited guest. She didn't want to lose herself and become Lo's shadow. That would quickly grow boring for the both of them. She felt renewed determination that moving to the ranch would not be the end of her aspirations but a springboard for them.

By the front door they shrugged into their coats and Gloria pulled on red woolen gloves, making her feel even more infant-like—a child of twenty-eight. She stuffed her hands into her pockets while Lo checked her reflection in the hallway mirror, scrunching her fingers up under her hair to create volume. She rubbed her lips together to even her lipstick, looked at Gloria in the reflection behind her, nodded sternly, and said, "Time to begin building our empire."

Gloria laughed. She felt like she was meeting a whole new person within Lo. "Can you drive in those shoes?"

"I used to. Long as the path outside isn't too wet. I need to feel like I'm eye-level with Peter today. We've stood across from each other in every conceivable way: at the altar, in court, at the dinner table, at Terrence's hospital bed—birth and death—and we've always done everything in the best interests of the union, or as close to as compromise would allow. It's different now, honey. I'm doing what's in our best interests." She reached up to the coatrack and pulled down a dark green beret and put it onto Gloria's head. "Oh, yes."

Gloria glanced in the mirror and adjusted the slant of the beret. "If you say so."

"Very much so." Lo opened the door and the cold air reached in for them.

Watching Lo climb into the big white truck in her heels and take the wheel was a juxtaposition that Gloria appreciated all the way into town.

Lo went into the office she used to share with Peter, and Gloria wandered the main part of town admiring the window displays and the decorations adorning the street. She found an art store and bought thick creamy paper and watercolors and brushes and knew what she wanted to give Lo for Christmas. Feeling inspired, she went to the car and hid her purchases out of sight in the back. As she walked across the street again, she saw Lo leaving the office carrying a manila folder. Gloria waved, and the way Lo lit up when she saw her made Gloria's breath swell in her chest. Lo strode across the road, her heels clipping on the slick tarmac, her hair bouncing against the shoulders of her navy woolen overcoat.

They linked arms, pressed against each other, their heads tilted toward one another as they hurried toward the diner.

"How was it?" Gloria asked.

"Interesting. Not what I expected. I'll tell you inside."

They sat in a booth and a waitress poured them coffee.

"I'll take a slice of pecan pie with cream on the side, lots of it," Lo said, tilting her face up to smile at the waitress. "We have a high-calorie situation on our hands."

Gloria hastily scanned the menu. "I'll take a mushroom and cheese omelet, thank you."

"Right away," the waitress said.

"Is it that bad?" Gloria asked, pulling her gloves off and reaching across to take Lo's icy hand.

Lo stared intently at Gloria's face, but Gloria had the impression her thoughts were elsewhere.

"To be honest," Lo said. "I'm still processing it. Peter said he wants to go back into business with me."

"Hah." Gloria's fingers loosened against Lo's hand and then a false smile sprang to her lips, like a placeholder while she processed her feelings. "Wow, that's great."

Lo let go of her hand and sat back against the seat. "Is it?"

"I mean, yeah, if you want to. It's not so unexpected, really." Gloria felt the cold seep from her skin into her flesh. It was unlike her to begrudge anyone anything, however it was a reversal of her expectations. She had braced herself for Peter's animosity but not for his offer of alliance. "What did he say?"

"Just that he has a lot of work and I could rent my old office space back from him and take on the overflow, new clients and so on. Basically, the less appealing jobs. We used to share a lot of the casework. I'd do a lot of the client intake and counseling, and he handled most of the negotiating and drafting. Once Terrence was born, Peter did most of the court appearances, but things would be different now, we would work much more independently." She picked up her coffee cup and raised it as if to take a sip, then set it back down. "He was quite friendly. It's been a while since we've had a pleasant conversation."

Gloria found she was suddenly interested in a toggle on her jacket. "So, what did you tell him?"

Lo let the words hang in the air until Gloria looked up and met her eyes. "I told him I'd have to think about it. I wanted to talk to you first." Her face was serious. "It'd be a shortcut to a client base, so it makes sense in that way, however I agree it could go pear-shaped."

Gloria realized she'd been holding her breath and she inhaled into the bottom of her lungs. "Does he know about us?"

Lo's gaze didn't falter. "No."

Gloria took another breath and the word hovered between them. Neither of them said anything and Gloria began to pick at the plastic of the toggle with a thumbnail while Lo observed her with a passive expression in the way she had surely perfected through her job. Gloria's toggle investigation grew more intense as she ran a conversation in her mind that she wouldn't have out loud. Lo watched her internal struggle without comment.

"Emergency pecan pie," the waitress announced, the plate cutting through the dense air across the table. "And the mushroom omelet. Can I get you anything else?"

"No," Lo said. "No, thank you." She waited until the waitress had retreated before saying, "Well, it's something to think about anyway. There's a lot to consider, the ranch as well. Peter would be entering a quiet period now, too, over the holiday season." She pushed her plate toward Gloria. "Try this."

Gloria shook her head, all the while thinking, *Don't be unsupportive.* "No, thanks." But she couldn't quite meet Lo's eyes. For some reason talk of Peter made her begin to shut down, like she was already preparing herself for the inevitable: Lo would realize she was a phase. To Gloria, Lo was almighty— clever, witty, strong, her emotions as vast and beautiful and ever-changing as the sky, bringing new weather, dictating the blooming of flowers, the birds in the trees, the flourishing or devastation of crops. She saw Lo not as a person, but as a state of being. She knew it was wrong to let anyone get all around her like the wind. She realized she was all clenched and forced herself to relax her shoulders.

Lo savored the pie, slowly pulling the spoon from her mouth. She gave her head a little shake. "I'm surprised this is legal, it's that damn good. I think you should try it. Just try it." She put the spoon back on the plate and slid it across toward Gloria.

Gloria looked at it a moment, willing herself to change emotional gears, before picking the spoon up and delving it into the gooey brown pie and then more lightly into the cream.

"I'm going to stop you there," Lo said. "Wrong ratio of cream. Half pie, half cream. Trust me, I know my pie. Here."

Gloria appreciated Lo's attempt to move them out of silence and she passed her back the spoon. Lo filled it correctly and Gloria obediently opened her mouth. Sweetness exploded across her tongue, tempered by the cool rich blandness of the cream. Lo was watching her expectantly.

"I wasn't aware there was a mathematical equation involved in eating pie, but that is perfect." Gloria covered her mouth and they laughed, breaking the tension.

An old woman at a table over Lo's shoulder was watching them with curiosity. Gloria pretended not to notice but she cast her eyes back down to the dark wood of the tabletop. She remembered how not so long ago Lo would barely eat, and here she was delighting in food as a sensual experience.

"When I was first married, I used to bake. I had this notion that I would be some type of Betty Crocker, churning out brownies and key lime pie. It lasted about three weeks before Peter got sick of desserts and I realized I couldn't look at another measuring cup without screaming. I was probably a disappointing wife." She shrugged slightly.

"Betty Crocker wasn't a real person, you know."

Lo licked cream from her lip. "Wasn't she some type of agony aunt?"

Gloria shook her head once. "Nope. Made up by a flour company or something."

"So, I aspired to wifely duties of an impossible standard. Sounds about right."

"You don't strike me as the Betty Crocker type." Gloria picked a mushroom up on her fork. "Were you happy with Peter back then?"

Lo twisted her hair into a bun, then let it untwirl back onto her neck. "Yes, very. I think he was just what I needed. Dependable, kind, ambitious. He was very cute with those big blue eyes. He seemed so centered compared to the other people I knew who were smoking pot or complete jocks, and I'd just come out of a rocky relationship. He was easy to fall in love with, I guess. There was little friction and that suited my own ambitions. We were young."

Gloria prematurely swallowed the mushroom, feeling it make its rubbery way down her throat. "Do you think if it wasn't for Terrence's death that you would have stayed with him?"

"Well…" Lo reached for her empty coffee cup and looked around for the waitress. "These waitstaff, they're all over you when you don't need them, and when you want a coffee, they're nowhere to be seen."

Gloria took another bite and watched Lo search the room for a diversion, the waitress busy flirting with a young man at a stool by the window.

Eventually Lo shut her eyes for a second and her teeth clamped over her bottom lip as they so often did when she was uncomfortable. "I don't have an answer for you, Gloria. I can't imagine a different life from that point, it's too painful. To think of a diverging reality where that day had never happened." She squeezed her eyes shut again and Gloria saw how Lo was so put together on the outside but underneath it all there was still a roiling terror.

"Hey, Lola." Gloria touched Lo's hand that had balled around its thumb. "My love, I'm sorry. You don't have to answer that."

Lo opened her eyes, and they were glazed with tears. "No, I'm sorry for you. Hard to play with a broken toy."

Gloria's breath left her as though someone had thumped her on the back. "A broken—"

"Excuse me," Lo called at the waitress, cutting her off. "Could we please have a refill?"

CHAPTER FIVE

Late that afternoon, Gloria sat at the dining table, plotting out a business plan for the ranch. To make things work she would need to be taking on horses for board, begin a better breeding program, get regular clients and horses to train. Her specialty had always been difficult horses. There were problems with this: she was unknown in the district, they had no indoor arena for the winter, and Lo—and surely Kip—might be hesitant about beginning a dressage horse training program if it meant cutting way back on their quarter horse stock.

Gloria chewed the end of her pen thoughtfully and looked across the table at Lo, who held a stapled sheaf of papers in her hand, reading intently, her lips working slightly as she brought the words from the page to her mind. She flicked the page, pressed the fold back against the stapled corner, and kept going. Gloria calculated how much money they could make if they sold off much of the herd at the yearly auction. There had been no auction last year, so the herd had grown larger and the profit wouldn't have been calculated into the ranch's forecast. It might be enough for a deposit on an indoor arena. An indoor arena would give them a good selling point for boarding other people's horses and for running training days and competitions. The horses were running wild, eating fodder that could be for the cattle, and no one had the time to put into them.

"Lo."

Lo's head snapped up and she pushed her reading glasses against the bridge of her nose. "Yes, my love?"

Gloria smiled, seeing Lo return to the room from wherever she had been. "Sorry to interrupt. Question: does the ranch have public liability insurance?"

Lo smiled and settled her glasses on top of her head. "Sure does. We can't have folk running around here without it."

"Cool-cool." Gloria glanced back toward her scribbled notepad. "I have a few ideas. What would you think about giving this place a little makeover and angling it more as a boutique dressage facility?"

Lo let the papers fall from her hand and leaned back in her chair. "I'm listening."

"Dressage is a growing sport, right? The ranch is beautiful, and we can still operate it as is, but if we ramped up the dressage aspect, we could market it that way and host events, competitions. People could rent the guest houses. Once competition season starts, Hamlet will build a name for us, maybe Sonnet too." She saw a shadow flick across Lo's face but she continued, "I can bring on young horses, work with problem horses, start teaching again."

"Are you creating a business case for me?" Lo asked, half joking. "Where would we get the capital? I mean, I have full faith that you can build a name for yourself out here and put the stables on the map, but that takes time."

"Sell off the excess stock, which would refine the herd anyway."

Lo inhaled slowly and began to bite her lower lip. "This time of year? Maybe we can revisit the idea in the spring."

"Fair enough, but if we could begin planning now then we can advertise and be ready for the spring."

"You're serious, aren't you?"

Gloria dropped her eyes to her blue scrawl again. "Yes." She slid the notepad toward Lo, much the way Lo had slid the pie across the table earlier that day. "I am."

Lo settled her glasses back on her nose and squared the notepad in front of her. "Where you've written 'Kip' with a question mark...does that mean how he would feel about it?"

"Yes. It'll be work in the short term getting them ready for sale, but cost and labor saving in the long term."

Lo nodded. "A consideration. If I have my business hat on here it all makes sense, although it's a big investment. It all hangs on the indoor arena and I'm just not sure we can afford it." She looked back up at Gloria. "I can see you're serious, though, and I want you to feel like this is your place too."

"Thanks. I just feel that there's something I may be able to bring, just this one thing. It could work out."

"I'll tell you what, you keep plotting out the way you'd like it to work and we'll give it the consideration it deserves. I said I'd read through this for Peter but if you still want to go to Rock's tonight, we can do that?"

"Really?" Gloria sat up straighter in her chair.

"Sure. How could I turn down an opportunity to get the gossip on Mallory? Besides, as Sue-Anne says, you're young and in need of male attention. Might need to marry you off."

Gloria stood up and walked around the table, Lo's head turning to follow her as she came to kiss the top of her head. "I'm quite happy living in sin, thank you."

* * *

Rock's was decked out in Christmas attire to match the rest of the street. Above the door, red glowing letters asked, "Naughty or Nice?"

"Do we have to pick one?" Gloria asked, her nose tipped skyward.

Lo pushed the small of her back and whispered, "I know which you are."

Gloria felt her stomach flip and she followed the cool blue skunk of Kip's aftershave through into the warm beer fug of the main bar. Country music pulsated and Gloria hadn't seen so many people in one spot since she first came to Wyoming. Lo let go of the back of her denim jacket which hadn't felt adequately warm in the bitter cold outside but now felt immediately unnecessary.

"This is a lot of people," Lo said, shrinking closer to Gloria.

Mallory, who turned out to be a pretty girl with high, happy cheeks and an infectious laugh, swept them straight to the bar and insisted they all have a shot. Kip and Lo didn't argue, so Gloria downed a tequila in good faith and spent the next twenty seconds coughing while the others laughed at her and Lo thumped her back. Kip seemed bashful and slightly awed by Mallory, which made Lo and Gloria turn to one another and smile knowingly.

"Can you dance?" Gloria asked Lo, to which Kip laughed.

"Can Dolores dance? She can but she won't."

Lo shrugged as though she'd been found out, but Gloria could see the way Lo was looking nervously at the faces in the room.

Gloria leaned back against the bar top. "You know what, you guys go and dance. We might grab a seat and have a drink. I'm hanging for some of those over-salted pretzels too. They're the only reason I came, really."

After Kip and Mallory bounced off to join the dance floor, Lo shot Gloria a grateful glance. "Thanks, honey."

Gloria winked. "Don't mention it, little lady."

"Let's go grab that booth before we lose it and before Hal, the dreary school principal, can bale us up."

Gloria was longing to take Lo's hand but she shouldered through the crowd instead. She always felt proud and self-conscious when she stepped out with Lo, like an explorer with a rare butterfly fluttering along behind. She saw another couple making for the booth and she quickened her pace, sliding in moments before they could claim it.

"Nice save," Lo said, sitting in the booth beside Gloria, so close that their legs were pressed together under the table.

"Thank god for the snow-season tourists or else I'd be avoiding—oh, hi, Hal!" Lo's voice became hearty and her fingers stopped stroking Gloria's thigh.

"Dolores, why, it's been a long time since I've seen you in town. How are you getting along? May I?" Before Lo could respond, Hal slid into the seat across from them. He was tall and broad with tanned jowls and basset eyes. He reached a hand across the table, and the grubby cuff of his work shirt pulled back, revealing thick blond hairs across his wrist. "Hal Bickle. I'm principal over at the elementary school where Terrence attended, god rest his soul."

Gloria's hand hesitated on its way to meet Hal's and she inwardly groaned. "Gloria Grant." She knew Hal wanted more but that was as much as she was willing to divulge.

"You're not from around here, are you?"

"Australian," Lo said hastily. "So, Hal, how's Wanda?"

Hal stifled a belch and rocked a little. "Better ask Clint Chisholm. She's living over there now."

Lo leaned forward. "Clint from the lumberyard?"

Hal's eyes closed a fraction too long. "Yep, living on Oak Street now. Never mows the lawn. Looks like a jungle. Wanda always hated when I left the lawns to get untidy. Huh." He rocked back again.

"Sorry to hear that."

Hal shrugged dramatically, his big shoulders caving in around his ears. A waitress came to take their order.

"No, no, no," Hal swiped Lo's money away, hitting her hand. "My round." He made a circle gesture over the table.

Lo shot Gloria a look and Gloria curled her hand firmly around Lo's thigh. They reluctantly ordered a beer and Lo whispered that they'd drink fast and excuse themselves.

"Where'd you say you're from, Denise?"

Lo and Gloria looked at each other in alarm and Gloria screwed her face up in an effort not to laugh.

"Denise is from Australia," Lo said, pushing her thigh up against Gloria's. "How's it going at the school? Has the library renovation finished?"

"Yeah, I wanted new sports equipment but you know how the board is crazy for books. Give a kid a ball and a team to be proud of, that's how they develop. You know, Dolores, I remember that time you came to the Easter recital in that skirt with the flowers." Lo's expression changed to shock and Gloria wasn't surprised when the next thing Hal said was, "I heard about you and Peter going your separate ways." He looked at Lo with gooey blue eyes. "I know, I mean I understand how lonely it can be. The ranch is a big place. If you ever—"

Lo cleared her throat. "Hal, I'm going to stop you right there. I appreciate everything you did on behalf of the school for Peter and I, but I am perfectly fine and can assure you I'm surrounded by too many good people to ever contemplate my loneliness."

Hal shrugged again. "I'm still in the house. It gets quiet, though."

The waitress arrived with three beers on a round black tray and carefully placed them on the table. "Hal, I brought you some pretzels."

"Thanks, Rita." Hal googled up at her. "Last one for me, I promise."

Rita gently touched his shoulder. "There's always tomorrow."

Hal suckled on the bottle like a baby and cast his eyes around the room. Lo took a long sip of her beer and ran the heel of her palm up the outside of Gloria's thigh. Gloria could see two men at the bar eyeing them with interest and she wondered where Kip and Mallory were.

Hal set his beer down decisively. "Well, it was nice seeing you again, Dolores. If you feel like a drink, you know where to find me. And good meeting you, ah…"

"Gloria," Gloria finished.

"Hmm, Gloria, yes. You too, with…I'll be seeing you." Hal braced himself on the table and stood.

"So long, Hal. Thanks for the beer."

They watched as Hal walked regally but unsteadily through the crowd, pausing to say hello to a woman in a purple shirt.

"Poor guy," Lo said. "He's aged ten years since I last saw him. This town is just a swirling soup of people, especially at

Rock's on a Friday night. I feel like the bread roll, just sopping it all up." She took another sip. "See, this is why I don't want to expose you to the small-town gossip. Instead of talking about Peter and me, it'd be you and me, and that is something I don't want for us."

Gloria pushed Lo's hair back behind her ear, revealing the small gold stud in her lobe. "Should we move to San Francisco?"

"Put some flowers in Hamlet's hair?" Lo smiled and moved her hand from Gloria's leg to begin peeling the label from her bottle. "A two-bedroom apartment, a room for you and me and one for Hamlet and Sonnet?"

Gloria nodded and rested her head on Lo's shoulder. Lo briefly leaned her head into Gloria's before they both straightened up.

"What about Kip, though? He'd have to come too. Better just to stay here, don't you think?"

Gloria formed a mental picture of Kip, Lo, and the horses all sitting on the sofa, watching television. "Good thinking, Ninety-Nine. Sonnet would be a terrible tenant."

"I just wanted to bring you out and show you some fun. Like Sue-Anne said, you're young and new in town."

In that moment, Gloria wanted more than ever to be at home, just the two of them, but they were here at the busy bar, so she said, "When did you start listening to Sue-Anne? And PS, I'm not that young."

"I try it every now and then. And PPS, compared to me, you're young." She finished her beer and said, "This could be my last trip to Rock's for a while, so what do you say we make the most of it and have a dance?"

"Are you serious?"

"Sure am. I don't want it to be gossiped about that Dolores don't know how to show a girl a good time."

They didn't hold hands and they didn't touch each other as they danced, but their eyes never strayed far and Gloria felt the energy coursing between them, setting them apart from Kip and Mallory and all the other people on the dance floor. Lo's body adapted to the music with the same grace it afforded everything else, and the fact that she had no idea how magnetic she was made Gloria all the more besotted. She wanted to take that pale face by its determined chin and kiss its beautiful mouth, she wanted to wrap her arms around Lo and touch her fingers to the damp skin beneath her fall of chestnut hair. It seemed she always wanted something she couldn't have. People knocked into them from all sides and someone stood on Lo's foot, then realized who Lo was and did a double take.

Lo's voice was breathy on Gloria's ear. "I'm going to visit the little girls' room. Sorry, awful euphemism, I know." Gloria reached out a hand but it was like trying to touch a goldfish in a pond. Lo was lost in the ripples.

"Is it time for a drink?" Gloria asked Kip and Mallory.

"Cocktails!" Mallory shrieked, making Gloria wonder if there was an off button. "Sex on the Beach! Come on, Gloria."

Kip looked at the ground and let Mallory drag him back over to the bar.

Gloria sipped on a nauseatingly sweet drink, half listening to Mallory's chatter as she scanned the room for Lo, wondering if she should go and check on her. There was probably a long queue for the bathroom. She rattled at the ice in her glass with her straw. After another minute, Kip, who was a good head taller than Gloria, tapped her arm and made a subtle pointing gesture. Gloria followed its direction and made out the copper crown of Lo's head above the crowd. She looked back at Kip and Kip gave an almost imperceptible shake of his head to indicate Gloria should stay. She trusted Kip; he was almost as protective of Lo as she was.

"They called me Celery at school," Mallory said, her eyes wide. She nodded emphatically. "They did. It wouldn't be so bad if my last name wasn't Salter."

Gloria burst out laughing and had to cover it with a cough and ended up dribbling orange juice. She was drunker than she realized. She wished Lo had been there to hear Mallory say that. She should find her. "Excuse me." She stepped around Kip and went to find Lo. Every time she thought *Celery Salter*, it was so ridiculous that she started grinning again.

Lo was standing by a high round table, talking to a neat-looking man of about forty with wire-rimmed glasses, wearing business attire. Lo was leaning in close, trying to catch what he was saying, one hand braced against the table. The man touched her wrist in a way that made Gloria's step falter and the grin fall from her face. Lo's shape, with its broad shoulders which hung a jacket so well and its long denimed legs which Gloria was touching only half an hour ago, was so familiar but so out of reach. What could she do? Go over there and interrupt? Demand an introduction with her presence? Although part of her was tempted to, she knew it would only make her feel worse to be introduced as Lo's friend, the guest staying out at the ranch. Lo crossed her ankle over the back of her other leg in a gesture that seemed so relaxed that Gloria stood, unable to move closer but unable to look away. It was good that Lo was talking to people; Gloria wanted her to feel comfortable. Lo's head tipped back and Gloria couldn't hear the laughter but she could picture it, and the man touched the small of her back, his hand lingering there. Gloria suddenly felt like a dirty secret.

"Excuse me, miss?"

Gloria looked up. "Oh, sorry." She moved aside to allow a stocky man with a square face room to pass.

"No, I meant, can I get you a drink?"

Gloria's mouth opened and she looked from the man to Lo and back again. "Sure."

"David." He offered his hand.

Gloria looked down at it before taking it. "Denise." She wasn't sure why she lied. She wanted to distance herself from the spite she felt, even as she embraced it by following David to the bar and accepting a beer.

"A woman who drinks beer, that's a rare find," David said, clinking his bottle against hers.

Gloria smiled, not quite meeting his eyes, and put her lips to the cool rim of the bottle. David was kind and polite, asking her questions and listening properly to what she said. He told her that he was involved in his family's canning business and that at the moment it was all about apples and cranberries, preparing for the holiday season.

"Denise," he said, making Gloria feel even more wormlike. "I just gotta say it, and maybe it's the Dutch courage, but you don't seem like most women." He blushed and looked down at his hand. "If you're not doing anything tomorrow night, would you consider going out for a drink? I know we're drinking now, but someplace else?"

Gloria couldn't take herself anymore. "David, thanks for the beer. I should actually find my—"

Before she could finish speaking, two things happened. She saw Lo and Kip walking toward her just as David leaned in to kiss her. She pulled back and apologized, putting the bottle down on the bar.

"No, I'm sorry!" David said, holding his palms up.

Gloria could see Lo's eyes flash with surprise and before Gloria could say anything, Lo had turned around and Gloria clutched David's forearm in apology and stumbled after her. She caught up to them outside. Mallory was trying to coax something from Lo who was looking stonily out into the street, but Kip was glowing with pride.

"Gloria, nicely done. David Strauss is a good guy. I'll set it up. What do you say, Dolores?"

"Seems Gloria doesn't need any help, she can figure it out on her own." Lo's tone was light but Gloria could hear the strain.

"It wasn't what it looked like. I was just talking and then…I said my name was Denise." Gloria rubbed her cheeks with the pads of her fingers, feeling trapped by Kip and Mallory's presence. She wanted room to explain.

Lo's movements were stiff. "Sorry, guys, I'm feeling beat. I think I'm going to head home." Lo leaned forward to hug Mallory.

Gloria felt awkward. She knew Kip and Mallory would think it was strange that Lo was making her own decision to leave without consulting Gloria. She could only play along so she said goodbye to them too and walked off with Lo, feeling the cold between them. Too late, she realized she'd left her denim jacket in the bar. Lo, who never missed a trick, stopped suddenly.

"Your jacket."

"I can get it next time."

"Don't be ridiculous."

Still Gloria hesitated, not sure if Lo would be there when she returned, but she could see by the set of Lo's jaw that Lo had made up her mind. Scuttling like a fearful beetle, Gloria ran back inside and gratefully retrieved her jacket from a kindly bartender, feeling weak with gratitude which only grew stronger when she saw Lo's solitary form in the street, her breath dancing in the darkness. Of course Lo had waited; she was decent and Gloria was not.

In the car, Gloria tried to explain to Lo's frosty profile but Lo asked if she could please just wait until morning. Gloria struggled not to cry, blinking back alcohol-infused tears. Why had she done that to Lo, given her a hard knock when all it would take was a feather touch to knock her down? Gloria rubbed her nose and tried to hide her almost sniveling.

Lo glanced sideways but not far enough to capture the sight of Gloria. "Don't cry. It's nothing to cry over."

Gloria had seen this side of Lo but never when she'd been the cause of it. "Lola, I'm sorry. It was honestly nothing!"

"Yeah, I know." The road had Lo's full attention, her movements purposeful. "Let's just go to bed and start tomorrow afresh."

"But you should never go to bed angry," Gloria said, reaching to push a strand of hair behind Lo's ear.

"No one's angry, Gloria."

"Okay." Gloria pretended to look out of the window, but she watched Lo in the reflection. It looked like she was on the other side of the glass.

CHAPTER SIX

It was dark outside when Gloria woke, too early even for the birds. Lo was still but Gloria could tell she was awake.

Gloria felt for Lo's waist, the incline to her hips, and shuffled closer to concertina herself into Lo's curled shape. She wrapped her arm around Lo's middle and kissed the nape of her neck.

Lo briefly squeezed her hand. "Gloria, Sue-Anne will be here soon."

Gloria slid her hand back and blinked sadly at Lo's gray T-shirt before rolling out of bed, stopping to pick her clothes up from the floor and going to the spare room, or her room, or whatever it was. She felt raw with lack of sleep but too alert to sleep. She tried anyway, lying in the cold narrow bed, feeling her goose bumps bristle against the sheets. On the opposite wall, the rising sun brought to life a painting of gun dogs splashing through a pond after flapping ducks. Gloria had never cared for the painting, showing the moment before the poor ducks' demise, but she knew Lo, who enjoyed hunting, had probably never viewed it that way. The sun stubbornly intensified against the curtains until she got out of bed and tried to revive herself with a hot shower. When she was feeling hurt, she was most sympathetic to her ex-fiancé, Mike, whom she had left before first coming to Wyoming. It made her feel close to him and conscious of the pain she had caused. The shower was like a tonic, warming her blood and bringing her to life. She put on jeans with the blue jumper with orange flecks that Sue-Anne had knitted her as a welcome back present. It was itchy around the neckline but was comforting. She almost bumped into Lo on the landing, heading to the shower. Lo didn't meet her eyes and Gloria went downstairs to make a hopeful cup of coffee in Lo's favorite gingham mug. She set it on the table at the place beside her own, on a coaster made of off-cut pine, bearing the ranch's brand. The kitchen clock ticked dolefully and Gloria strained for sounds of anyone. Eventually Lo appeared, her eyes still bearing the stubborn sooty marks of last night's makeup.

"Morning," Lo said without enthusiasm.

"I made you a coffee." Gloria patted the chair beside her.

"Thanks." Lo folded herself into the seat and wrapped her hands around the mug.

Gloria tapped her fingertips silently against her own mug, trying to find an opening into the conversation they had to have. "About last night, I'm sorry that I upset you. To be honest, I probably wouldn't have accepted a drink from anyone, it's just that I saw you talking to that guy at the table and the way he was touching you, I just felt like, well, like no one."

Lo looked at her for the first time. "No, I'm sorry too, Gloria. I shouldn't have left you with Kip. On my way back from the bathroom, I ran into Nick. He's an old friend, more a friend of Peter's than my own. It's been so long since I've seen any of those guys, before Terrence died, really, and now I never see them because their loyalty is to Peter. It's no excuse, though, and you're not no one." She let her knuckles fall to the table for Gloria to take her hand. "I think it was a combination of everything, running into Nick, seeing all these people I haven't seen for ages, being stared at, then seeing you talking to David from the stupid canning plant. It was a lot."

Gloria clutched Lo's hand. "I didn't think of that. I reacted out of jealousy but that's not how I want to be. In fact, I've never been the jealous type, ever."

"That makes both of us. You should be able to have a beer with anyone you choose."

"And you should be able to talk to anyone you choose."

Lo smiled thinly. "I know. I don't want to keep you in the shadows, but I can see I'm not ready."

"I thought you wanted to go out to Rock's."

"Only because I thought you wanted to. Next time, you and Kip go paint the town. I'll wait here to hug you when you come to bed."

Gloria smiled down at their hands. "I only want to be where you are." She met Lo's eyes. "Apparently, Mallory used to get called Celery at school. Celery Salter, that's her name."

Lo's brow furrowed and she laughed. "What? Celery Salter. I bet the kids didn't mean to in-Salter."

Gloria shook her head but she was grinning. "Can't you be Celery-ious for one moment? She told Kip and I at Rock's and I laughed and had to pretend to cough and spat juice everywhere."

Lo shook her head. "I'm sorry I missed that. You know I'm going to think Celery every time I see Mallory now."

"I know, that's why I told you. I can't stop it, it's running through my head all the time. Celery Salter."

They both turned to the sound of the front door opening and let go of their hands with one last squeeze. A few seconds later, Sue-Anne appeared, the tip of her nose red, her hello booming in the quiet kitchen. She had a string bag of produce over one forearm. Gloria stood up to help her.

Lo looked back over her shoulder. "There's fresh coffee, Sue-Anne. Come sit with us."

Gloria took a mug from the cupboard and filled it with coffee as Sue-Anne began taking groceries from the bag.

"Now, Beth has been puréeing veggies, even though I told her Hayley needs solids now, but she buys too much at once. So, here's a turnip—good for soups—and a bunch of celery."

Gloria put Sue-Anne's coffee on the table with a thump and she and Lo looked at each other and began to laugh. Sue-Anne looked from one to the other.

"There's some peppers too, Hayley won't eat it. What on earth is so funny?"

Lo had tears streaming down her face and she flapped her hand at Sue-Anne. "Nothing."

Gloria felt so bad for Sue-Anne that she tried to explain about Mallory-Celery but Sue-Anne only shook her head.

"I'm just glad you're wearing the sweater I knitted. That color is very becoming, Gloria."

Gloria wiped her eyes and tried to pull herself together. "Thanks, Sue-Anne, it's my favorite."

Sue-Anne ignored her coffee and began rifling through the fridge. "Good, I'm glad. I made Hayley a little vest with the leftover wool. Dolores, isn't it today you're meeting Claudette?"

Lo groaned. "I haven't forgotten. It's always so busy in town on a Saturday, I don't know if I can face it again. I should have told her to come here."

Gloria felt she knew why Lo hadn't asked her mother over—because she didn't want to explain Gloria. She could understand, but it was still a sore spot. "I had better go and get started with the horses," Gloria said, taking her cup to the sink.

She didn't wait for an answer or to give Lo a chummy goodbye. In the mud room, she pulled on her boots and coat and a faded blue baseball cap. The sun outside was dazzling against the glittering fields. There hadn't been any snow for a few days and there were spots where the ground showed through like gray shadows on the earth. Instead of fighting the cold, Gloria tried to embrace it, let it wake her mind and body. She could see Clarence bringing the tractor from the barn to take hay out to the cattle who were out by the stream as it hadn't frozen over. She gave him a wave on her way to the stables, but he looked away.

Hamlet, Sonnet, Firecat, Bugsy, and Freddy down the other end of the stable, were all rugged up and waiting eagerly for their morning feed. The stables were warmer than outside but it was still cold enough that steam rose from the horses' nostrils. Gloria fed them all and began cleaning out their stalls, starting with Freddy, wheeling the barrow full of stale sawdust back and forth to the muck heap. It was the closest she got to a workout these days.

It was after eleven by the time she had finished, and she was warm and hungry. She took Freddy out into his field to let him blow some steam off and watched as he hurtled around, skidding through the snow. She reflected that being a stallion must be a lonely life. Then she took the others out to their respective fields and let them go. Firecat was quick to skitter around, flicking up snow, but on the other side of the fence Hamlet stood waiting for more treats, and Sonnet and Bugsy watched Firecat's goings-on from a safe distance. Gloria walked back to the house feeling frustrated. She wanted to be doing something productive. She loved the challenge of a new horse. By the time she got to the house, Lo had already left to meet her mother and Gloria felt both sad and relieved. The kitchen was empty, so Gloria made herself a peanut butter sandwich and went to the living room to sit by the fire. Her skin tingled when she drew close to the heat, and she felt colder rather than warmer. She wasn't sure if Sue-Anne had left for the day or if she was burrowed away in another corner of the house. Gloria looked at the Christmas tree and remembered Lo's present. She hadn't drawn in a long time, but she set herself up with her watercolors and paper on the coffee table. Images stayed strong in her mind's eye, and even as dense jaundiced clouds rolled across the sun, dimming the light inside the room, Gloria's pencils created life on the page. She set her drawing to dry on the table and, feeling quite satisfied with the result, she poured herself a glass of red wine and sat on the couch to watch the fire. She had been so absorbed in her art that she hadn't given Lo and Claudette's lunch date much thought. She didn't want to find another reason to feel anxious after last night's hostilities. She wanted to feel connection to the world here like she had back home. She thought of her best friend June, who had been her sounding board since high school, and of Klaus, who was grumpy and strict but had offered her endless networking and socializing opportunities. She had even grown fond of Monica the surly groom, who had become instantly more pleasant once she realized Gloria was going to move to Wyoming and give her back her status as queen of the roost. She missed her parents and being able to jump in the car and meet friends for coffee or a beer. She missed the buzz at the stables with regular clients and the staff, but she realized what she was missing most was the ease of unfiltered actions.

She poured herself another glass of wine and watched the sun fight its way from behind the clouds. She didn't want to mope, she wanted to be grateful for what she had, so she got a fresh sheet of paper, folded it into a card size, and drew the view through the window of the snow-capped mountains and the pine trees with the sun striking the river in the distance. The cattle were tiny black splodges and the barn a bright splash of red. She would send it to her parents. For Klaus she drew Hamlet's head in a holly wreath. She was just wondering what June would like when she heard the rumbling of an engine and realized it must be Lo returning from lunch. She scooped up the drawings and paper and hastily shoved them under the couch and grabbed the drawing supplies, knocking her wineglass over. She dumped them all at the dry bar and took some paper towels and thanked her lucky stars that nothing had dripped onto the floor. She mopped up the wine and threw the paper towels into the fireplace and was sitting down on the couch as Lo came into the room.

"Oh, there you are." Lo went to stand by the fire and extended her hands toward the warmth. Her brows pulled together. "What are you doing?"

"Just sitting here where it's warm."

Lo looked at the empty wineglass. "Some lunchtime drinks?"

"Don't tell me you didn't have a wine with lunch?"

Lo huffed a breath out. "I had to endure that somehow. All my mother is interested in is rehashing the past. As if I'm not fully aware of what a fuck-up I am now, she likes to trot out my kid, my marriage, my career. It's like she's comparing me to my more talented sibling, only the former me is the sibling!" She went to sit on the armchair opposite Gloria so she could stay by the fire. "She was only slightly mollified when I told her I'd be taking on some work for Peter."

Gloria stood up. "Wine?"

"Yes, please. I think I need a cigarette or something."

"I can't help you there, but I can get you a drink." Gloria went to crack open another bottle of red. Seeing the tin of pencils and brushes, she rearranged some liquor bottles so they were mostly out of sight.

"It's okay, I have an emergency pack hidden in my desk drawer." Lo accepted a glass of wine. "Thank you, and don't judge me. I've managed to largely avoid cigarettes despite everything, it's just that my mother brings out the defiant teenager in me."

"By all means. I might even join you."

Lo looked at Gloria. "Will you?"

"Sure."

"Oh, god, you're the absolute best." Lo put her glass down on the mantel and scurried off to retrieve her secret pack of cigarettes. Gloria peered under the couch to make sure the drawings were concealed. She was curious about Lo's mother with her city boyfriend.

Lo returned, already pulling two cigarettes from the pack. She held the tip of one to the fire, then used it to light the next and handed it to Gloria. She took her wineglass and sank back into the armchair. As she took a deep drag, she watched Gloria and Gloria felt like her organs were yanked up an inch.

Gloria couldn't help staring. "How do you manage to be so good at everything you do?"

Lo exhaled. "Where were you at lunch when I needed a cheer squad?"

Gloria put the cigarette to her lips and drew back on it, her head instantly swimming. "I wasn't on the guest list."

Lo leaned forward and flicked her ash at the fireplace. "No, that's true. Should I tell my mother I'm a lesbian too?"

"She might stop worrying about what you did in 1985, but I'd probably go with bisexual."

Lo took a slug of wine. "I'm not sure that's true. I'm only into one person and that's you. Let's go label-free, shall we?"

Gloria smiled. "But you've made up your mind about working with Peter?"

"Well, I think it is an easy way to pick up work and start generating an income."

"Ouch!" Gloria felt that statement like a blow to the chest.

"Not you. Come here." Lo patted her lap and Gloria looked at her angrily before caving and going to sit on her knee. "You've just arrived," Lo continued. "It's my job to look after you. You'll find your feet. Winter is just beginning and things have shut down." She looked up at Gloria with her earnest autumn eyes and Gloria nodded, wanting to believe her. "I think you were right about having people over. How's this: I'll ring up every person I know from the dressage scene and we'll have a get-together." She pushed back a lock of hair that had fallen over Gloria's forehead. "I'll even call Caroline."

"Caroline Bandiana?" Gloria asked skeptically. She knew Lo hadn't spoken to Caroline since Terrence died when Peter had threatened to sue Caroline for poor training of Sonnet, the horse he had been riding.

"For you, I would speak to her." Lo leaned forward to set her wineglass on the table and take one last drag of cigarette before throwing it into the fire. Gloria felt every movement of Lo's body through her own, down to the little jerk as Lo flicked the cigarette. Lo wrapped her arms around Gloria's waist. Her breath was smoky but there was that ever-present hint of burnt vanilla and citrus.

"That would mean a lot." Gloria meant it. She put an arm around Lo's neck.

"She does have an old indoor arena. She's not on Klaus's level, but she knows Hamlet and she's a good trainer and she knows everyone there is to know on the dressage scene." Lo leaned her head into Gloria, nestling in below her chin and Gloria held her close. "We could put the horses in the trailer and take you over there."

"Will she want to make amends?"

"We can only ask. She is pretty stubborn and Peter was way out of line, but you'll need her as an ally if you want to get involved in her world. She often judges at events."

"I need to be doing something to feel like I'm moving toward a goal. I had this momentum with Klaus. Say what you want to about the man, he is a good trainer and he just sort of lends you this energy. I have to carry that through here and get something happening."

Lo worked her fingers into the band of Gloria's jeans to touch her skin. "Give Caroline a try. I think you'll win her over. She's a little abrupt, but you get along with all types."

"I'll make it work. Can we call her?"

"Now?"

Gloria stood up and took her wineglass to stand in front of the fireplace. "Why not?" She took a log from the basket by the fireplace and dropped it onto the fire. Orange sparks shot up toward the flue.

Lo looked at the phone on the side table. "There's no way she'll answer the phone on a Saturday, she'll be busy with the horses."

"Please, just try. We can leave a message."

Lo reached for the cigarette packet. "Gloria, I'm just calming down from dealing with my mother. Can we call her tomorrow?" She took a lighter from the packet and lit the cigarette then lay back into the chair and put her feet up on the coffee table. "My mother wants to set me up with her doctor."

"Let me ring her, then."

Lo looked surprised. "My mother?"

"No, Caroline!"

"Oh, if you have to do it now. Her number is in the directory there." Lo's fingers with the cigarette pointed toward the well-worn phone book. She took a gulp of wine as Gloria flicked through the pages. "You know, after you left to go back to Australia, I called once."

Gloria looked up.

"I found the number for Klaus's yard." Lo shook her head. "You answered and I...I hung up."

"You never told me." Gloria's hand had paused with the book held open. She blinked at Lo.

"I heard your voice and you sounded so far away. I had rehearsed what I would say to you but I was completely petrified. I just hung up."

Gloria stared for a moment. "I don't remember that. What would you have said?"

"Oh, I don't know. That I was sorry, that I missed you. I guess I wasn't ready, I still had a lot more work to do on myself before I could back those words up." The fire crackled and something burst, making Lo jump. "Anyway, you're here now. Go on, call Caroline. It looks like I might be at the office at least a couple of days next week, but Thanksgiving is coming up and I'll definitely be home then. It's just so I can get my head around what needs doing. I'm not going to abandon you every day, I promise, and it'll be good for you to be around a horse person."

"You're a horse person." Gloria felt like her own voice was far away.

"A real horse person on your level."

Gloria returned her attention to the book full of various pen scrawls in Peter's unimaginative round hand and Lo's familiar slant. There was Sue-Anne's writing, the pen pressed firmly into the page, and Terrence's attempts at numbers and letters. She found Caroline's number. Her first name had a red scribble across it and Gloria wasn't sure if Terrence had done it or Lo. She could feel Lo's gaze on her, but after a moment Lo stood to refill their glasses. She touched Gloria lightly on the head. Gloria slowly entered the numbers, an unfamiliar sequence to the phone numbers back home, and looked at Lo for reassurance. Lo winked and sat back in the armchair. Gloria listened to the ring tone, the wine making everything feel fuzzy around the edges.

There was the sound of someone picking up and a woman's voice said, "Hello."

Gloria's mouth opened and she looked helplessly at Lo, who flapped her hand and mouthed, *Say something.* "Hello, Caroline?"

"Speaking."

"Hi, my name is Gloria Grant and I'm staying at Heaven's End with Lo—Dolores—Ballantyne. She said, well, I'm looking for a dressage trainer and I—"

Caroline cut her off. "The Australian. Yes, I know who you are. Sorry, I'm booked out."

Gloria hadn't been expecting that. "If you could find an hour?"

Caroline interrupted again. "Not at the moment, sorry. Goodbye, Gloria."

Before Gloria could respond, the phone had gone dead. She slowly took the receiver from her ear and placed it back in the cradle. "I guess not."

"Don't worry, we'll figure something out."

Outside the wind had picked up, pulling at the bare branches of the fruit trees in the garden. Clarence's hunched form battled to close the big barn doors.

"I'm not giving up that easily."

"Ugh, I have reached my limit." Lo tossed the cigarette into the fire and stood to take her wineglass to the kitchen. "Have you had enough?"

"More than enough. I feel like I am the chimney." Gloria passed Lo her glass. "In fact, I think I need to brush my teeth."

"Let's brush our teeth and go to bed."

Gloria smiled. "It's three in the afternoon. Straight from teenage delinquent to old woman in need of a nap?"

Lo paused and ran her eyes down Gloria's length. "Oh, I have no intention of sleeping."

"In that case, I won't bother putting my pajamas on."

"Excellent decision."

Gloria's attention snapped toward the window. "I still have to put the horses away."

"We'll worry about that later. Come on, cowgirl."

CHAPTER SEVEN

In the morning, while Lo was still in bed, Gloria took her drawings from their hiding spot and looked at them again. She wanted to show Lo the cards she had made but she didn't want to give her Christmas surprise away. She took the supplies back to the spare room and hid them in the bottom of the wardrobe. The cards she tucked under a book on the nightstand to write when she had finished them all to post. Creating artwork had connected her back with her sense of self, reminding her that she had a connection with the world around.

The house was quiet. Even the wind, which had scuttered the garden path clear of snow, had stopped. Gloria lit the fire so that the living room would warm up. Seeing that the wood basket was low, she wrapped her robe tighter around herself and went outside to grab an armful of logs from the pile Kip had left on the back veranda. She knew no one else in this house would be mad enough to dash outside without shoes on, but there was no one to witness it. She tidied the living room and made some coffee. She missed the café lattes back home in Melbourne. She endured the taste of the ranch coffee rather than enjoyed it, but it was hot and strong and available. She pictured June saying, "Just how I like my men," and smiled to herself.

Lo was still in bed when Gloria finished getting dressed and Gloria called softly to her back from the doorway but she didn't stir. Outside, she could see Kip and Samuel walking to the barn. She yanked on her boots and grabbed her coat and ran down the path, hoping to catch them. She yelled as she ran, almost slipping on an icy puddle. Samuel turned, then Kip, and Gloria arrived at them laughing and panting.

Kip lifted his hat. "It's been at least three days since a woman has chased me down like that."

Gloria always felt her mood lift around Kip. "Oh, I don't know. Mallory"—she had to remind herself not to say Celery— "seemed pretty keen on Friday night." She bumped him on the arm with her shoulder. "Hey, Samuel."

"Morning, Gloria."

Kip wrenched open the side barn door. "She can near drink me under the table, but, say, what was up with Dolores?"

Gloria's eyes adjusted to the dimness in the barn as the overhead lights stuttered to life. "It may not have been the best idea, going to Rock's on a Friday night."

"She needs to get back around people again. You watch now, she won't leave her room today. She'll cry her eyes out all over again."

Gloria sent her mind back to Lo's sleeping form and thought how unusual it was that Lo who didn't sleep much was lying in bed after Gloria. "She was fine yesterday."

Kip shook his head. "She burns bright for a short while then she dims right down. Even now that she's leaving the house, big crowds don't jive with her. People are forever bringing up Terrence or they go the other way and avoid her because they don't know what to say. Gloria, help load that hay onto the back of the trailer."

Samuel set about coupling the trailer to the tractor and Gloria began lugging bales of hay over for Kip to throw onto the back. As she thought about the afternoon before, Lo coming home drained from lunch with her mother and hitting the wine bottle, she began to see the day in a new light.

Gloria paused for a moment to squeeze her hands open and shut and Samuel came to take over. "You need gloves next time."

She looked down at her reddened hands. She had been in such a hurry to catch up to them that she hadn't brought hers.

Kip's face was red. "Gloria, if you want to help us feed the stock, we'll finish loading here while you get your gloves. If you can do the hay with me, it'll free Samuel up to take out Freddy."

"Sure, I can do that."

All the way up the path, Gloria looked at the house, wondering if Lo was watching her through the kitchen window. She hoped Kip was wrong, but the house seemed to be holding its breath. The snow had been scoured from the roof by the high winds and the eaves were dripping with melting ice. Gloria skipped up the steps to find her gloves. She opened the door to the kitchen, hoping Lo would be at the table reading her briefing documents over breakfast, but she could see the kitchen was at she left it. She found her gloves on the bureau by the front door next to the red poinsettia that Sue-Anne had brought; they were much the same hue. She couldn't resist running upstairs to check on Lo. She let her feet fall heavily on the stairs, hoping to rouse Lo, but when she went into the bedroom, the blinds were still drawn and Lo was a curled lump under the bedspread. Gloria hesitated in the doorway, knowing Kip would be waiting, but she had a bad feeling in her stomach.

"Lo." She went to sit on Lo's side of the bed and placed a hand where she guessed Lo's hip was. "Lola, are you okay?"

Lo opened her eyes and looked at Gloria. She nodded. "I'm okay. I just feel tired."

"Do you want to help feed the cattle with Kip and me?"

Lo closed her eyes. "No, thank you. You go."

"Okay." Gloria lingered a moment longer, but when Lo didn't open her eyes again, she stood and walked back downstairs, hurrying more with each step.

The tractor was already grumbling outside the barn, the trailer stacked high.

"Get in beck!" Kip yelled from the driver's seat. "You can climb, can'tcha?"

Gloria hoisted herself up and sat on the carpet of hay bales, holding on to the rattling cage as they slowly headed toward the pastures. With the cold wind in her face and the sweet smell of homegrown hay all around, Gloria took in the mountains and the trees and the white fields. The idea of Lo going into town for work seemed unfeasible, but she knew Lo was the type of person who equated work with value. In the distance she could make out the dark shapes of cattle, who, hearing the clattering of the hay wagon, began to amble closer. She tried not to wish herself back at the house, but anxiety rode along in the trailer with her. As they rode up farther toward where the river slushed black and icy, Kip called back for her to start throwing hay down. The cattle flocked around, heedless of the tractor's steel power.

"How much?" Gloria yelled over the engine.

"All of it. We'll load up again for the horses." Kip drove forward and Gloria kept throwing biscuits over the side until he climbed down to help her.

Once the hay was surrounded by cattle, they motored back toward the barn again, the empty trailer bouncing along behind.

Gloria was chilled to the bone by the time they got back. The clouds had rolled in, bringing a gentle sifting of snow. She went to check the horses but she couldn't face the idea of going out again. She thought of all the times she had complained about cold back home and wondered what all the fuss had been about. Still, she guessed, cold was cold.

The house was heavenly after the biting air outside. The pipes groaned as Gloria filled the kettle. She took two pieces of bread and shoved them into the toaster, her hands inarticulate with cold. She held them over the orange heating element. She had a craving for Vegemite, but peanut butter would do.

Gloria took her plate into the living room where the fire was now cold ashes. She looked at it sadly for a moment, knowing what it meant, then arranged the kindling the way Lo had taught her. She sat and ate, each bite bringing her less and less satisfaction. The telephone looked blindly at her. The directory fell easily open at Caroline Bandiana's number. Gloria peered upward toward the bedrooms, feeling she was doing something wrong, but of course Lo didn't appear. Caroline's voice came to life down the phone line and Gloria opened her mouth to speak but soon realized she was hearing a recorded message. She left a brief message asking Caroline to call her and hung up. She sat back down on the couch with a thump and threw her crust into the fire. She felt too uninspired to finish her drawing and she knew that there was never an end to work to be done outside, so she went back out into the snow to work Hamlet and Sonnet in the barn.

That evening she tuned the radio in the kitchen to golden oldies and made spaghetti. She slid around the kitchen, bopping to "My Girl" by The Temptations as she set the table for two and, like an apparition, Lo appeared in the hall doorway, looking bleary-eyed and much like she used to when Gloria first arrived at the ranch. Despite willing her there, Gloria was surprised to see her.

"You've been cooking," Lo said, her voice rusty. She came to stand by Gloria who was filling up a pitcher of water. Her sweatpants puddled around her ankles and her top must have been an old one of Peter's.

Gloria put the pitcher down and her eyes glowed at Lo. "You're awake."

"I have those papers to finish for the morning. I'm sorry, I'm not very good company. Something smells delicious, though."

"I hope it will be. Come, sit."

Gloria dished out two bowls and placed them opposite each other at the large table. Lo picked hers up and took it to the spot beside Gloria's.

"I want to be next to you. I've missed you."

Gloria pulled their chairs in close. "I've missed you too." She poured two glasses of water.

Lo's hand shook as she reached for one. "Thank you, this looks wonderful."

"I helped Kip feed the cattle this morning."

"Did he put you up in the trailer?"

Gloria nodded. "I can't wait for calving season."

"You're turning into a regular little ranch gal, ain'tcha? Once the real snow hits, we won't be able to use the trailer, just the tractor or the Gator. If there's a blizzard, the roads will be closed off. You'll be stuck here with me. Can you handle it?"

Gloria looked out into the darkened skies as though a blizzard was already brewing. "Just you and me, I think I could handle that. What about the cattle?"

Lo spun some spaghetti on her fork and regarded Gloria. "They won't be invited."

Gloria rolled her eyes. "Do they stay in the barn?"

"Yes, they have shelter and that's not for you to worry about. Let Kip and Samuel and Clarence worry about that."

They finished dinner and Lo insisted on clearing up while Gloria went to phone her parents. Her father told her that she was about to be an aunt again. Gloria rarely saw her brother or his family as they lived thousands of miles away in Perth. She adored her little niece but found her sister-in-law overbearing. She always managed to interject Gloria's shortcomings into every conversation. Gloria's mother was beside herself with excitement, which again triggered the well-worn conversation around why Ben lived so far away, which of course created a new opportunity for segue into when Gloria was coming home. Lo brought her briefing papers into the room and sat on the couch, a smile playing on her lips as she listened to Gloria trying to convince her mother that she was happy where she was.

"Mothers, hey?" Lo said after Gloria hung up and slumped back into the armchair. "I've been relieved of the obligation to annoy adult children, but I can begin to see how the dots join."

"I am about to become an aunt again. So much easier to be a cool aunt than a cool mother, although I'm sure you never let a thing like motherhood make you sweat."

"Helps that I wasn't particularly cool to begin with."

Gloria smiled, glad Lo had found her sense of humor again. She just wanted to squeeze her sometimes, even though Lo was too aloof to court squeezing. Gloria wondered whether to tell Lo that she had called Caroline again but as Caroline hadn't responded, she decided against it. Lo put on her reading glasses and returned to her papers. After poking at the fire, Gloria retrieved her notepad to continue her business plan. It really all hinged on warmer weather and a better arena. Her eyes wandered to Lo, legs curled up, one elbow on the arm of the couch, and she began to sketch her instead.

Lo folded the first page of the document back on top and took her glasses off. "I'm going to go into town early tomorrow so I can get in there before the crowds. I feel nervous enough about starting work again, I'd prefer not to deal with a hundred well-meaning questions too. Don't look at me like that. I know I'll have to get used to it, but Friday night showed me that I'm not there yet. The only way I've been coping is by ignoring people, but I know it's not healthy."

"Is that why you've been in bed today?"

Lo's eyebrows lifted. "I must drive everyone crazy. I drive myself crazy!"

Gloria turned the notepad over so Lo wouldn't see the sketch and patted her knee. "You drive me crazy. Come here, I want to be Santa this time." Lo smiled and came to sit on Gloria's knee and they wrapped their arms around each other. Gloria breathed in Lo's shampoo. "Be gentle with yourself. For what it's worth, maybe you should start seeing someone again."

Lo leaned back to look at Gloria. "A shrink?"

"If you were your client, what would you say?"

"Ugh, I hate it when you're right." Lo ran a finger over Gloria's cheekbone.

"Do you want to redeem yourself over a game of cards?"

"There's no satisfaction there, you're too easy to beat."

Gloria wriggled her knees side to side, making Lo sway. "Can you think of any other satisfying ways?"

Lo bent forward to kiss her mouth then cupped her face. "I have spent many hours thinking of those satisfying ways, however I feel too nervous about tomorrow."

"Do you want me to come in with you?"

Lo laughed and hugged Gloria to her. "That is a sweet offer, but I'll be okay."

"Will you think about it?"

"What?"

"The shrink."

Gloria heard Lo's lungs empty with a sigh. "Yes. I'll give Doctor Linley a call tomorrow. I'm going to take up swimming again. I need something solitary that isn't lying in bed all day. Or maybe running. Both."

"Okay, Miss Wyoming," Gloria said. "What's the brief about?"

"There are four here but they're not long. They just talk to the various cases Peter has coming up. He told me to pick a couple to take on as he's booked out. I'm thinking I'll go with the embezzlement and the contract breach. I don't want to deal with the family court."

Gloria grimaced. "Maybe you should take up cake decorating instead."

"I tried baking, remember? I have neither the passion nor the skill. It'll be okay. I've always enjoyed work. I'm like a dull cart horse that needs to be shackled to a plow."

Gloria laughed. "We already have one of those. Hamlet has been shuffling around like he's sleepwalking. I gave him a dig with the spurs the other day and he just farted, didn't even bother to speed up."

"I'll try not to be so vocal in my apathy."

CHAPTER EIGHT

Kip negotiated the icy roads while Gloria marveled at the landscape which was completely altered from the last time she had traveled the highway. The green fields were now white. Mounds of snow sat atop the fence posts and everything was hushed. The pale sky was almost the same color as the ground it lay upon.

"Everything looks so closed off now. Even the pastures have shut for winter."

Kip waved to the driver of an oncoming truck. "That's Ethan Priestly from town, which reminds me that I have to be back by twelve for the forecasting meeting."

"I don't think we'll be long."

"How does Dolores feel about you seeing Caroline? See that's her place up ahead."

Gloria sat up straighter and cleared a spot on the window to better look through. "She doesn't know."

Kip shook his head.

"Caroline doesn't even know."

Kip sucked in his cheeks and made a popping sound with his lips.

"Well, she wouldn't answer my calls."

"All I can say is that I'll have the truck turned around toward the road so we can make a quick getaway."

"You're not coming in?" Gloria took hold of Kip's elbow. "I thought you could be my icebreaker, you know, talk me up a bit."

"Gloria, you know what separates a steer from a bull?"

Gloria let go of his arm and flopped back.

"Yeah, well, I'd like to keep mine." Kip indicated left and turned onto the tree-lined drive that led to the long house that sat in front of a cluster of buildings. A dirty smudge of smoke from the chimney was the only sign of life. True to his word, Kip turned the truck around so it was facing the road and grinned at Gloria. Gloria scowled at him and slammed the door, instantly regretting it as a bird startled from a hanging feeder on the front porch and flew skyward. Gloria cleared her throat and rang the doorbell. It made no noise, so she pressed it again.

"I can hear you!" came a voice from beyond the door as the latch scraped back. A figure appeared beyond the screen door. "You're not that annoying Australian are you?"

"Yes, hopefully not annoying."

"Well, you just slammed your door loud enough to scare that finch off my feeder."

"Caroline, may I please come in? I promise that's all the slamming I'll do today."

Caroline opened the door and stepped back. "You're also letting all the cold in."

Gloria wondered if Kip had heard the conversation. If so, he was probably warming himself with laughter.

The front door opened straight into a living area with jumbles of furniture spread across the red rug like an antique obstacle course. The walls were just as cluttered, with various framed art works, many paintings of horses or livestock, and the occasional photo. Caroline was not a big woman, and she walked with a stoop but she had a fierce look about her. Her hair was shades of soft gray and her eyes were a sharp blue. The source of the chimney smoke was a fireplace flanked by two red velvet armchairs, one of which contained a sleeping cat. There was no television.

"I would ask you to sit down but Cleo looks quite happy. You can just as easily do your spiel standing up, I suppose."

Gloria took that to be her cue. Fortunately for her she was used to Klaus's dismissiveness and his arrogant clientele. "Caroline, the reason I'm here is that I've moved into Heaven's End and I've been training Hamlet, and to a degree, Sonnet, for the best part of a year and I need a good trainer. I thought because you know the horses and you coached Dolores that you might consider taking me on."

"As I told you on the phone, I'm not taking on new clients."

"Caroline, would you please reconsider, just this once?"

Caroline shook her head. "Things ended badly between the Ballantynes and myself, and if there's one thing I hate, it's drama."

"Would you see me ride? Just give me one shot. If you still think I'm not worth investing in, then I'll leave you alone."

Caroline looked at a stack of envelopes on an oak bureau. "I don't need to invest, I have enough students."

Gloria had one trump card left in her pocket. "Not like me you don't. I'm Klaus Hofmann's protégé."

Caroline squinted at Gloria. "What are you doing here then?"

Gloria's eyes slid to a portrait of a young woman holding a rose. "Love. I came here for love."

Caroline rolled her eyes. "Well, that was stupid, wasn't it? All right, Love Fool, I'll give you half an hour on my mare. If you can get anything out of her, I'll think on it."

A smile flew across Gloria's face. "Thank you!"

She waited while Caroline pulled on a jacket covered in cat hair then spent another few minutes searching for her sunglasses before locating them the pocket of her jacket. She put her scarf on and marched Gloria outside where Gloria had to rapidly plead her case to Kip, who looked boot-faced but didn't protest.

"Your behind all the way to Diamond Rock River for Keaten Preston?" Caroline vaguely waved at the truck. "Could find better suitors queuing to pay a fine at city hall."

Gloria didn't make any comment as she crunched her way along the path to the stables.

Caroline gestured around the neat stable block with the names of horses painted in pale blue script on plaques on each half door. "Here you go, Love Fool. It's not fancy like what Klaus must have. Not sure what you heard about me, but I'm about the holistic approach, horse and rider. I like my riders to sit quiet on a horse and not interfere." She stopped outside a stable door that read *Rarity*. "This is Rarity. She's an old gal but she still knows all the tricks. You'll find her gear on the peg in there. I'll see you in the arena in ten minutes. I'm going to need a thermos of something hot if I'm going to sit and watch you. You want me to bring your fella in?"

Gloria was patting Rarity's gray face. "He's not...no."

Caroline was already walking away.

Rarity was almost as large as Hamlet but finer boned. She was patient with Gloria and stood four-square by the mounting block while Gloria climbed up. Gloria kept her moving at a brisk walk around the arena while she waited for direction from Caroline. Lo was right, the arena was old and in need of resurfacing, but at least it was sheltered. The mare had a fluid stride and she listened well enough to Gloria's aids. Caroline sat on a folding beach chair at the end of the arena with her thermos and said nothing. Realizing that Caroline was merely going to observe, Gloria made sure to warm Rarity up before she asked anything of her. Where Hamlet was obedient if unimaginative, Rarity twitched away from Gloria's leg and overinterpreted signals to mean something more than they were.

Caroline leaned forward in her chair. "You ask for collection in the trot, she gave you passage. I told you, I like my riders quiet in the saddle. You ask for too much."

Gloria felt uncomfortable in her jeans on an unfamiliar horse who clearly wasn't happy. The mare's white tail swished and her canter was choppy. Eventually Gloria slowed her to a walk and returned to where Caroline was sitting.

"Klaus lets his golden girl ride around like a mannequin placed on a horse? Being quiet doesn't mean stiffening up like you're made of plastic."

Gloria patted Rarity's neck. There was no point arguing. "She's a lovely horse. I'm sorry I didn't do her justice."

"I trained her but she's an old hand. She anticipates the answer before you've asked the question. Still, if you're a big deal like you say you are, you should be able to adapt to any horse you're on."

Gloria slid down and Caroline stood slowly and with effort. They began walking toward the stable, Caroline swinging her thermos by her side.

Gloria looked at her watch. She had forgotten poor Kip. "Caroline, I really have to go. Will you work with me?"

"Go put her away and make sure you pack up after yourself. The Monday morning arts show started five minutes ago on the radio and I make a habit never to miss it." Caroline turned and waved over her shoulder.

Gloria stared after her but could see it would do her no favors to make Caroline late for the radio program, so she took Rarity back to the stables and made sure she was rugged properly and left things as she'd found them. When she got to the car, Kip was pacing back and forth, about ready to shout. Instead, he clenched his fists and raised them to the heavens.

"Sorry, Kip. I promise I'll make it up to you. I'll do all your chores for the rest of the day."

"You're going to do the forecasting with the accountant and create a new budget based on predicted yield?"

Gloria was careful not to slam the door this time even though the finch hadn't returned. "No. But I'll help you fix the spotlights on the Gator and I'll do the horses' breakfasts every day this week. Oh, it's nice and warm in here."

"You can also tell Dolly that I was an ignorant and unwilling party in this excursion."

Gloria drew a smiley face on the window. "I'll definitely tell her the ignorant part."

"I mean it, Gloria. I don't want blowback from this."

"Okay, okay."

As soon as they got back to the ranch, Kip hurried off to get ready for the appointment and Gloria went to check that the horses were okay and look at the list of odd jobs on the whiteboard in the feed room. If she could cross off all the ones she could do today, maybe she wouldn't have wasted Kip's time. She wasn't sure yet if she'd also wasted her own.

Lo was already sitting at the kitchen counter, helping Sue-Anne chop vegetables by the time Gloria came in with Kip for dinner. Lo winked at Gloria while Sue-Anne was wrestling a chicken into the oven and Kip was helping himself to a beer. Outside, the sun had begun to melt down the horizon, falling from the clouds for the first time that day.

"I was telling Gloria she needs wraparound sunglasses. Snow blindness is a real thing, ain't that right, Sue-Anne?"

"I'll fetch you some from the store tomorrow," Sue-Anne said.

Gloria didn't bother protesting. She knew once Sue-Anne had a mind to provide, she would. "How was your first day back, Lo?" she asked instead.

Lo puffed out her cheeks. "I got through it, that's probably what I can say about it."

Kip took a chunk of carrot from the tray Sue-Anne was about to put in the oven and bit into it. "How was Peter?"

Sue-Anne was saved from scolding Kip by her interest in the situation. "Was it like old times?"

"I'm not sure which of the times you're referring to, Sue-Anne. He was civil. We spoke for a while about what I was willing to take on and what he felt I could do, then I went into my old office and he stayed in his and we both did our work. I said bye on my way out."

"Give it time, honey. Things will work out the way they were meant to," Sue-Anne said.

"Yes, exactly." Lo turned to Kip. "Is that bottle of white still in the fridge?"

"I'm off now," Sue-Anne announced. "I've set the timer on the oven for the roast. Don't forget like that time you let the beef go dry, Dolores."

Lo rolled her eyes. "One time, and I still ate it."

Sue-Anne left and Kip said he'd prefer to go home and eat something from the freezer than wait for Lo to burn the chicken, so he took a slice of Sue-Anne's spiced apple cake and put his jacket back on. As he slid the door open, he gave Gloria a meaningful look which meant he wanted her to tell Lo about Caroline.

As soon as Kip shut the door behind him, Lo tipped her head back and let out a long breath. "If Sue-Anne is going to interrogate me every evening, I may have to let her go."

"She'd still keep coming back."

Lo took a sip of wine. "I know. I've tried to let her go. She won't."

Gloria went to check the timer. "Thirty-seven minutes. I'm going to have a shower. My back is aching and I can't get warm."

"Okay, my beauty. I'll try not to burn anything."

On her way through to the bedroom, Gloria stopped to listen to the voice messages on the machine. There was one about accommodation during the ski season but nothing from Caroline.

At the table that evening Lo carved herself a generous portion of chicken. "How I'm going to eat a whole chicken on my own, I have no idea."

Gloria had been unusually quiet, stifled by the words she had to say but couldn't.

Lo put the knife down. "Gloria, are you all right?"

Gloria kept her gaze steady. "Yes."

Lo helped herself to salad and pushed the servers around the bowl toward Gloria. "Are you worried that I won't cope with work?"

"Not at all." Gloria took a gulp of wine. "I made Kip drive me to Caroline's today."

Lo's hand paused on the pepper grinder. "So that's why the little rat didn't want to wait for dinner. I thought it was weird he would opt to eat leftovers." She picked up the pepper grinder and cracked it over her vegetables. "Why didn't you tell me you wanted to go?"

"I don't know. I tried calling her but she didn't pick up, so I thought it might be better in person."

"And was it?"

Gloria's mouth twitched to the side. "I still don't know."

Lo picked up her knife and fork but her attention was on Gloria. "I don't get why you didn't tell me."

Gloria crushed a roast potato with her fork. "I didn't want to upset you."

"Nothing's really changed has it? You don't trust me to manage my own emotions, like I'm a child."

Gloria felt her stomach drop. Her head tipped to the side. "I was scared. Just as your emotions are yours to manage, so are mine."

"That's fair but, at a minimum, truth is the ground on where all else stands."

"Is that written in a courtroom somewhere?"

"No, but there would be a whole lot less divorce if it was understood at the beginning of a relationship."

Gloria finished crushing the potato and moved on to cauliflower. Too easy a target. "We can't even be honest with people about our relationship."

Lo reached for her wineglass. "I knew you'd say that. It's not the same thing. I'm in a relationship with you, not with Joe Blow from the store."

Gloria didn't want to fight. It brought to mind tensions between her parents at the dinner table, her mother tired after work coming home to a messy house, her father not caring about the messy house. How she had tried to make herself small and stay out of the line of fire. The cauliflower gave way under her fork and she speared a crescent of tomato instead. "It doesn't matter anyway. Caroline didn't think much of my riding." She scraped the tomato from her fork with her teeth and bit down decisively.

"Did you take Hamlet with you?"

"No, she put me up on Rarity. She didn't go so well for me."

Lo's head pulled back. "She's not an easy horse to ride."

"You've ridden her?"

Lo nodded. "She taught me all the dressage movements. She's a good schoolmaster."

Another tomato fell victim to Gloria's spear. "And then you taught Hamlet. The circle of dressage life."

"I can't take any of the credit for Hamlet. Anything he does well is in spite of me, not because of me. What did you think of her setup?"

"Like you said, it's a bit run-down but it was bliss to ride under cover. Maybe she'll let me hire the arena if she won't take me on."

Lo swallowed a mouthful of chicken. "Did she mention me?"

Gloria peered into the salad bowl for more tomato. "She said she didn't want drama."

Lo laughed. "Did she say that about me?"

Gloria shrugged. "I believe she referred to 'The Ballantynes.'"

"I guess I don't blame her. I'm changing my name back anyhow." She scooped up her tomato wedge and plopped it onto Gloria's plate.

Gloria looked up. "What is your maiden name?"

"Anderson. I'm sure she'll call you, don't worry."

Gloria tried the name in her mouth. "Anderson. Dolores Anderson." It was plain, but Lo was one of those people who needed no adornments. The more she dressed down, the more obvious her beauty was. To Gloria, anyhow.

"Actually, this chicken is a little dry. I'm a terrible cook. It's almost a crime to ruin Sue-Anne's preprepared meals, but somehow I manage it." She poked fretfully at a drumstick. "Thanksgiving on Thursday. Don't let me near the turkey."

"This Thursday?"

"Of course," Lo said.

"You haven't said much about it."

One corner of Lo's mouth lifted and she pushed her knife and fork together. "The holidays are scaring me a bit. Thanksgiving, Christmas, it's all about children and family. I don't want to be a downer for anyone or a reminder of sadness."

"What do you usually do for Thanksgiving?"

"Well." Lo looked down at her plate and picked up her fork to toy at the drumstick she'd discarded. "The family. Of course, usually there's Peter and Terrence." She put the fork down again and placed her hands in her lap as though she'd been caught doing something naughty. "My mother. Last year she brought Casey. Kip most years, but Sue-Anne and Samuel will be with their own families. That's it." She looked up. "We could do something, you, me, Kip, my mother, I guess."

Gloria smiled. "I'd like that."

CHAPTER NINE

Gloria spent Tuesday ducking in and out from the stables, checking to see if Caroline had rung, but the only messages were regarding ranch accommodation for the ski season. Lo was resolute she didn't want any guests until the new year, and she and Sue-Anne began a game of hide-and-seek with the booking diary, which Sue-Anne kept putting by the telephone and Lo kept finding hiding spots for: the desk drawer, the shelf under the coffee table, anywhere but where it could be used for its purpose.

On Wednesday, despite Lo's assertion that she was a terrible cook, she came home from work with a tub of cranberries and a desire to cook cranberry sauce from scratch. Kip had sourced a turkey from his friend who owned a turkey farm and refused to even let Lo see it lest she should burn it with her gaze. Sue-Anne left them with piles of vegetables and strict instructions with cooking times down to the minute.

The idea of meeting Claudette made Gloria feel nervous and excited. Lo hadn't said much more about her mother coming other than Claudette was known for her pumpkin pie. To Gloria, who had never tasted pumpkin pie, the two became intertwined. Claudette, who sounded sweet but a bit much, seemed too similar to the idea of the pie. Lo was quiet and terse when Gloria tried to ask her how the day had been, so Gloria let Lo toil away at her cranberry sauce and instead went to help Kip fix the spotlights on the Gator as she'd promised she would. Kip made her drill through the grill and screw the new lights on while he drank a coffee and pointed out imperfections in her work. He hadn't quite forgiven her for making him wait at Caroline's.

"You know, we need to talk about a wage for you," he said once she'd finished.

"A wage?" Gloria asked, standing back to admire her work. "Look at that. It's beautiful."

"Yeah, sure. Isn't that why you're here? I mean it's a condition of your green card or whatever, right?"

Gloria dusted some metal filings from the hood. "I guess, I mean…" She glanced up at Kip but she couldn't read his expression.

"Unless there's some other reason you're here that you want to tell me about?"

Gloria felt heat rise to her cheeks. "I should probably talk to Lo first. About the wage, I mean."

Kip held out his hand for the drill. "Course, no problem." He looked as though he might say more but he returned his attention to the Gator.

Gloria followed the countless footprints back along the path to the house as the sun's dying rays struck the curve of the land. In the kitchen, Lo's cranberry sauce was cooling on the stove top and the counter had been wiped down. Gloria went through to the living room, and as she walked past the telephone she saw a scrap of paper with a message written on it. *Gloria, Caroline Bandiana called.* Gloria felt suddenly afraid to hear Caroline's verdict. She stared at the digits of Caroline's phone number and she didn't recall telling her fingers to move but the phone was ringing on the other end and Caroline's voice came clearly down the line.

After Gloria rang off, she sat looking into the glowing embers of the afternoon's fire. She prodded at it with the poker, then threw a log on top, then another for good measure. On the mantel was a black-and-white photo of the ranch when the house was smaller and the path was only what was worn into the ground by boots and hooves. Three men on horseback were in one corner, caught midstride through the long grass, mountain bound. Gloria was struck by the many lives and events those mountains had witnessed. She was part of the story, but a blade of grass in the great big plains. She walked upstairs purposely and Lo was lying on the bed, facing the doorway, the covers clutched in a knot under her chin. Gloria went to sit beside her and smoothed the little hairs away from her temple. Lo moved a hand to the inside of Gloria's knee.

"Do I need to beat Peter up?" Gloria asked.

Lo nodded into the pillow. "Yes."

"Is work too hard?"

"Yes."

"Do you want to quit?"

"No."

Gloria sighed and folded herself around Lo. "I didn't think so."

"I love it, but I find the interactions so difficult, and Peter and I keep setting one another off." Lo sniffed.

"That's understandable, it's all new." Gloria waited for Lo to go on.

"He doesn't give me much, but today he smiled, and he looked so much like Terrence that it just brought those feelings back."

Gloria's lungs palpitated an extra breath. She wanted to know which feelings Lo meant and she didn't want to know. "You've known each other almost your whole adult lives. There'll always be something there." She tried to keep the resigned regret from her voice because she didn't regret Lo's love for anything, not really.

"Those were easier times, when Peter was cheerful and I knew how to make people happy. I used to stand in front of people and have the right words, now it's like there's empty space in my mind where there used to be matter."

Gloria took her hand. "The words are right there, you're using them now."

Lo raised Gloria's fingers to her lips. "With you. What did Caroline say?"

"She said her arthritis has flared up and she can't take on any more clients."

Lo kissed the back of Gloria's hand. "I'm sorry, my love."

Gloria breathed deep. "She also asked if I would be interested in taking on her existing clients for the meantime and helping out at the stables because her usual stable hand has moved away. Apparently she is friends with Fiona Hammond, who trained under Klaus. I broke in both of Fiona's horses and brought them on into the young horse division. In Caroline's words, I must be less incompetent than I look."

Lo wriggled from Gloria's embrace and sat up. "That is a big deal!"

Gloria laughed. "Not really."

"Oh, honey, after a full day with Caroline, you'll realize that it is." Lo pulled the floppy neck of her sweatshirt back over her shoulder. "I'm sure we have some nice champagne somewhere. Come on, let's take a celebration where we can. Tomorrow we'll have Claudette and Casey and who knows who else and we'll give thanks for what we have, but tonight let's drink to you. We have to get you up in the truck now so you can have some independence." Lo's eyes were lively and she was out of the bed before Gloria stood. "Up. Oh, I know what I have. Peter gave me a bottle of something French that a client gave him. He announced at lunch today that he doesn't drink anymore."

* * *

The next morning, stumbling around the stables, shoveling manure into a wheelbarrow, Gloria could only think that Peter was on to something. Sonnet had no respect for Gloria's hangover and tried to nip her on the arm when she was fixing her hood. Kip was in and out of the house fifteen times, checking on the turkey, and Lo was bustling around, suddenly concerned with smudged windows and dust on the skirting. Gloria had wanted to appear bright and likable to Claudette, but when Kip walked in ready for dinner, freshly showered and smelling of cologne in his neatly pressed blue shirt, Gloria felt worse for wear. Lo had put on a dark gray woolen dress which looked quite un-Lo-ish but Gloria could only assume was something her mother had bought her. Gloria went into an internal panic that her sweater knitted by Sue-Anne with her jeans—at least they were clean—wouldn't stand up to scrutiny. Madly, she rifled through the clothes she had brought with her from Melbourne, which weren't many as she had decided she was a whole new person, and pulled out the same black slacks and black top she always wore when she didn't know what to wear. She wriggled into them thinking that she was lucky the old her had hesitated at throwing them out and that the old her really wasn't that different from the new her after all. She had no shoes to wear, so she went and took Lo's black ankle boots. She looked away from her own reflection feeling less than tip-top and reminded herself that she was Lo's friend, a friendship struck up that had led to a second visit, that was all. It made her feel even more stifled than she already felt. Omitting the truth was one thing, but outright lying was another. The doorbell chimed and Gloria gave herself a stern look in the mirror then tried on her smile. "Oh, why, hello," she said, imitating Lo's accent. "How I love your pumpkin pie! Just so sweet." She grinned and shook her head at her ridiculous reflection. There were footsteps and voices downstairs. It occurred to her that if she didn't hurry up, she would be making a grand entrance down the staircase like some type of debutante dressed for a funeral. When she peeked from the landing, the living room was empty. She tried to step lightly down the steps, but the boots fought her every footfall. Fortunately, Claudette, Casey, and Lo had congregated in the dining area, admiring the sharp blue day through the windows where the sun struck every glistening grain of snow, sending shimmering arcs of light across the room. Lo turned toward

Gloria, her face painted in a river of rainbow. Part ice queen, part faery. Claudette turned around to see what Lo was looking at, and the rainbow was gone.

Lo's introduction was assured and professional. Gloria shook Claudette's hand and had her arm pumped by Casey, a tall thin bald man wearing a vest and tie. In Claudette, Gloria could see Lo's bone structure and the haughty tilt of the chin, but Claudette's orderly features had been given the passionate strokes of the artist on Lo's face. Claudette was dressed in a periwinkle blue shirt and a black woolen skirt that showed off her still slender legs. Lo suggested they go and sit in the living room, and as they filed through the hall, Gloria noticed the absence on the bureau of the photo that Kip had taken last summer of Lo driving the pickup truck, one arm hanging out of the window, looking back grinning while Gloria stood up on hay bales in the back, wearing what she called Lo's "cowgirl" clothes: shirt tied at her waist and denim shorts and boots. Gloria could bring that moment to her mind's eye as vividly as if it had happened that day. The smell of warm grass, Lo beginning to unfurl her petals in the sun of Gloria's love, looking at her with a smile that lit Gloria up like she was the only star in the galaxy.

"So, this is your first Thanksgiving dinner, Gloria?"

Gloria looked away from that empty space on the bureau and into the wintery eyes of Claudette. "Yes. Lo tells me you make a fabulous pumpkin pie. I look forward to trying it."

Claudette laughed, a disconcertingly similar laugh to Lo. She paused in the entrance to the living room. "Dolores refused to eat it as a child. She had some idea about jack-o'-lanterns being squashed into a pie. Remember that, Dolly?"

"No, it was after Jeremy Foster up the street dared me to eat a piece of the jack-o'-lantern that had rotted on their porch. I couldn't look at pumpkin for years."

Claudette went over the fireplace to study the photo of the ranch. "What possessed you to eat that thing, I'll never know."

Lo's voice was soft. "I was a kid. It was a dare." Her gaze slid over Gloria and she turned to fix them some drinks.

"It's amazing how much the ranch has changed," Gloria said, keen to steer the conversation to neutral territory.

Casey went to place a hand on Claudette's back. He peered at the photo. "I bet this place is made out of those pines."

"Much of it, yes," Lo said. She held up two wine bottles. "Red or white?"

There was the sound of Kip's boots clipping across the floorboards and he appeared in the doorway. "Have I missed anything?"

"Oh, Keaten!" Claudette said, her voice immediately growing playful. "Good to see you."

"Miss Claudette, Happy Thanksgiving. I must confess, I could smell that pie as soon as I came in." He kissed Claudette on the cheek and shook Casey's hand.

Gloria and Lo looked at each other. Gloria could see Lo's mouth twitch and she had to look away. Gratefully she accepted a glass of red from Lo and took a sip to hide any smiles.

When they were all seated, Casey turned his hawklike gaze to Gloria. "So, Gloria, how do you fit into the picture here?"

Gloria wasn't expecting such a direct question and she quickly dredged up her friendship story, but Kip jumped in for her.

"Gloria here is a wonderful horsewoman. She was so great with the horses over spring that we wanted her back, so she's come to stay. Ain't that right?"

"I'm not sure about the first part, but it's so beautiful here and Kip has taught me a lot about horse training. Dolores was so hospitable—"

Claudette laughed. "That surprises me. Dolores was going through such a tough time, we won't talk about that, but I suppose it is different from whatever activities you're used to in Australia. Not really the season for it here, though. I can't imagine how you fill your days."

Lo cleared her throat. "We're lucky to have Gloria here. She's highly sought-after. In fact, she's going to work primarily with Caroline Bandiana, taking on her students."

Claudette squinted. "Caroline Bandiana?"

"She trained my horses."

Claudette opened her mouth and looked at Kip for backup. "The woman who trained the horse Terrence was riding? Well,

I'm not sure why you would have anything more to do with her."

There was a silence that was eventually interrupted by Kip exclaiming that the turkey must be ready. Lo's expression was blank and Gloria could see her receding into herself by the minute. As they filed into the dining area, Claudette leading the way, Gloria ran a hand across Lo's back. A tension groove had carved its way along Lo's jaw. When she shot Gloria a look, her eyes were full of anger.

As Kip was reverently placing slices of turkey on plates, Lo madly sipped on her red wine and Claudette noticed that Gloria's plate only held vegetables.

"You don't like turkey?"

"I'm a vegetarian, but it looks wonderfully cooked. At Christmastime my mum always complains that it's difficult to get turkey right."

"Are you one of those animal activist types?" Claudette blinked at Gloria.

Gloria spoke hastily, aware of Lo opening her mouth to say something she might regret. "Not really, I've always loved animals and I made a choice years ago. Veggies are great anyway."

Casey threw his hat into the ring. "You're missing out on the homegrown beef."

Claudette placed her hand over Casey's and looked at Lo. "Doll, he is still talking about that barbeque we had in July. Only the other day I heard him telling the O'Briens about it, didn't you, honey?"

Casey nodded. "Oh, yes."

Just as Gloria thought the meal couldn't get more awkward, the front door slammed and everyone swiveled to see Peter enter the room in a navy overcoat, his blue eyes bright with cold. Before he could finish unfurling his burgundy scarf, Claudette stood up to welcome him with open arms. Gloria looked at Lo, who had surprise written on her face, but there was also something else: guilt. Peter came to kiss Lo on the cheek and then Gloria. He took a seat next to Casey and Gloria stood to help Kip create another placing, then they each gave a thanks. Gloria felt her voice was not her own, and she said how grateful she was to be at the ranch and how welcomed she had been made to feel. When Kip offered Peter a glass of wine, Peter merrily accepted and Gloria wondered what happened to his alcohol abstinence.

"Thank you," she said as Kip offered her Lo's cranberry sauce, even though she had no turkey. She wanted to leave the table, go outside, and ride out over the new snow into the cold, feel a more pressing sensation that would override the dread she was feeling now. Canter into the bracing wind and let her mind rest from the conflicting emotions. She tried to be present, listen about the work Peter and Lo were doing, pay attention to Casey's stock market tips, answer all of Peter's questions about the intervening months, but her heart was heavy. Kip's expression was soft when he looked at her, but she looked away, unable to take it. Claudette was beaming now, finding the positives in everything and Lo seemed to relax.

As soon as the pie had been eaten and vigorously praised, Gloria excused herself under the pretense of checking the horses. Lo touched her knee under the table but Gloria ignored it and went to change into her outdoor clothes. She went out through the laundry and tramped her way through the barren garden, not wanting to see another person. Hamlet and even Sonnet greeted her with enthusiasm and Wilbur the dog came from the barn, stretching as though she'd woken him from a long sleep.

"Ah, my horse-people." She rubbed Sonnet's forehead under her hood and fed her an apple she had taken from the fruit bowl.

Hamlet rattled his door with his teeth to get her attention. Sonnet had tired of Gloria's fussing anyway. She scratched Hamlet behind the ears and kissed the soft skin between his nostrils. Gloria looked through the stable doors out into the glistening day. It was a day for riding. She went to get Hamlet's gear and saddled him up, leaving a rump rug on him so he wouldn't get cold.

The freedom of open spaces, Hamlet's snort as the cold air entered his lungs, helped calm Gloria. The snow was thin enough on the ground that the track was visible and the only sound was the striking of Hamlet's hooves against the hard ground. He was a cold-blooded horse, bred for these winters. Gloria, thin skinned and not made for Wyoming winters or motherly inquisitions, needed to pick up the pace, warm her body, and clear her mind. Full of feed and kept indoors, Hamlet was happy to oblige, cantering until they lost the fence line and found the thickets of trees. Cattle came eagerly, looking for fodder or excitement. Hamlet, who had seen them countless times, suddenly decided they were an alien species and arched his neck, jumping sideways away from them. Reluctantly, Gloria turned for home, the shadows already lengthening like spilled ink.

CHAPTER TEN

Gloria timed it well enough that Claudette and Casey had left but, to her surprise, Kip, Lo, and Peter were in the living room drinking whiskey. Lo had produced one of her post-Claudette cigarettes and was standing by the fireplace to use it as an ashtray. Peter sat beside Kip on the sofa with his feet up on the coffee table. Gloria's hair had curled with moisture and her cheeks and nose felt red. She felt even more separate and desperate-looking in her farm clothes beside this elegant trio.

"Gloria, come stand here." Lo beckoned her over by the fire.

Gloria held her tingling hands toward the heat and Lo slung a casual arm around her shoulders. Gloria could smell whiskey on her breath and feel the wool of her sleeve against her neck.

"Gloria," Peter said a little too loudly. "It seems you have a lot of talents. Lo tells me you managed to get Caroline to take us off her hit list. I always felt bad about the way I reacted but she's such a prickly person. All's fair in litigation and war. I thought she'd hate us forever."

Gloria wasn't sure what Peter was even doing there, like he still owned the place. "She is okay with me, but for all I know, she still hates you."

Lo snorted, which turned into a cough and her hand slipped from Gloria's shoulders. Peter looked at Gloria in surprise, but he smiled. "You may well be right." He turned to grin at Kip. "I like her." He beamed back around at Gloria. "Ever thought of being a lawyer, honey? With that sharp tongue all you'd need are a few cocktail parties with the right people under your belt. Dolly, remember the parties we used to have when we lived on Tyne Street?"

Lo exhaled a ribbon of smoke toward the ground. "That was a long time ago."

Peter wasn't to be deterred. "Even at the ranch in the early years. Kip, that time Maurice Eild insisted on showing off his riding skills and was bucked off into the rose bushes? The courtroom smelled like a distillery and Maurice had a scratch running right between the eyes. Bill Palmer opened his mouth for his closing argument and a belch came out. It was chaos but Dolly stood there, giving everyone her ice maiden impression until Maurice brought the room to order. Kip, did that plant ever flower again?"

Kip laughed good-naturedly. "Takes more than that to kill one of Sue-Anne's rose bushes. There sure have been some good times over the years."

"Ah, but the sand keeps slipping through the hourglass. Times change, don't they?" Peter drained the last of his whiskey. "Life has a way of taking intentions and turning them into surprises. This week has been one heck of a ride. Dolly helped me settle a case that was looking like a stalemate. I'd almost forgotten how she has this way with people." His eyes were bleary and he shrugged. "I honestly thought I'd never see the woman I married again."

Lo puffed her cheeks out and stared at the ground like she was counting the fibers on the rug. Gloria just wanted the day to end.

Kip looked from Peter to Lo to Gloria. "Pete, I'm heading into town to do some visiting. I'll drive you home."

Peter looked at his watch then glanced up at Lo. He seemed to waver in his decision before setting his glass back on the table. "Sure, Kip. I guess I drank too much. Just enjoying fine company and a celebration for our little win this week." He stood up and went to kiss Gloria on the cheek, then Lo. Lo stood close to Gloria, their shoulders touching. "Dolly, if you drive my car in to the office tomorrow, I'll drop you home after work."

"We'll figure something out," was all Lo would commit to.

Peter stopped in the doorway, looking at a new floor lamp that Lo had put in the corner to brighten up the room in the winter months. "I like it," he muttered.

They heard the sounds of the men putting on coats and then the heavy front door opening and closing. Lo passed Gloria her whiskey. Gloria took a sip then handed it back and went to sit on the couch. The seat was still warm from Peter.

"That was a bit weird."

Lo tossed the cigarette into the fire and went to sit beside her. She slumped into the couch with her head flopped back and stared up at the wooden beams of the ceiling. "Being friendly postdivorce seems harder than being enemies."

"If you're working together, you can hardly be enemies."

Lo turned her head to look at her. "The amount of messy divorce proceedings I've been witness to, I should be grateful things didn't get too ugly."

"He wants you back."

Lo's eyes were solemn. "Gloria, don't."

Gloria shrugged. "Doesn't take a clairvoyant to know that. I've never seen Peter so messy."

"He's my colleague now, nothing more. The separation was his decision too, not mine alone." She sat up and reached for the cigarette packet on the table. "Is that why you left after lunch?"

"There was no need for me to stay. I hate pretending to be your friend or some hick from down under who has come to work with the horses." Gloria hadn't meant to sound so harsh but found as she said the words, she meant them.

"I'm sorry, I don't want to hurt you, you're not a hick from down under, you're my sweetheart, but I don't know what to do." She took Gloria's hand, pressing her fingers against the plastic of the lighter. "This is why I've tried to keep my mother separate from you."

Gloria looked down at her chapped hand in Lo's silky palm. "Yeah, well, you might find it easy to turn our relationship on and off like a tap, but all this pretending is starting to feel like it's not."

Lo threw the cigarette and lighter back onto the table and took hold of both of Gloria's hands. "My feelings aren't pretend." She shook them. "Hey, look at me."

Gloria reluctantly met her eyes. "I don't want to be a dirty secret when the love I have for you is pure." Gloria could almost see her love for Lo like pure white light in the form of a heart, alkaline, clean, shining like pearl. It radiated through her, liquid in her veins, aura in her lungs. Her eyes grew moist and her face screwed up with her sudden baring of the soul.

"Oh, my little romantic, come here." Lo pulled her into a hug. "Peter and I were broken long before you."

Gloria let go first. "Did you know he was coming?"

"Not really, I mean I did mention that he would be welcome, but he said something about seeing his brother and I thought that was the end of it. I was as surprised as you."

Gloria doubted that. The effects of the huge meal, tense relations, and frosty ride were taking their toll. Outside, the sun was beginning to lower its rotund form into the trees. Gloria yawned. She had told Caroline she would work her horses tomorrow and had agreed to show Kip that she could manage the truck on the icy roads by herself. She squeezed Lo's knee.

"It doesn't matter anyway. Let's clean up the kitchen and let the afternoon put some distance between lunch and dinner."

CHAPTER ELEVEN

Christmas was pulling them closer to its frosty embrace and to Gloria everyone seemed preoccupied with their own affairs. A few times she'd asked Lo to meet her in town for lunch but Lo had been apologetic about being too busy. Despite the long days that Gloria was putting in with Caroline or her students, she still tried to help around the ranch, but Kip seemed preoccupied and rushed. Relations were not improved when he filled the barn with extra hay and told her he had to be blizzard ready so she could no longer use it to ride in. It made more sense to move Sonnet and Hamlet to Caroline's anyway as she was spending more and more time there. She had to admit it was easier with Caroline's arena and, after an initial upset and return to her old vicious ways, Sonnet accepted her fate as long as she knew Hamlet wasn't far away.

Caroline was different to Klaus but their work ethic was the same. Gloria took on most of Caroline's less advanced clients and worked her horses and, when Caroline was up to it, she would coach Gloria on Hamlet or Rarity. Any time Gloria made an error or underperformed, she called her Love Fool and made her canter serpentines with simple changes on each bend because Rarity particularly detested it and would give Gloria a hard time. Caroline loved comparing Gloria's talent, or lack thereof, to her nephew, Oliver, who lived in Iowa and apparently rode like god's gift to dressage. Gloria was sick of hearing about him and Caroline knew it so she tested Gloria's patience and manners on the subject, ascribing to some philosophy on mental willpower. Gloria had to work her own horses, because they were hers as much as Lo's now, before her workday started or on her lunch break if she could get one, and she was often so exhausted when she sat down to dinner that holding a knife and fork seemed beyond her. Lo was usually just as late; her idea of part-time work was long hours at the office, which only increased the more Gloria was occupied. Gloria felt that the story that they had made to explain their relationship to others was becoming true. They barely had time together and much of it was spent preparing for the next workday. Gloria was used to working through the Christmas period as it was usually a busy time with horses, but she was looking forward to a couple of days break around Christmas to spend time with Lo. As brief as their time was in the evening, there was so much to say. Lo wanted to hear how Gloria was getting along with Caroline and how the students were going, and Gloria was endlessly fascinated with the legal upsets of the community. Sue-Anne was less than impressed with the both of them, worrying that they were wearing themselves out, particularly Lo, whom she liked to keep an eye on. Gloria felt most of Sue-Anne's fussing was because she was missing having their company at mealtimes, but Lo didn't want her driving back and forth in the winter weather so she banished her, apart from the two days she did the housework.

Both Gloria and Lo were trying to reinvigorate their careers and it was taking all their energy, but Gloria was thrust back to the spring when she'd first met Lo and the times spent together were parceled out into little bursts of heaven where Gloria would will time to stand still. Gloria knew how precious they were, and she spent every moment present and appreciative. It felt like she was back there, her heart bursting with the privilege of sitting beside Lo as Lo chewed buttered toast and read the morning paper with a crumb sitting gloriously on her chin just for Gloria. In those moments that were as everyday as they were intimate, Gloria understood the pain of losing someone you loved most. Sometimes in the evening, they would sit and muster interest for the late news or a comedy special and Lo would hold Gloria's legs on her lap, absentmindedly stroking them as they tried to eek another few minutes from the day. Her hands would pause, caught up in what she was watching, before she'd huff with laughter or shake her head at some horrible event on television and then her hand would resume its pattern. It was their own private world and Gloria didn't take it for granted because she felt it was only just in her grasp. Any further upset might send it crashing to the floor. They were used to long hours, but Gloria noticed chinks in Lo's armor. Often Lo wouldn't sleep or she would drink to put herself to sleep, delaying the insomnia by an hour or two. It seemed she had found another way to stop herself from feeling and that was to never give herself a spare second. Somewhere in the desert of the midnight hours she must have walked the tightrope of emotions, but if she did, she kept it to herself. Still, she tried for Gloria. She took up swimming at the Y, made sure she had a coffee with Gloria before she left for Caroline's, and often brought home flowers or a cupcake from the bakery. These efforts were not lost on Gloria, who looked for evidence of life in their love. She could endure a lot but to be emancipated from Lo's heart would be to have the door of the inn shut in her face. She could handle the manger as long as Lo was with her.

Gloria had sent off her handmade Christmas cards and finished the watercolors for Lo, getting them framed in town. She wasn't sure if Lo would like them, but it was too late now; she had nothing else to give her.

Kip was on constant blizzard alert, preparing the ranch for heavy falls and deep snowdrifts. Gloria knew if they had weather like that no one would be taking their horses to Caroline's and she wouldn't be expected to visit the regulars she had picked up, which required a juggling act of vehicles. They were putting off buying another car because Gloria was earning pocket money. Although Caroline's pupils were initially skeptical, most people had warmed toward Gloria, and she was feeling the beginnings of community. When clients heard that she was living at the ranch, she would see their faces become doughy with sympathy and their voices would slide downward to end on a quavering note. It was the questions they didn't ask that were most telling. She had a glimpse of what it must be like for Lo, to have her son follow her almost more insistently in death than he had in life.

The morning of Christmas Eve snuck up on Gloria like it always did. It seemed to be so far in the distance and suddenly it loomed. As soon as Gloria stirred, Lo was awake, her eyes snapping open, immediately alert. The one blessing of their early mornings was that the threat of Sue-Anne arriving before they were out of bed was gone. Gloria felt they should be able to do what they liked in their own home but she had let it be; there was no point spending their time together arguing.

The digital clock on the nightstand said 5:03 and before Gloria could bring herself to peel back the covers, Lo was already pulling on sweats over her swimsuit. Gloria watched her, the familiar transformed in the half-light. The unapologetic way the firm muscles clung to her bones, her skin shaded with dawn shadow. Gloria loved that stubborn boyish body, just as she loved that quick but stubborn mind. It scared her slightly, that she could need something that could neither be tied nor corralled but rather kept free of will by her side. She liked doing that sometimes, watching Lo in the true skin of self. Often Lo would lapse into pensive moments, pulled into herself by her thoughts, lost with her gaze in the distance, her face softened into an expression that it reserved for those moments. Now, though, she was all brisk, businesslike movements, already impatient with the day. Gloria knew her mind would be running through all the things she had to do, ordering them into a timeline of priority, her day a running sheet to tick off. Gloria's own day was more loosely encapsulated, driven by the changing moods of nature: the horses' feed times, the weather, client bookings, the drive to Caroline's. Gloria extended her legs to the still-warm spot where Lo had been lying. A bed wasn't Lo's home, she was too restless and full of purpose. Often Gloria would wake in the night to feel Lo loosening the covers to go wandering, or if Gloria was in a deeper sleep, she would wake to find a cool vacancy beside her. Unlike Gloria, Lo was unafraid of meeting the morning cold.

"Are you getting up?" Lo asked, alert to Gloria's movement. "Yes."

"You want a coffee?"

"Yes," Gloria said again, stupid with sleep.

Gloria sat at the table with her hands wrapped around a mug, a last five minutes before she landed in the world outside where Kip and Samuel would already be bustling around and horses would be banging impatiently on stall doors for breakfast. Lo touched a hand to Gloria's head as she rounded the table with her gym bag over one shoulder, her keys already in hand.

Gloria tipped her head back to look up at Lo. "What time will you be home?"

"I'm going to leave early, promise. Can you get away from Caroline's to meet me in town for a late lunch?"

Gloria was surprised. "Sure."

"Come pick me up from the office and we'll go to the diner. I was thinking we could pick out some presents for the ranch hands and Sue-Anne."

Gloria nodded. "Kip's got his eye on an embossed browband for Bugsy from the saddlers."

"Good thinking."

Gloria watched Lo's shadow slip out the door behind her. Without giving herself time to think, she took her dishes to the sink and grabbed the bag of almonds that Lo had left for her and filled her thermos with hot sweet coffee. Sometimes things felt almost normal and sometimes she missed home, June, her family, and even Klaus so much that it brought her to tears.

CHAPTER TWELVE

Gloria sat in the bland comfort of the office waiting area along with a man in a gray suit who was leafing through some papers. At the end of each page, he would raise his finger to his mouth with a little flourish, lick it, and turn the page decisively, making a near inaudible grunt of satisfaction. Gloria was so absorbed in watching him, it was only when he looked up at her that she realized Candice, the receptionist, was telling her that Lo was in a meeting and wouldn't be long. Gloria made sure to redirect her gaze to the art on the walls. There was the alpine slope that Peter's mother had painted and another of a pink sunset over the mountains, surely the work of the same hand. The details were created in broad strokes, not the minute shading that Gloria favored for her own work, but the colors were bold and so lifelike that they gave the image power.

A woman came through from the corridor and went to speak to Candice, who asked after her grandchildren. Gloria listened with mild interest as the woman explained about the struggle of having daughters who were feuding at Christmastime and how she just wanted one Christmas where they could all enjoy one another's company. Candice made sympathetic noises as she set up another appointment. Lo appeared in the doorway and motioned for Gloria to come through into her office.

"Sorry, honey," she whispered. "Give me five."

Gloria sat opposite Lo, looking around the sparsely furnished space. Lo's desk was stark, no photos or personal items, only framed certificates hanging on the walls. It struck Gloria that, like at the ranch, there was no evidence that Terrence had ever existed.

Lo settled her glasses on her nose and began furiously tapping on the keyboard of her computer. The phone rang and she stared at it a moment, her fingers still rattling, before answering it in one swift motion. She looked at Gloria but her face bore the passive expression of someone imbibing information. She said yes twice, then smiled and said she would put the caller through to reception. She began hanging up before she'd even said goodbye.

She looked at Gloria properly this time. "If it rings again, I promise not to answer. You look beautiful, by the way." She returned to her typing.

Gloria had been feeling very unbeautiful in her riding clothes and big brown coat next to Lo in her black contoured dress with threads of silver through it. As though Lo had read her mind, she looked up from the keyboard and said, "You're like a breath of country air in here. Did you get a ride in with Kip?"

"No, he was busy. There's a branch down over the fence in long meadow but Samuel brought me in on his way home."

"Never a dull moment. Someone needs to tell the cattle that it's the holidays. Come on, let's go."

Gloria was relieved. She was too scared to look at her boots in case they had manure on them. Lo slipped into her jacket and they left without bumping into Peter.

No matter how often she left a warm room to go outside, the cold still shocked Gloria and she stuffed her hands into her pockets. The street was busy with last-minute shoppers and there was a line of cherry-cheeked children and impatient parents coming from the toy shop where Santa sat on his holly-decked throne. They crossed the road to avoid the congestion outside the post office and Lo pretended not to notice two women waving at her. She looked instead into the keen wind from the mountains that was snapping her coat and tugging at her hair. The diner was busier than usual, and they waited to be seated. This time Lo could not evade the well-wishers. As always, she smiled graciously and introduced Gloria, although now Gloria was finding some faces were familiar. She knew Hilda and Reg Brown from the grocery store and some of the clerks from the bank. In the background, crooners sang the joys of Christmas on repeat, and the sound of the till and the door jangling open and closed played backup. The waitstaff wore red hats with white trim on their heads and one waitress, having the audacity to have perspiration on her face in this weather, wiped down a newly vacated table by a window so that they might sit. Lo slid into the booth and seemed to hunch down. Before the waitress could leave, she asked, "What's the soup of the day?"

The waitress looked around. "Uh…oh, it's tomato with a side of herb bread."

Lo looked confused for a moment, then said, "Sure. Gloria?"

"Just give me a mushroom omelet with a side of spinach, thanks." One side of Gloria's lip curled up. "You in a rush or something?"

"It's a big day. Lots to do."

"As long as the browband is still there we can get it for Kip, and I know Sue-Anne loves that homewares shop where everything looks off-white."

Lo peeled her coat off. "How do you know all this?"

"Intel gathered from conversations in the barn or kitchen."

Lo briefly took Gloria's hand and squeezed it. "You've obviously been listening." She glanced over Gloria's shoulder. "There's Janis again. I just finished a meeting with her. I couldn't get her to leave. Peter charges the minute anyone goes over time, but I don't have the heart anymore."

Gloria snuck a glance and saw the woman who had been at the office. "I heard her telling Candice about the rift between her daughters."

"Why she doesn't staple a poster to a pole, I don't know. It would save her a lot of time."

Gloria grinned. "You're awful."

Lo rolled her eyes. "I have a professional and personal policy on gossip. I don't want to feature anywhere in the supply chain. I've known some lawyers who have shared confidential information in a CLM."

"What's a CLM?"

Lo smiled. "A Career-Limiting Move. Plus, you know how I feel about people talking behind my back, so why would I do that to anyone else?"

Gloria could see how seriously Lo took privacy. Her respect for both her own and that of others was immense. Gloria was grateful for Lo's integrity even as she pushed against it, wanting her expressive freedom.

"It's too loud in here to spread gossip anyway. Something smells good though...coffee and cinnamon?"

Lo took an appreciative sniff. "Yes, maybe gingerbread? I would love to be one of those women who makes neat gingerbread houses."

"I think I'm one of those women who likes eating gingerbread houses," Gloria said, staring longingly at the pretty little houses in cellophane behind the counter. "They remind me of Hansel and Gretel. I had a picture book as a child and I was too scared to read the story, but I used to cover the words with my hand and look at the picture of the gingerbread cottage."

Lo was staring at her with her head tipped to the side. "God, I love you, you strange girl."

Gloria almost fell into Lo's dark pupils, like warm pools of calm desire. "I love you too, Miss Wyoming."

The waitress brought them back from the plane they were on by delivering their food. Gloria tucked into the fluffy omelet and buttery mushrooms, realizing how hungry she was. "I think I'm going to have dessert too. I can't stop eating in this weather."

Lo tore some bread off and dipped it into her soup. "How about I buy you a gingerbread house and we get going?"

Gloria's chewing slowed, then she swallowed a lump of mushroom. "It's Christmas Eve, can't Peter do without you for a few hours?"

Lo reached across and stole a mushroom from the edge of Gloria's plate. "Peter's not my boss."

"I know," Gloria said, offering Lo a forkful of omelet. "It's just that you've been working so hard and not sleeping, and well, it's Christmas."

"All of those things are true, that's why I took the afternoon off to spend with you. So, eat your lunch, and then I'm taking you somewhere."

A slow smile spread across Gloria's face. "Are you? Where?"

Lo raised her eyebrows and took a bite of Gloria's egg before passing the fork back. "You'll find out soon enough."

Gloria ate quickly and forwent a second cup of coffee. As promised, Lo paid for a gingerbread house and Gloria ummed and ahhed over the one with the blue frosting shutters or the house with the little green trees and eventually chose the green trees. Before they left, the cashier gave them each a red-and-white-striped candy cane. Out on the street, they crossed the road again and Gloria put the gingerbread house in the car so it wouldn't be ruined. She tried asking Lo again where they were going but Lo pretended she couldn't hear her. Lo linked her arm through Gloria's as they battled the wind along the main street.

"In here," Lo ushered Gloria into the beauty parlor.

"Here?" Gloria asked, balking in the doorway.

"Both of us. Get in there."

Gloria walked in, conscious of the dirt under her nails and her wind-burnt face. She had never paid much attention to the salon on her trips to town, but it was bright white inside with peach-colored seats in front of mirrors, a glass chandelier hanging from the center, nail stations by the window, and hair washing sinks up the back. Lo spoke to a blonde who told them to have a seat in the chairs in front of the mirrors. Gloria slipped out of her jacket and looked across at Lo as they both sat down.

"Bubbles?" the woman asked, clasping her hands together.

"Yes!" said Lo. "Times two."

"What are we doing?" Gloria hissed.

"Everything."

Gloria accepted a glass of champagne and regarded her reflection. She had to admit she looked like someone who had been outside in the elements spending more time with animals than people. Despite the weather or because of it, her nose was sunburnt and her cheeks were red.

A young woman with hair streaked the color of wheat came up behind Gloria and floated a black cape across her shoulders and clipped it at the nape of her neck, then she pulled the hair elastic from Gloria's ponytail and fluffed her hair out with her fingers, all the while staring at Gloria in the mirror.

"Hello, Gloria, I'm Laura. What are we going to do for you today?"

Gloria blinked against the bubbles rising into the back of her nose. "My hair? Ah, a trim?"

"Sure. How much would you like off?"

Gloria indicated to just above her shoulders.

"We can do that. You have a lovely rich color, but how about just a touch of red as a base under the black? It'll just add a little shine in the light."

Gloria glanced across at Lo, who smiled.

"Okay, why not?"

"Help yourself to some magazines on the ledge there, and I will mix that up for you."

Gloria thanked her and listened to Lo describing exactly the layers she wanted in her hair. "Oh, you know how I usually have it," she told the woman.

"Absolutely, Doll, I do." The woman called for Laura to mix her a color also. "Are we doing manicure and pedicure today?"

Lo nodded. "We are." She looked at Gloria. "Both of us."

"Aren't you two adorable? I'll tell you what, once we get that color in, we'll get you straight over to the nail technicians while it sets." She looked over to where two women were attending to clients at the nail station. "We have been so busy today. Doll, I can't say that it may not be because of you."

Lo almost choked on her champagne and waved her hand in front of her face. "Helen," she eventually spluttered.

"Oh, sorry, honey, let me get you a tissue."

Laura returned with the colors and Gloria relaxed as Laura began painting the mixture onto her head. Lo's eyes closed and a soft smile stayed on her lips. Gloria watched her indulgently. How had she gotten here, in this place, orbiting this burning star? She let Laura carry her champagne flute over to the nail area and she picked a glittery gold because it reminded her of a Christmas bauble. Lo picked a shade the hue of holly berries called Dare To Be and they sat down, feeling fun but ridiculous with their heads in wrap and their finger and toenails being painted.

By the time they left, Gloria wasn't sure if it was the bubbles or the varnish fumes, but she was feeling lighter. Her newly washed and blown hair bounced in neat waves that framed her face and her nails shone in the sunlight.

"This way, honey." Lo took Gloria's elbow and steered her down the street. "We're not done."

Gloria had stopped questioning. She thought back to the woman she had first met at the ranch last spring, who was thin and bitter and living in the shadow of life. Still, Gloria had seen through that to Lo's steely resilience and sharp wit below. Now, this elegant, expensive-looking woman looked so different on the outside but Gloria knew she was the same reasonable, intelligent, kind person she always had been. Like a tree turning its leaves in autumn, letting them fall and regenerate, it was just the seasons of life changing through the weather.

In front of the clothing boutique, Lo briefly took Gloria's hand and led her inside. "New clothes. Choose whatever you want."

"Is this my Christmas present?"

"No."

"Can we afford it?"

"Yes."

Lo went straight to say hello to Cathy, the woman who owned the store. Gloria remembered the last time they had been in the store. The feeling she had that day, Lo just venturing out in public again, just being in her presence. That feeling hadn't entirely gone away, but now she felt Lo's love, steadfast and sure against her. With the sound of Lo and Cathy's chatter in the background, Gloria went to choose new jeans and an olive-green sweater so she could give the one Sue-Anne had knitted a rest. Cathy went to assist a customer who was buying a gift and Lo came to see what Gloria was choosing.

"I like that sweater. Get the dark purple one too, it suits your coloring."

"What about you?"

Lo crinkled her nose. "I have too many clothes. Now, let's choose you a party dress."

"A party dress?" Gloria asked uncertainly.

"It is the party season. I like dressing you up."

Gloria wasn't convinced that she'd have much call for a dress, but they did have such pretty things. She let Lo rifle through the rack.

Lo stood back with her hands on her hips. "No, I'm thinking black. A little black dress. What do you think?"

Gloria shrugged. "I like black."

"This blue dress is neat, but it's not wow, is it?" She turned gratefully to Cathy. "Cathy, we need a party dress for Gloria."

Cathy's eyes twinkled. "I know what you like, Dolores, and I think I have something that would suit Gloria. Give me one minute."

Gloria's attention was taken by rubber boots and Lo continued assessing the other dresses. Cathy returned, beaming, with a black velvet dress draped over both arms.

"Just came in today. I ordered some pretty things in for New Year's parties. This should fit."

"Go, try it. We want to see how it looks."

Gloria took the dress from Cathy and locked herself in the change room. She held the dress up against herself and ran her fingers along the velvet. It had been a long time since she'd gotten dressed up. In fact, since she'd been out with Lo, Peter, and Mike last spring. She began to peel off her winter layers and shivered her way into the dress.

"Here," Lo called. "Try it on with these." A pair of shiny black heels were shoved under the door.

Gloria slipped into the shoes and looked at her reflection. The dress had wide straps that came down to a blunt neckline. It hugged her body, ending at mid-thigh. There wasn't much of it. Gloria wasn't sure.

"Come on out," Lo called, then said something to Cathy that Gloria couldn't make out.

Gloria hesitantly opened the door, pulling the hem down as much as she could, but she needn't have worried. Lo's eyes shone when she saw her.

"Oh, yes," Lo said softly.

Cathy came to adjust the shoulder strap. "It's very becoming on you, Gloria."

Lo was nodding. "What do you think, Gloria?"

"I'm not sure where I'll wear it."

"You'll wear it," Lo said assuredly.

"Will I box up the shoes too?" Cathy asked.

Lo was quicker than Gloria. "Yes, please."

Gloria was feeling a bit puzzled about Lo's sudden desire for them to be made over. Back in the change room, she sniffed under her armpit—no, all fine—and ran her hand along her thigh—a bit bristly but passable—and could only surmise that she had been in a self-care slump. Perhaps Lo was feeling fitter since she'd taken up swimming, and she was putting on makeup and nice clothes for the office. Gloria pulled her comfortable warm clothes back on, noticing Rarity's gray hairs all over her breeches. Okay, she could definitely try a little harder. No wonder Lo was choosing Peter's company.

On the way home, Lo hummed happily to herself, their Christmas shopping on the seat between them. Kip's browband was in a gift bag from the saddler's, and they had found a porcelain angel holding a pink rose that was just the type of thing Sue-Anne would love for her cabinet. She watched over the gingerbread cottage wrapped in cellophane. On Gloria's lap sat the pink paper gift bag containing her shoes and clothes, including the dress, which was folded on top of everything.

"Now," said Lo as they turned through the ranch gates. "What you're going to do is go straight inside with the clothes and leave the rest to me. I'm going to pour you a glass of something nice and come up to our room, just wait there."

Gloria looked at Lo. "What is going on?"

"Look at this beautiful blue day. You're home for Christmas and it's our first together. I want it to be special." She parked the truck and picked up the items on the seat between them. "Now, be a good girl and do what you've been told."

A crease formed between Gloria's eyebrows, but she allowed Lo to usher her inside and straight up to their bedroom.

"Do you want to have a lie down?"

Gloria put the bags on the foot of the bed. "I'm not a toddler."

Lo placed the rest of the presents on the floor beside the dresser and came to wrap her arms around Gloria's neck. She kissed her lips. "I would never ply a toddler with alcohol. What do you want to drink?"

"Do I have to stay here?"

"For five minutes, yes."

Gloria sat on the edge of the bed and looked at the little pine cone sitting on Lo's nightstand. Beside it was Lo's half-drunk glass of water and a book called *Ruminations on Morality* that she must have begun in the night because it was now on top of *Art and Meaning*, which she had been reading the day before. Since cracking her shell painfully open, she refused to let her time be wasted. Even her insomnia was a chance for productivity and learning. Gloria picked the book up and began reading the back cover but outside there was the humming of a heavy engine and men's voices yelling. She stood up to go to the window.

"Here you go!" Lo said, coming into the room. "Right this way, honey." She stood in the doorway with an arm swept out to the landing.

"I'm allowed out now?"

"Only to the bathroom."

"The bathroom?" Gloria couldn't keep the dismay from her voice. She returned the book to the nightstand.

"Don't grumble yet, I'm about to make you take your clothes off." She took Gloria by the hand.

"Were the horses just a ruse to make me join your sex cult?"

"You've discovered my dark secret."

Gloria smiled. "Why does this keep happening to me?"

In the bathroom there were candles around the tub and the bath was filling with frangipani-scented water. Sitting on the tiled edge was a glass of champagne with a cranberry in the bottom.

"What else would you like? A book? Music?"

"Is this all for me?"

"And the other sex slaves." Lo's face was deadpan.

Gloria unbuttoned her breeches. "Are you going to stand there and watch the show?"

Lo arched a brow. "I would love nothing more, however I have a few things to do. This is for you. How about some music?" She went to the digital radio that sat on a shelf beside the mirror so she could listen to the music in the shower. She changed the tuning from the local country station to an easy listening station. "Do you like this one?"

Gloria pulled her top over her head. "Sure."

The mirror was beginning to fog up, and Lo drew a big love heart around their reflection before turning to look at Gloria. "You are lucky I am busy or else you'd be in trouble."

"Who are you?"

Lo went to turn the running water off. "Remember way back when, how I said that you were getting to know me when I don't exactly feel like me? Or words to that effect. Well, every day I feel more like me, just normal. I have to live with the past and some days that's too much, but you helped me realize something, and that's that it also just is. It would be more of a sin not to live the life I have." She took Gloria's wrist and peeled the hair elastic over her hand and reached up to tie Gloria's hair in a bun. "But, that is not a discussion for now. I want this to be a happy moment, one we can talk about next Christmas and the one after."

"Are you going to make me have baths then too?"

Lo kissed her and undid the back of Gloria's bra. "No." Then she turned and walked out, closing the door behind her.

Gloria stood with her bra hanging open, staring at the back of the door. She hoped Lo wasn't entering some type of manic mental breakdown, but she seemed so together. Gloria let her bra slither to the floor and dipped her fingers into the water. It had been years since she'd had a bath. On the radio, a woman sang, *"Your heart crashed into mine and went boom."*

CHAPTER THIRTEEN

Gloria emerged from the bathroom smelling and feeling like she was a flower raised in a greenhouse. Lo must have heard the bathroom door open because she appeared in the corridor.

"Go put on your new dress."

"What for?"

"Let's get dressed up."

Gloria wiped moisture from under her chin with the corner of the towel she was holding around herself. "I just want to put my sweatpants and robe on."

"It's Christmas Eve. I want you to put your dress on so I can unwrap you like a present."

"Can't you unwrap my robe? I'll tie the belt in a bow."

"Put some makeup on too. I'm going to have a quick shower, then I'm coming to check on you."

Lo gave Gloria a stern look and moved around her to get into the bathroom. She shut the door and Gloria shook her head. She wasn't sure what had gotten into Lo. Maybe it was one of the self-help books she'd been reading. Surely they weren't at the stage where their sex life was stale, as it had only just started. Gloria contemplated putting on her comfortable clothes but couldn't bring herself to disappoint Lo when she was trying so hard to do something nice. Instead, she sat down in front of the vanity with her robe on—temporarily only—and did her makeup. By the time Lo reappeared, Gloria was in the dress and shoes, combing her hair in front of the mirror. Outside, the sun was slipping behind the mountains, striking the window with hard pink light, making it impossible to make out the pastures below.

Lo smiled. "You look beautiful. I must have been good after all because Santa is giving me exactly what I asked for."

"What else did you ask for?"

"Only world peace and that I not encounter Judge Belvedere next year. Now, what about me?" She opened the closet. "This green one?" She pulled the hem of her olive-green silk dress out to show Gloria.

"What's that red one?"

Lo unhooked a knee-length dark red dress with a split up the side. "A bit sexy don't you think? Peter bought me this one but I never actually wore it. It probably doesn't fit."

Gloria's eyes narrowed. "Too sexy for what? For me to unwrap like my present? It looks exactly like a gift to me. Try it on."

Lo slipped the dress from its hanger and threw her towel on the bed. Her body had already begun to harden into the athletic form of a swimmer. The dress fit her easily, diving down her cleavage, clinging to her torso and falling loose along her thigh until she moved and the fabric parted like a theater curtain, showing the length of her left leg. The bright red fabric clashed beautifully with the orange tones of her hair.

"Excuse me," Gloria said. "Chanel called, they want their cover girl back."

"It's not too *Pretty Woman*-ish?"

"No, just enough. You need some diamonds, though."

Lo grinned. "You're on board then?"

"I've been on board all afternoon, I'm just not sure what for!"

"Soon, my darling, soon."

There was more yelling and banging outside. Gloria peered toward the window and began to walk over for a closer look, but Lo grabbed her arm.

"Diamonds for both of us. Here, earrings. That's all you need for that dress."

"What is that?" Gloria asked. "Do you think one of the horses is kicking out the shed?"

"Let Kip worry about that. Here, put these on." Lo handed Gloria a pair of diamond studs that Gloria had worn once before. "I love these on you." Lo held a diamond drop earring to her own lobe. "Too much?"

"Stop saying 'too much.' You're like a very beautiful clothes rack. Anything you wear looks like it was made for you." Gloria took the earring and slipped it into Lo's ear then kissed the edge of her jaw.

"Perfume!" Lo said, making Gloria laugh.

Lo busied herself with the last of her preparations, spritzing them both with perfume and applying red lipstick.

Gloria watched her from her seat on the bed. "Can I put my pajamas on now? We could eat popcorn and watch a Christmas movie?"

Lo glanced at the clock on the side table. "That sounds wonderful and we will do that tomorrow, but now we are going downstairs to have the rest of that French champagne. Wait, wait." Gloria stood up and Lo took her by the shoulders and turned her toward the mirror. She curled a strand of Gloria's hair back behind her ear. "Look at you."

Gloria's reflection blazed back at her with more intensity than she felt but, as she looked, her confidence rose to match the woman in the mirror. Her ordinary features suggestive of beauty, her eyes fearless and her mouth quick to smile, her hair the richest shade of brown that was saved from looking black by the true black of her lashes. "I'll do."

"No." Lo squeezed Gloria's shoulders and her eyes were serious. "Don't be flip. This is what you look like to me all the time. There's no one on this earth as beautiful as you are to me."

Tears filmed Gloria's eyes. She wanted to explain to Lo what Lo meant to her, but every word seemed inadequate or like a poorer version of what Lo had just said to her. "Lo, you're the only one for me."

Lo smiled. "I know, honey. Now don't ruin your makeup. Let's go."

Gloria wanted to hold on to Lo and weep. To be looked in the eye and seen down to her soul. She knew that was a rare and defining moment. She was suddenly grateful the occasion was marked by a formality the clothes afforded. She held Lo's hand and they walked down the stairs together. Gloria could hear the sound of engines and car doors slamming outside in the twilight.

"What's going on?"

Lo led her to the front door and pulled their coats from the rack. "Put this on, stand here, and don't peek. I will be back in one moment."

Gloria leaned against the bureau and stared at the lengths of wood that made up the opposite wall, the knots and the ribs in the grain. She thought back to when Lo had come to find her in Australia, the week they'd spent at a cheap motel, too scared to pour their hearts out but too scared to leave things unsaid. It had taken them until the last day to tell one another what they really wanted. And now here she was. Outside she heard sounds of vehicles and voices, and something else...bells?

The door opened again and Lo reappeared. "Okay, come on." She didn't take Gloria's hand but she held the door open for her.

Lined up with the front step was a red sleigh with gold paintwork curlicues. Her old friend Duster the horse was hitched to the front, tolerating the reindeer antlers that someone had fixed to his harness, and Samuel was in the driver's seat wearing a Santa hat. The front drive was full of parked cars and people clutching jackets around themselves and watching the sleigh.

Gloria turned to Lo. "What is this?"

"You ask too many questions. Just get in."

Samuel helped Gloria and Lo in, and they sat down and pulled a thick red faux fur rug over their knees. Samuel chirruped to Duster and they moved off to the sound of bells. Gloria felt like she was experiencing an alternate reality as she noticed more and more of what was going on. Lights were strung around the front porch and in the fir tree to the right of the house. Duster plodded dutifully along, taking them around the house and leading them down on the path toward the stables and the barn. Inside the lit-up barn, Gloria could see people dressed up like they were. Live music from a country band drifted on the still night toward them and Gloria thought she spotted two of her students, and she couldn't be sure but it looked like Kip carrying a laughing Mallory along the path so her high heels wouldn't be ruined by snow or mud.

"Samuel," Lo said. "Take us up a little ways first. You can turn around at the long meadow gate."

Samuel nodded and Kip turned to the sound of sleigh bells and Mallory shrieked and clung to his neck as he took one arm off to wave at them. Once they were clear of the barn, Samuel said, "Hi-yup," to Duster, who broke into a trot and Gloria held Lo's hand under the rug as they jiggled along.

"Thank you. This is…" Gloria was lost for words again. She looked up at the stars which had begun to penetrate the new night. "Magical."

"Your first Christmas barn dance."

Samuel and Duster brought them around in a slow arc and back to the barn.

Samuel helped Gloria and Lo down where there was a mat leading to the doors. "I'll continue bringing more people down to the barn. It's getting busy now."

"Thanks, Samuel. Can I get you a hot drink?"

"No, ma'am. Thank you, but I have a bottle of bourbon in my pocket."

Lo laughed. "That'll keep you warm, just don't tell your mama that you're drinking on my watch."

"I'll be eighteen in April!"

"Exactly!"

Gloria could already hear the laughter and chatter that was spilling from inside. Samuel urged Duster on, and she and Lo were left standing on the rubber mat. Things were suddenly making more sense to Gloria. The reason Kip wouldn't let her near the barn, why Lo had dragged her around town getting made up, the reason Lo had almost choked on her champagne in the salon.

"I can't believe you pulled this off in secret. I am truly the dimmest person. Even all the banging outside."

But Lo was staring into the barn at the revelers the way deer looked at them when they rode out by the forest. Her aura had switched again from someone in command to that of one in terror, and Gloria knew that panic had sprung in Lo.

Gloria squeezed her hand. Lo nodded and they were enveloped by a cloud of people wanting to hug Lo. Lo stood stiffly for a moment but there was nothing Gloria could do; she couldn't comfort her the way a lover would or a wife would, she could only watch as Lo was swept away. Within the next second, Kip and Mallory, who was now standing on her own two feet, were upon Gloria, Kip telling her how pretty she looked and Mallory exclaiming over the strings of lights overhead. Catering staff in white shirts with black ties and black pants were carrying trays of food, and a young man with long brown hair in a ponytail stopped to offer them chicken drumettes with sticky sesame marinade. When Gloria refused, stating she didn't eat meat, the man told her that he would find her something.

"We'll be by the bar!" Mallory said.

A man and a woman stood behind a bar made from hay bales with slabs of wood on top. Gloria had been drinking sparkling champagne all day, so she thought it would be safest to stay on that train. She looked around the barn and was surprised that there were many familiar faces. Helen from the salon was talking to Barrett, Kip's mortal enemy from the hardware store. Cathy from the clothing store was standing with Reg from the grocery store. Little children ran around with their hair neatly combed, wearing their best. Two of her students, looking very different in evening gowns, were chatting with two other men who were possibly their husbands. One looked over and noticed Gloria, then waved enthusiastically and made a thumbs-up and nodded to indicate Gloria looked good.

The waiter returned with a fresh tray of finger food. "These arancini are vegetarian."

Gloria beamed at him. "Oh, thank you. You just keep 'em coming." The waiter had been blocking her view of what was rapidly becoming the dance floor, but as he moved off toward the next cluster of people, Gloria could see Lo over on the other side, standing in a group of people whose clothes marked them as upper class or professionals. Gloria could only assume they were Lo's legal peers. She imagined the tall man with gray hair and his hands stuffed in his trouser pockets was a judge by the way he seemed to preside over the conversation. He laughed and the sound rang out over the music. Lo had a glass in her hand and she joined in the laughter. Gloria relaxed a little and turned back to Kip and Mallory.

"The barn looks beautiful, Kip. I can't figure out how you pulled it all together."

"We almost didn't. Sam, Clarence, and I weren't enough, we had plenty of town folk who chipped in. Cleaning this barn out wasn't easy, especially with the short notice Dolores gave. She'd been so adamant that there would be no party this year, but she did a backflip and we had to get all the hay out and tidy up, plus grade the path, organize the food and alcohol, the decorations, get the word out, all in two weeks and without you knowing a thing. I tell you, we could have used your help but she couldn't be swayed. It's been a long time since I've seen Dolores try to please anyone on anything."

Gloria felt a blush creep up her cheeks and she glanced back across at Lo. "But this happens every year, right?"

"Not last year. Christmas was canceled at the ranch."

Gloria watched two little boys trying to climb up one of the supporting beams. They were probably the age Terrence would be now and she wondered if they were his classmates. She looked back over at Lo and saw Lo's eyes were also on the boys. As if seeking assurance, Lo's gaze found Gloria. Someone in Lo's group must have said her name because her attention snapped back to the conversation and Gloria tuned back in to Kip. She pulled at the hem of her dress out of habit but realized she wasn't cold at all. She thought it was more to do with the alcohol than the heaters.

Gloria finished her drink and began on another as Mallory dragged Kip onto the dance floor. It was getting crowded by the bar and, as Gloria went to find a quieter spot, she was discovered by her student Julia, who was around the same age as Gloria and was delighted to see her out of context. As they were talking about Sonnet's hip that had been worrying Gloria, she did another visual check-in on Lo and saw that she looked happy and animated. It took her only a split second to realize that she was talking to Peter. Gloria felt a physical heaviness in her body and she watched the comfortability with which Peter and Lo interacted with their professional peers. Gloria knew she was doing the same, talking to Julia, but it was more than that. It was the way Peter claimed propriety over Lo and Lo didn't resist. Peter had ended the marriage at Lo's request, but he had ended it when Lo was withdrawn from the world, including from him. Now that she appeared much as she must have when he was happy in the marriage, of course he viewed her differently. He had been so desperate for her to be the same confident, assured person he had first met that he had set about introducing tools and assistance to get her there, not realizing that what she needed was time and love. Now that he was willing to give her that, Gloria could see that things might be different. Gloria nodded at what Julia was saying about equine physiotherapy and watched Lo excuse herself to greet more people. Peter stayed where he was but his eyes trailed after Lo.

"Look, Gloria, it's Caroline!" Julia said, grabbing Gloria's forearm and almost spilling her drink.

Caroline walked toward them with her limping gait. She had on a long, dark green chiffon dress that looked a decade out of fashion, but she had the type of matter-of-fact, no-fuss attitude that gave her an air of refined dignity.

"Gloria! Julia! Have I missed the food? For two years I have been craving those sweet and sour pork balls."

Julia looked around. "I haven't seen any balls at all."

Gloria managed to keep her laughter down to a grin and she instinctively looked for Lo to share the joke. She saw Lo was standing talking to a petite woman in a white dress with blond hair falling down her back. She looked familiar and she gave Gloria a slightly uneasy feeling, like the woman was insincere, but Gloria wasn't sure why. The woman sparkled up at Lo like a hard little diamond, touching Lo's hair and the strap of her dress. Gloria asked Caroline how the cold was affecting her joints, but she couldn't stop sneaking glances over Julia's shoulder at Lo. The name came to her from a filing cabinet at the back of her mind: Kelly Armstrong. The same woman who had tried to hit on Mike when they'd had dinner. It seemed Gloria was not the only one bothered, for the next moment Peter was striding over to get among the female flesh spilling from brief fabric. That'd be right; smooth Peter would know Kelly Armstrong, the advertising executive.

"Gloria," Caroline was saying. "This is my nephew, Oliver."

Gloria blinked in surprise. Caroline's annoying nephew from Iowa was standing beside her, a glass of liquor in one hand and a mini pizza in the other. "Hey, Gloria, sorry, I would shake your hand, but…" He raised both hands as evidence of their occupation.

Gloria was aware that Julia had gone silent, staring at all six foot two of broad-shouldered, square-jawed Oliver with his flop of honey-brown hair falling across one eye. The fact that he was so good-looking just irritated Gloria further. Of course he was. He could have that over her too. As a waiter walked past with champagne, Gloria whisked a glass from the tray and smiled. "That's okay, my hands are full too." She raised her hands in the same gesture Oliver had made. Everyone was starting to annoy her. "If you'll all excuse me, I had better go and see if Lo wants some help."

Lo didn't look like she needed any help at all. In fact, she and Peter both seemed to find whatever Kelly was saying extremely funny. On her way over, Gloria finished one champagne, set the glass down on a bar table, then took a sip of another.

"Gloria!" Lo smiled. "Have you met Kelly? In fact, Kelly said they are scouting for a location to shoot an ad for cologne and the barn might be just the thing."

Kelly nodded. "Hi, Gloria. Now, I'm no location scout, but I do try and get involved at all levels of a project."

Kelly obviously didn't recognize Gloria, and why would she? She hadn't registered Gloria at all at the restaurant that night. Kelly was the kind of person who everyone noticed. She was just that little bit more in every way than anyone else. Gloria didn't want to think ill of her, so she smiled and attempted shorthand for *let's be friends*: "That's a gorgeous dress."

Kelly lifted a shoulder toward her chin. "Thank you, Gloria. Gino Fiorantello made it just for me."

Gloria had no idea who that was but she was obviously supposed to be impressed, so she made an appropriate face and was saved by Peter stopping a waitress to offer them drinks. He was always so darn tuned in, commanding things, changing atmospheres. Gloria wished he'd go away.

"What do you do?" Kelly asked, clearly not caring but wanting Gloria to ask her the same question in return.

"I just mess around with horses. Nothing much."

"But you're from Aus-tra-li-a?" Kelly said it slowly as though Gloria couldn't speak English.

"Yup." Gloria made a popping sound with her lips. "With the brumbies and the kangaroos."

Kelly turned to grin at Lo. "That is just so sweet. And I thought you wouldn't take in guests again, Dolly. I mean, how many times have I had to pester you about opening up your ranch to our location team?"

Peter laughed. "You'd better ask her again tomorrow after the alcohol has worn off."

"No," Lo said sharply. "Gloria isn't here as a guest, she's moved here, into the house."

"Gloria has been so helpful to Dolly, better than any therapy. I just knew that getting out with the horses again would give Doll some type of emotional reset. Animals seem to have a natural healing ability. I'm not very good with them myself, but Dolly always was."

"Fascinating," Kelly said. "I never mentioned it, because I don't like to pry, but when you disappeared completely after you-know-what, well, I think I speak on behalf of the whole of Diamond Rock. We didn't know what to do. I mean, Doll, you were so skinny, and not good skinny, but like a corpse. It just wasn't right. I'm so glad you're better now. We prayed for you at church, you know. Miracles do happen."

Lo's face was taking on a passive expression like a calm before a storm, but her eyes were glittering topaz and agate. Gloria slipped her arm around Lo's waist, not caring who saw. "What," Lo said, "is the miracle you're referring to?"

Peter interjected. "Dolly's back at the office now too. Not a miracle, we just put one foot in front of the other and it gets a little easier each day."

Lo held up a hand to silence him. "Nothing to do with the death of my son was a miracle, and unless he gets up from his cold frozen grave and walks through those barn doors right now, there are no miracles."

Kelly looked helplessly to Gloria, finally at a loss for words.

Gloria leaned into Lo instead. "Let's go see if Samuel needs a break."

Lo stood unmoving for a moment, her anger holding her there. Gloria didn't care if Kelly endured the force of it, but she didn't want Lo to regret anything. After a second, Lo let Gloria guide her toward the doors, even though she could feel the quivering intensity of Lo's emotion. They walked outside into the cold night and stood just outside the doorway. Samuel and Duster were nowhere to be seen but the sleigh was sitting pressed up against the wall of the barn. They walked over and climbed in, and Gloria wrapped the cold blanket around them. They both shivered but they needed quiet. Over to the left the house was dark, like a lantern that had been switched off for the night.

Lo spoke first. "It's like no matter how well I think I'm doing or how far I think I've come, it's raw nerve. Someone hits it and I lose my cool."

Gloria shrugged, the goose bumps on her bare arm grating against the goose bumps on Lo's. "Your son died and that will never be okay."

"But I have to pretend it's okay or else I'm not functioning, right? There will always be a Kelly Armstrong with nosey questions or opinions, especially around here. At least at work they come in more concerned about themselves and I can create a professional barrier, but socially..." Her voice cracked. "Sorry."

Gloria felt her own heart cracking. "Don't be sorry."

"I am, Gloria. I wanted tonight to be perfect for you."

Gloria felt for her hand under the blanket and the vibration of their shivering pulsated through the seat of the sleigh. "The whole thing is perfect, you're perfect. I'll take you any way you are. I wonder what the time is. Is it Christmas yet?"

"Christmas," Lo said. "I'd almost forgotten. It can't be that late."

"Should we go in and have some dessert and dance?"

Lo glanced at the smokers by the barn door, but no one was paying them any mind. She slipped her hand around Gloria's waist and drew her close and kissed her. "Okay, now we can."

Lo and Gloria danced and laughed, and to any onlookers, Lo seemed fine. Peter cut in and asked to dance and Gloria let him, not wanting any more conflict. She realized her feet were hurting anyway. She found a hay bale and sat down, easing her heels out of the shoes.

"Gloria." Gloria looked up into the assured face of Oliver. "Mind if I sit?"

Gloria moved over slightly and made a futile attempt to cover some thigh with her dress. "Be my guest."

"What's it like working with my aunt? She make you canter serpentines too?"

Gloria turned to look at him properly. "Yes!"

"So, it's not just me?"

"Oh, she's all right. If there's one thing I've learned, it's that every trainer has something to offer, just take the lesson and use it to improve. Caroline is no slouch, her methods are working on my horses."

"I've heard." Oliver placed his hands either side of him on the hay bale, his index finger grazing the side of Gloria's bottom.

Gloria was too drunk to care. "About my horses?"

"She called me up and said there's a girl over here, she's your age and she makes you look like you just got your first pony." Oliver laughed at the memory.

Gloria's mouth dropped open. "Caroline said that to you about me?"

"Yes, ma'am. She also said if I didn't stop hopscotching around the ski slopes and come help her with the horses, she'd take back Leonite."

"Who's Leonite?"

"The horse she bred for me. He's out of Rarity. So here I am. Looks like we'll be seeing more of each other."

"I doubt it. I don't usually hang around the stables. I'm out on the road or in the arena working." Gloria turned away and saw the band had stopped and Lo and Kip were making their way to the microphone.

"What do you think I'll be doing? Dusting my aunt's artifacts?"

The singer adjusted the microphone for Lo and she scanned the crowd of people who had all turned to see why the band had stopped playing. Someone whistled and another person yelled, "Hello, Dolly!" Lo smiled and Kip stood beside her with his hands in the pockets of his jeans, as though daring anyone to do or say the wrong thing.

"Hi, everyone," Lo said. "Firstly, I'd like to say thank you to everyone for coming and making it such a great night on short notice, I sure do appreciate it." She paused and looked from face to face. "As you all know, Peter and I tragically lost our son, Terrence, about a year and a half ago, well, sixteen months and three days ago, to be precise. This is a small town and we have all touched each other's lives in some way over the years, whether it's Mary with her delicious preserves, Helen visiting our homes to cut hair when we can't go out, Peter taking on legal work pro bono…there is a sense of community here and I wanted to host the party tonight in your honor. Now that you're all gathered here, I do have a small request." She looked over at Gloria and Oliver sitting on the bale of hay and then back across at Peter, who was standing off to her other side. "I know it's the off season for farming and things may be tight." She looked into the crowd and smiled. "Not for the ski resort owners, though." There was a titter of laughter. "But there is a cause near to my heart. The Diamond Rock Hospital is in dire need of life support equipment. Perhaps if it was better equipped, Terrence would still be with us today. Peter and I have a sheet of paper here." Lo indicated toward Peter with a hand and Peter held up a clipboard. "And we would love if you would pledge a donation, no amount is too small, and to get the ball rolling, the Ballantyne firm has pledged the first donation. We think this is a cause we can all get behind that will benefit the whole town." The smile fell from Lo's face. "Thank you, and Merry Christmas to you and yours."

Peter held the clipboard overhead again and called, "The pledge board will be on top of the bar here. We know where you all like to be."

After that, someone put a CD in the sound system and the band began to pack up to the sound of Faith Hill. Oliver stood up and reached a hand down to help Gloria to her feet. Gloria reluctantly slipped her feet back into the heels. She had to admit she was feeling a little left out of Lo and Peter's donation drive. When she'd arrived, Lo had said this was her place, too, but she still felt like a secret guest. She let Oliver pull her to her feet.

"I had better go and make a pledge or Aunt Caroline will skin me alive. You coming?"

"Maybe later." Gloria really wanted to go back to the house, put her sweatpants and robe on, and watch mindless television. She missed Hamlet. Whenever she needed a shoulder to cry on, he was always there. He was a great excuse to escape from the humans when it all got too much. "You heading off? I'll go and say goodbye to Caroline."

"Nice meeting you, Gloria. I'll be seeing you at Caroline's. She thinks you've been working too hard and she tells me that's my job. She thinks I was born with a silver spoon in my mouth and need to learn the virtues of hard labor."

"Hi-ho, Silver. See you around."

Oliver shook his head but he was grinning. "You're even scarier than Aunt Caroline made out. Have a great Christmas."

Gloria watched him join the people by the bar, then she sifted through the crowd, looking for Caroline's green chiffon. She spotted her sitting on a bale of hay across the floor, talking to Lo. Gloria picked her way across the room. People had already begun to leave. It was Christmas tomorrow and there was food to be prepared and presents to wrap. Children were asleep on their parents' shoulders and Gloria heard the sound of jingling as Samuel and Duster faithfully ferried people back to their cars.

"Gloria, sit down. I was just telling Dolores how much of a help you've been. I couldn't have kept going without you, but I think it's time for me to pull back. My health isn't getting any better." She turned to Lo. "She's a good girl, don't tell her I said that, though. It's such a nice thing you're doing for the hospital. I said to Oliver, if I ever get so bad I'm bedridden in hospital, just shoot me like a horse, right between the eyes." Her gaze found Oliver among the pledgers at the bar. "My sister spoiled him. He's here to get his hands dirty and help his aunt. You make sure you give him all the worst jobs, Gloria. He doesn't know it, but if he wants to improve his riding, he needs to toughen up a bit."

"Caroline, if he's anything like you, I'm sure he's plenty tough."

Caroline shook her head. "Dolores, he's as milky as a cow's tit."

Lo laughed. "Oh, I have missed our chats."

"Gloria, help me up, please." Gloria helped Caroline to her feet. "Dolores, you are welcome any time. I don't want to be charged with kidnapping your horses too."

"They're Gloria's horses now."

"Just like that?" Caroline looked from Lo to Gloria and back. "Whatever you say, Dolores. She rides 'em better anyhow. You've got a good gal here."

Oliver arrived to take his aunt's arm. "I told you to wait for me."

Caroline waved her cane in the air. "I have this. I'm not old, just a cripple!"

Oliver raised his eyebrows. "Thank you, Dolores. It was a great party. No rest for the wicked, though. As you both know, horses still want their breakfast at the crack of dawn, especially yours. That big fat gelding never stops eating."

"Just like someone else I know," Caroline muttered. "Dolores, I'll see you tomorrow. You too, Love Fool."

Oliver made a gesture like tipping his hat even though he wasn't wearing one and gave Gloria a wink.

"Tomorrow?" Gloria asked as Oliver and Caroline slowly made their way to where Samuel was waiting with Duster.

Lo smiled apologetically. "It's Christmas, Love Fool. I couldn't say there's no room at the inn."

Gloria smiled and leaned her head into the crook of Lo's shoulder. "Not you too. It's nice, I'm just surprised." Gloria liked the idea of having Caroline over for lunch. Even though Caroline could be a crosspatch, Gloria loved absorbing her wisdom about horses and occasionally other things.

"Tell me again why you're a love fool?"

Gloria looked over at Kip, who was helping Mallory into her jacket. "She thinks Kip is my boyfriend, which in her eyes would make me a fool. Although if he was, he wouldn't be the most faithful over there with Mallory."

"Hence the fool. I did tell Caroline that we aren't doing anything fancy, just a roast."

"Speaking of roasts, where is Sue-Anne?"

Lo tugged the bottom of Gloria's dress down for her. "She said it's too cold and she has too much food to cook. Can you imagine Christmas dinner at her place?" She glanced at the groups of people milling around, waiting for a break in the conversation to say thank you and goodnight. Kip was helping the waitstaff collect glasses and Gloria decided to leave Lo to it and pitch in by picking up discarded napkins and paper plates. Sharing another meal with Lo's mother and Casey wasn't high on the list of things she wanted to do, but family dinners back home were often just as awkward. The missing ingredient was possibly children to make things light. She would miss the birth of her new niece or nephew. She had always assumed she would be a mother, but she accepted that it would probably never be the case now.

At last, after the final merrymakers had been persuaded toward the door and the staff had been paid, Kip said he would close up. Despite having his girlfriend, Amy, up front beside him, Samuel was looking fed up. Gloria didn't blame him. All she could think about was getting into the house herself. She was feeling grateful that she had been uncharacteristically organized and wrapped the framed watercolors. She planned on retrieving them from their hiding spot in the spare room and putting them under the tree when Lo was getting ready for bed.

CHAPTER FOURTEEN

"Hey, sleepyhead."

Gloria opened her eyes to see Lo's hazel eyes fixed on her. "What time is it?"

Lo glanced behind her at the clock. "Five fifty-three in the morning."

Gloria closed her eyes. "Too early. Still dark."

"It's Christmas morning!"

Gloria threw her arm over Lo's ribcage. "Even more reason to give yourself the gift of sleep."

Lo kissed Gloria's cheek. "Don't you want your present?"

Gloria could see that Lo wasn't going to give up. "Okay, okay, I'm awake." She rolled right on top of Lo and lay her head in the crook of Lo's neck. She kissed her collarbone. "Are you sorry you woke me now?"

"Oh, that feels good. It's like a massage. Is this my Christmas present?"

Gloria kissed the hollow of her throat. "It can be."

"Post-lunch entertainment. Hop up, I want to give you yours!"

Lo struggled out from beneath Gloria and threw the blankets back. Gloria always admired Lo's lack of regard for the cold. Lo began putting on warm clothes. "Come on!"

With only the light of the torch bobbing in front of them, Gloria let Lo lead her down toward the stables, struggling on a step behind. Where the path veered off toward Kip's cottage, Lo dragged Gloria. She banged on the door and they heard the sound of footsteps and Kip's voice saying, "I'm coming!"

He opened the door dressed in his work clothes and Lo peered around behind him. "You got company?"

He shut the door behind him, but he was grinning. "Never you mind, Dolores. Merry Christmas, Gloria."

Gloria wished him a Merry Christmas. As they walked on toward the stables, Lo and Kip were whispering something, their foggy breath giving them away, Gloria looked around at the stark trees and the slushy drive, ghostly in the beam from the flashlight.

"Why are we here? I thought I was getting a morning off from the horses," Gloria grumbled.

Kip opened the stable door and turned the light on. Wilbur, who bedded in with the horses for the night, yawned and stretched then came over, blinking his eyes against the light. There was the sound of rustling as the horses who had been lying in the sawdust began to wake up. Hamlet's and Sonnet's stalls were empty, of course. Gloria missed them a little. Down the end, Samuel's mare, Firecat, began whinnying, eager for her breakfast.

"Close your eyes," Lo demanded.

"Do it!" Kip added.

Gloria stopped in her tracks and shut her eyes. "It's too cold for games." She heard the sound of one of the locks being pushed back and more whispering and rustling then laughter. "Can I open yet?"

"No!"

She heard something clatter and Kip swear then Lo laugh.

"Now?"

"No!" they both yelled.

There was the sound of someone running. Wilbur sat by Gloria's feet in solidarity, and she blindly reached down to pat his head.

"Okay, now," Lo said.

Gloria opened her eyes but it took her a moment to take in what she was looking at. There, with a big red bow around his neck, wearing woolen rugs, was a beautiful chestnut yearling colt with a broad blaze and two long white stockings on his hind legs. He was nuzzling at Lo's arm.

"What's that?" Gloria asked.

"This is Picante, but he goes by the name Pogo."

"But what is he doing here?"

"He lives here."

Gloria was still standing in the same spot, one hand on Wilbur's head.

"Aren't you going to say hello to him?"

Kip had less patience. "He's your horse. Give him a hug. I've been instructed to take a photo."

Disbelieving, Gloria went over to touch the colt to see if he was real.

"Say cheese."

She turned toward Kip and hoped she smiled as the camera flashed. Kip took another for good measure and Pogo squealed and flinched at the unfamiliar flash. Instinctively, Gloria put a hand out to steady him. Wilbur came to sniff at Pogo's muzzle and Kip took one more picture then said he was going to do the feeds and go back to bed.

Gloria wrapped one arm around Lo. "But how? Why?"

"Oh, my love." Lo breathed warm against her neck. "You've never had your very own dressage horse to train and compete. This is for you. No one will take him away or sell him, and if he begins to turn out well, you've got your first stallion standing at your dressage stud. Look at this." Lo pulled up the edge of Pogo's dark green rug to show Gloria the gold embroidery.

"It's a pine cone!"

Lo smiled. "A gold pine cone, just like the one you gave me. That's the symbol of our stables, and look, beside it says Heaven's End."

Gloria shook her head. "This is unbelievable. You are full of surprises. I honestly can't keep up." She ran her hand over Pogo's fluffy baby neck. "He is just the most exquisite thing I've ever seen. But how?"

"Oliver brought him down this morning. He's by Ti Prego out of a lovely imported mare. I think he's a special one. Wait until you see him move."

"I just can't believe it," Gloria said. "Thank you!" She swept Lo into a hug. "I want to bring him into the house like a puppy. But how did you…how did you pay for him?"

"With money. I see him as a good investment for the future of our stables."

Gloria had the feeling that Lo was trying to spare her any guilt over the cost, but she was too excited to worry about it. She could see the future so clearly, the beginning of her dressage dreams with her very own horse and her own stables, where finally she would be working hard toward her own goals instead of someone else's.

"Do you want to put him away and we'll have some breakfast and watch him go in the daylight?"

Gloria agreed even though she wanted to keep looking at him. Kip was mixing up the feeds and Pogo could hear the feed bins being opened and closed. Gloria put him back in his stable and gave him a kiss on his satiny pink nose. He jerked his head up, unused to all the fussing. She could tell he was going to mature into a nice size horse, not quite as big as Hamlet but almost. Finally, she tore herself away and she and Lo made their way to the house. On the path there was the odd damp napkin or discarded toothpick from last night.

Inside, Gloria poured coffee into a cup. "Can we eat the gingerbread house?"

"Absolutely."

Gloria placed it in the center of the table in all its cellophaned glory. "Now, would you like your present before or after you destroy this?"

Lo was sitting at her usual place at the table with her hands wrapped around a mug, but she sat up straighter. "You got me a present?"

"Sort of."

"I want to see."

Gloria drummed her fingers on the tabletop while she considered whether or not it was a good idea to give Lo the pictures or not. Too late, she had committed. "Okay, is that a strong coffee?"

"Always, darlin'."

"Right." Gloria nodded once then pushed up from the table with both hands. She had forgotten to put the gift under the tree so she walked back to the spare room and retrieved it from the closet, not the craftiest of places but she didn't think Lo would be rummaging around the house looking for gifts. The three paintings were in a box, wrapped in red-and-white-striped paper with a metallic red bow on top. Lo had given her a horse and she was giving her this? She walked quickly back down the stairs. Lo's gaze was expectantly on the doorway and her eye followed Gloria as she came to sit on the chair beside her. Gloria held the present in both hands then thrust it at Lo. "Here. You might hate it."

Lo shook her head. "That is not what you say to someone as you hand them a gift."

Gloria watched Lo use her fingertips to wedge under the corner of the paper and neatly undo the wrap while leaving it intact. She folded the paper in half and placed it on the table and gave the box a gentle shake. She lifted the lid off, encountered more tissue paper, and looked up at Gloria and smiled. Finally, she unwrapped the first picture just as precisely as she had the box and placed the paper on the table in much the same way before turning her attention to the picture in its black frame. The picture itself was only ten inches by ten inches and it was of the view from the back porch in spring when Gloria had first come to the ranch: the vivid blue green of the grass, the red barn, the gravel path, the glass snake of river and the purple mountains and black pines against the boundless blue sky. The vivid colors were what she remembered most when she looked out now at the gray dawn. Lo held it out at arm's length and looked at it. "This is just magnificent. The detail, oh, look at the shadow of an eagle over the grass! Who did this?"

Gloria clasped her hands between her knees and pressed against them. "Open the next one."

Lo gently set the picture on the table and opened the next image. All three were the same size and this one was of the river, the special spot where Lo had taken her, a place she had liked to play with Terrence. Lo was staring fixedly at the picture. She touched a finger to the glass. "A dragonfly." She looked up at Gloria. "Who drew this?"

"There's one more."

"But how could they know about the spot? Did you draw this?"

"Open the last one."

Lo placed that frame beside the other and picked the last package up from the box. She held it, her hands shaking and somehow Gloria knew that Lo knew. Lo tried to pass it to Gloria. "You do it." But Gloria made no move to take it from her. Lo eased the paper away, pausing. She pulled one corner off and started to cry. Gloria felt it had been a huge mistake. She should have stopped at the landscapes, it was enough.

"You don't have to."

Lo held one hand to her mouth and she made an animal keening sound of pain. She pulled the wrap farther then stopped, then finally pulled it all off. Gloria knew she had captured Terrence's likeness. Even though there were no photos displayed of him in the house, Gloria knew where there was a bundle in a drawer. She didn't know much about him, but she knew he loved the outdoors and animals and particularly horses, and that he was a fine rider. He had one arm slung around Sonnet's neck and his face pressed against hers, smiling right at them. In his other hand he held a dandelion clock. Blurry in the background was the spring grass. Sonnet looked calm, her dapples deeper with youth. Terrence looked peaceful and happy, even though he had his mother's somber features. Lo put the picture down then picked it up again, her mouth pulled back in a grimace as she tried to contain any sound. Gloria had expected that she might be sad or angry, but not this primal grief.

"Lo." Gloria placed a hand on her arm. When Lo didn't respond she gave it a little squeeze. "Lo," she tried again. "My

love. Lola." She gave her arm a shake then tried to take the
picture from Lo, but Lo clutched it to her chest and began to
sob so Gloria wrapped her arms around her and let her cry.
They sat there, Gloria holding Lo and Lo holding the picture,
until finally Lo began to sniff instead of sob and Gloria kissed
her cheek. The sun had started to pierce the kitchen with white
light and Gloria stood to make some fresh coffee. She returned
with the two steaming mugs and Lo was still holding the picture
but she was staring at the table. Her eyes were red and puffy and
her mouth bleary. Her lashes were clumped together and tears
had streaked her cheeks and darkened the front of her red-and-
black flannel shirt. Gloria sat back in the chair beside Lo and
put a hand on her thigh.

"Are you okay?"

Lo shrugged. "I can't tell anymore." She swiped at her nose
with the cuff of her shirt. "It's been so long since I dreamt about
him. He used to come to me in dreams and I wouldn't want to
wake. It's the insomnia, he can't find me. But this morning, I
had been dreaming that it was school photo day and he said to
me, 'Mommy, I posed for one more.'" She cocked her head and
looked at Gloria. "Isn't that strange? But now I see that he did.
Even the dandelion, he used to love blowing them and making a
wish. Always for his own horse, that's all he wanted." She sniffed
again and blinked back more tears.

Gloria stood to get the box of tissues from on top of the
fridge and offered the box to Lo, who pulled a tissue out but
balled it in her fist without using it.

"How did you get this? Even his hair, that's just how it was
with those red bits in the light. And Sonnet, she was like that.
She was so calm with him, she adored him." She looked at Gloria
with a heavy question in her eyes.

"I drew it for you. It's just that there are no photos around
and I think it would be nice if he was around, just his picture, I
mean."

Lo nodded. "You're right. He should be here with us. I just
don't know how you made these, they're incredible." She stood
up and carried the picture to the wall opposite where they were
sitting and held it up to see what it would look like. "There

used to be a family portrait here but I would like to hang them all here so people can look out at the view you've painted as the scenery changes. Remind me to get the tools from the shed when we go and check on Pogo. If it wasn't so cold, we could have put him in the yard out here." Lo came to sit down again.

Gloria took a sip of her coffee. It was getting cold again. "You know you don't have to go all out for me. The surprises, the horse."

Lo had started to hiccup. "I—hup—know. Sorry." She hiccuped again and held her breath for a few seconds, then continued, "It's just that I've learned a few things in the past two years and one is that life is short. Have the party, buy the horse." She blinked back sudden tears. "You are so full of life, the uncompromising way you see the world, it helped me see that life is right here and I wouldn't be serving Terrence any better if I wasted it. So, if I choose life, then honey, I should choose to live. The horse was part of our plan. I had a solid year or more there where I didn't plan a thing, not even whether I would get out of bed that day. Now, I'm getting up before the sun, even if it is just to cry." She smiled and Gloria smoothed a tear from her cheek.

"You're a strong woman, Lo." Gloria looked outside at the winter-blanketed fields. It was strange how the cold could arrive and seemingly extinguish life but come spring, the grass would grow, the flowers would bloom, the rivers would rush, and the animals would come out of hiding. A flower that was so delicate and fragile in appearance had the resilience to regenerate and endure. She thought back to last night, Peter and Lo's fundraising efforts. She still had so much to say, so many things she was unsure of. Lo was right, Gloria didn't like to live life by halves. But things were okay, weren't they? Lo was, for the most part, happy and strong and Gloria's wobbly plans for a dressage stable were slowly taking shape. But it did bother her, the sneaking around like they were doing something bad. Gloria didn't care what anyone else thought and she wasn't scared of gossip. She had a feeling it was more than that—it was Peter. Lo didn't know how to disappoint him again. Gloria didn't want to be that jealous person, she wanted to celebrate Lo's wins, but why was he everywhere all of a sudden? Once, months ago, Lo had told her that she felt some type of emotional debt to Peter, and Gloria knew that type of debt could never be repaid. If Peter felt he held power over her, Gloria wasn't sure, but she would feel better if he moved on. If she was honest with herself, she wished Lo would draw more of a line in the sand, but now was not the time to bring it up. Lo's tears were still damp on her cheeks and Gloria really just wanted to enjoy the day.

Lo took one shuddering sigh and pulled the gingerbread house closer. "I've done the huffing and puffing. Time to demolish it?"

"Tear that fucker down, baby."

Lo laughed thickly and pulled at the green bow that was holding the cellophane closed. She undid it just as neatly as she had the wrap and smoothed the cellophane open around the house. "You first."

Gloria broke away a little green tree and took a bite. She wasn't usually into sugar for breakfast, but it felt like a long time since she had woken up. "What time are Caroline and Oliver arriving?"

"Around midday. This is good gingerbread. We probably should have saved it to share."

Gloria licked her fingers. "It was a sugar emergency level five. We have Sue-Anne's plum pudding in the pantry."

Lo winced. "There's something else."

Gloria raised her eyebrows.

"I asked Peter."

Gloria closed her eyes for a long moment, gathering herself so she wouldn't respond in anger. "Doesn't Peter have family he wants to see?"

"Gloria, he had family, and I took that away."

Gloria looked at Lo in disbelief. "Firstly, no you didn't take anything away. Accidents happen every day and it wasn't your fault. Secondly, Peter has family! He has his brother, his parents, he has friends." She couldn't help herself, she was angry.

"I do feel somewhat responsible for him, I mean, he is my colleague and, I hope, my friend."

Gloria had thought that her outburst might make Lo cry, but she felt tears threaten her own decorum. "It seems to me that being friends with Peter is more important than being with me."

"What's that supposed to mean?"

"Why did you want me to come? You don't want to share your life with me, I'm like classified information that you keep in your briefcase." Lo's chin snapped back like she'd been hit and Gloria knew she should temper her words but she'd been holding them in for too long. "Do you know how much I missed you after you left Australia? Now I wonder why I bothered." She was already horrified with herself. She wanted Lo to yell back but instead Lo looked at her a long moment, then stood up and nodded. Her gaze shifted to the empty wall opposite and she nodded again, one hand wrapped around her abdomen in a gesture Gloria knew so well, then she pushed her chair in and walked out through the hallway. Gloria stared after her and the tears broke free. She wiped her eyes, seeing smudges of last night's makeup on the tissue. Coming to Wyoming had been a journey of faith but her love for Lo had been her guiding star. Now that the clouds had rolled in, she was lost, bobbing out at sea, unable to find true north.

Just as carefully as Lo had unwrapped the gingerbread house, Gloria sealed it back up and took it to the pantry. The wrapping paper she shoved under the kitchen sink and the watercolors she left where they were. There was no use crying, it didn't change anything. Lo was prepared to love her by halves, and she wasn't sure that was enough for her. *Don't do it*, she cautioned herself. *Be brave.* But she could already feel the armor closing around her heart.

CHAPTER FIFTEEN

Gloria had been too busy sulking at the stables to help Lo prepare the food, but Lo had done a beautiful job on her own. The table was presented like a *Country Living* magazine cover with her grandmother's white tablecloth and a centerpiece of pine cones and greenery with gold candles. The watercolors were nowhere to be seen, but Gloria was glad; the last thing she wanted right now was people to comment. Gloria went to get changed in the spare room. She remembered the first day she had ever arrived at the ranch, looking through that same window at the mountains, no clue of the future that was in store. She felt just as unsure now. She tried to look back over her life—had she always felt this way? She was pulled to thoughts of Klaus, taken by a longing for his forceful methodologies and the path she walked on with him. She didn't want Klaus romantically or sexually, hadn't in a long time, but there was certainty there. She knew it was just a weakness, a longing to collapse against a solid foundation. Klaus always told her what to do and mercilessly picked on her to shape her into the product he wanted. It wasn't a connection to her soul, just an identification of the traits and abilities in a package he could work with, the same way he would find a promising horse, the right temperament, confirmation, trainability. He was willing to offer Gloria an exchange: his power for her loyalty. She had already said no to him and she knew why. She had to forge her own path, not walk in his shadow.

Gloria was pulling on her new black jeans when she heard Lo's quiet knock on the door.

"Can I come in?"

"Yes."

Lo opened the door but stood in the doorway, hesitating like she used to. She had on white jeans and a pale gray angora sweater, her hair hung over her shoulder in a braid. Gloria buttoned her black jeans and sat on the bed to put her socks on.

"You're still coming to lunch?"

Gloria looked up, careful to keep her expression neutral. "Why wouldn't I?"

"You seemed upset, and I gathered you didn't want to see Peter. It's too late to uninvite him, you know."

Gloria picked at a ragged edge on her thumbnail. "I never said I wanted you to uninvite him."

"Okay, good, because they'll be here any minute. Sue-Anne said we can pop in later if we want to."

"I probably won't," Gloria said, still finding great interest in her nail.

"No problem."

From the corner of her eye, Gloria saw Lo wait another second, then turn and walk away. She knew she was standing at a crossroad. She could take Lo in her arms and apologize, or she could let the cool harden to cold. The doorbell rang. She gouged off the rough piece of nail. Even if she wanted to hug Lo, she couldn't.

The silence between Lo and Gloria went unnoticed at the crowded table. Kip sat at the opposite head to Lo with Mallory on his left, who was next to Gloria who was next to Oliver, then Caroline, then Lo, then Peter then Casey then Claudette. It was an odd mix of people and the conversations went in clusters, which was just fine for Gloria who was speaking to Mallory about a crime novel they'd both read. Every now and then Gloria looked over at Lo and Peter talking about something to do with work. She heard the occasional phrase to do with an injunction. The roast pork and vegetables were cooked with Lo's misjudged attempts at precision.

Oliver leaned in confidentially to Gloria. "I only just realized those two aren't married still. I thought he lived here."

Gloria, who was taking a sip of champagne, raised her eyes toward the ceiling and made a grunting noise.

"You don't like him?"

Gloria smiled. "Am I that obvious? Actually, he's not a bad guy but no one else will be able to contribute to that conversation about his injunction, will they?"

Oliver shrugged, his eyes on Lo and Peter. "It takes two to tango."

"I guess."

"Does that mean we can't talk horses?"

Gloria took the redirection of conversation. "Speaking of, I want to hear all about Pogo. When did you bring him here?"

"You like him?"

"He is absolute perfection. I love him. I am in such disbelief that he's mine."

Oliver helped himself to more mashed potatoes and plopped a dollop on Gloria's plate without asking. "Your name is on the paperwork, he's registered to you, so it's all official. My friends Louise and Karl Jensen bred him. When Caroline heard what Dolores was looking for, I thought they might have something. You know why his stable name is Pogo?" Gloria shook her head. "You haven't seen him trot yet then. He has incredible lift. That'll translate well to a good piaffe and passage. He has that natural head carriage too. I think he's a winner."

Gloria looked at Oliver with a new sense of interest. "You know your stuff, don't you?"

"You can see for yourself tomorrow. If that gelding doesn't stop eating and do something with his fat rump he might explode, so you'd better exercise him."

"Stop picking on him, he is the absolute best."

Oliver looked Gloria in the eye but pointed his fork at Lo. "Why'd she buy you the horse?"

"When I left last summer I didn't take any wages. Might be her way of clearing a debt."

Oliver picked something from a back tooth with his tongue. "Might be." He made a sucking sound against his teeth then stabbed at a circle of roast carrot. "You going to take me for a walk to look at your new colt?"

Gloria was ready to say no but she looked across at Lo listening intently to Peter. "After dessert."

Once the meal was over, Gloria felt the weariness kick in. It had been a late boozy night, an early morning of excitement, an argument, and now a heap of food. Claudette had made brandied custard to go with Sue-Anne's pudding. It appeared Caroline had forgiven Lo but she wasn't ready to let Peter off the hook.

"Dolores, Hamlet goes well for Gloria, doesn't he?"

Lo nodded. "Far better than he did for me."

"That's true, but only because she's motivated. You have promise, you just won't put the time into cultivating your talents." Lo smiled vaguely and began serving out the pudding, but Caroline was not to be deterred. "Gloria, did you find Dolores improved with you?"

"With me?"

"Under your coaching." Caroline gave her a meaningful look, which seemed to be more to do with Kip and Mallory than anything else. "Did Dolores improve with Hamlet under your tutelage?"

"Oh, I've never taught Lo."

Kip looked up from pouring custard all over his pudding and smirked at Gloria, who realized what she had just said and how it created an unexpected twist in the story she was supposed to be sticking to.

Lo cut in quickly. "Gloria was here to train the horses."

Caroline waved away an offer of dessert. "What for if you won't ride them?"

Peter sighed. "We don't know yet, she might pick it back up. Isn't that right, Doll? Give it until the summer and then if not, get rid of them. They are a drain on resources when there are other horses sitting in fields begging to be ridden."

Gloria's eyes narrowed and she swiveled in her chair to face Peter. "The horses aren't even here, they're at Caroline's, and I'm looking after them, so you needn't worry that they are draining anyone's resources."

Caroline seemed more than happy to take Gloria's part. "Gloria works for their board so it's all taken care of. Sport horses will rarely show you any capital for your investment, I'm afraid."

Peter nodded. "I originally arranged for Gloria to come here in the hope it would encourage a sense of normalcy or interest if Lo took up the sport like she used to. I mean, there are various types of investments. There is no price on mental health, so in that way it's valid. Whatever Doll wants, I guess."

Gloria was aware of Oliver engrossing himself in the task of eating to stay out of the conversation, but Claudette had no such reserve. "Peter, I always tried to dissuade Lo from those dressage horses. You're absolutely right, there are hundreds of horses here that she could ride." She turned to Lo. "Doll, you always bit off more than you could chew. I think it's great that Gloria has taken on the horses. Now you can focus on work and self-care."

Gloria hated the term "self-care." She knew she looked unamused but she'd had enough and she didn't know why Lo wasn't shutting the conversation down. She dropped her spoon back onto her plate and pushed her chair back slightly. "I'd better go check on the colt. He's not used to this environment yet. Lo, thank you for lunch. Everything was perfect."

Oliver stood with her. "Yeah, great food, Dolores. I'm gonna...yeah." He pointed toward the door as though that offered explanation enough.

Gloria didn't care if anyone thought she was rude. They had no hope of knowing who she was anyway. How could they? She was living a lie.

Oliver held his tongue until they got outside. "Well, that was awkward."

Gloria marched on toward the fence line that ran down to the stables. "It's an odd grouping of people."

Neither she nor Oliver had taken jackets and Oliver clutched himself against the cold.

"I'm trying to piece together the puzzle here. Dolores and Peter are divorced?"

"Something like that." Gloria didn't want to talk about it. "What about you, are you married?"

Oliver's huff of laughter sent a fluffy cloud into the afternoon. "I think that's a way off for me. One day I'd like to have a wife and kids, but I like my lifestyle."

Gloria could feel the damp seeping into her boots. "Is that code for something?"

"Not code, but I do like the bachelor lifestyle. Don't get me wrong, I don't treat women badly or anything. I just don't have time to commit to one woman, so I don't."

"How noble of you."

Oliver shrugged. "What about you? No secret husband in Australia?"

They had reached the stables. Gloria laughed and unbolted the door. "Not at all. Look, here he is!"

Pogo looked at them, his eyes wide. Oliver went to pat him. "He's got a kind nature. He'd only been in a horse truck once but he handled it okay on the trip over. You got a spot here where we can take him out and let him strut his stuff?"

"There's only the barn that's indoors."

"That'll do."

Gloria brought Pogo through to the barn which was still set with tables and hay bales from last night. She turned the fairy lights back on and let Pogo go. He was more interested in snatching mouthfuls of hay than showing off his paces, so Oliver took him by the headcollar and trotted him out for Gloria who sat on a hay bale to watch. Oliver was right—Pogo moved like he was floating in slow motion. After a couple of laps back and forth, Oliver was breathing hard. He came to sit beside Gloria.

"Running after three plates of food isn't the best idea." He sat up straight and undid his belt a notch, then settled back down. Gloria was clutching her knees to her chest for warmth.

"How long are you planning on staying at Caroline's?"

"As long as she needs me. To be honest, her spinal arthritis has degenerated rapidly. She doesn't talk about it much, but she's in a lot of pain and she misses riding. I think that's why she's so hard on me, and probably you. Her career was cut short so she can't fathom anyone who would waste their ability, especially Lo. She takes it so seriously that she can't understand how Dolores can take it or leave it."

Gloria absentmindedly watched Pogo investigating the planks of wood that had been used as the bar top. "Lo's relationship with horse riding is fraught now. She still loves it but won't actively participate in it. She's busy with work again anyhow." She pulled at a flowery stalk of hay and ran it up and down her thigh.

"To live out here"—Oliver swept a hand to indicate around the barn—"she must love it. It would take a lot of work to run this place."

Gloria had had enough. "Yeah. She has staff. Kip manages the place and there are a couple of guys who work under him." She stood up. "I should get Pogo back into his stable where it's warm."

After everyone had left, Gloria and Lo cleared up in near silence. To break the silence, Lo made a valiant attempt at small talk.

"Oliver seems nice. It's good of him to help his aunt."

Gloria squeezed the sponge she'd been using into the sink. "Yeah, he's all right. Apparently, Caroline's back has degenerated a lot."

Lo pushed all the chairs in neatly around the table and placed the fruit bowl that had been relegated to the counter back into the center. "Is that what you guys were talking about at the stables?"

"Yeah, I guess."

"It sounds like she needs help with the day to day, not just the horses."

"She gets around okay. You know how stubborn she is."

Lo nodded and straightened the tea towel which was hanging on the oven door handle. "How about we watch that Christmas movie? We could make popcorn?"

"Will there be one on?"

"There usually is a Hallmark movie or something."

Gloria wiped around the sink. She still had her back to Lo. "Why don't you go on in and see if you can find one? I'll do the popcorn."

"Okay."

Gloria's head was bent over the suds in the sink but she watched Lo wrap her arms around herself and bite her lip in the reflection. After a second Lo bowed her head and walked out of the kitchen. Gloria knew she was hurting her, and she didn't feel any better for it. She threw the sponge into the sink and turned around, leaning against the counter. She had said she would make popcorn so she would, but everything felt pointless. Lo could kiss her and hug her but Gloria knew she wasn't okay with the way things were. The life she wanted was right there but every time she thought she could grab it, it moved out of reach. Standing around overthinking things was helping no one. She found a bag of popcorn and put it in the microwave. She took out a red bowl and put the kettle on to boil. With each action she reminded herself to be present in the moment, not to go worrying or jumping ahead. It would be just like her to throw it all away because she was scared it might be thrown away.

She found Lo in the living room by the fireplace, flicking through television channels with the remote. Lo hastily threw the cigarette she'd been smoking into the flames and swiped at the smoke in front of her face. "Sorry. I tried to hold off on my post-Claudette cigarette, but I lost the battle."

Gloria placed the tray with the popcorn and hot cocoa on the coffee table. "Why do you see her if she stresses you out that much?"

"You know me, just a glutton for punishment. The irony is, she's the one who made me so paranoid about opinions, always expressing hers so freely. I try not to care what she says because I know it'll only hurt me, but she's my mother."

Gloria handed her a mug. "If you keep listening to her opinions, she'll keep giving them to you."

"What are you suggesting I do?"

Gloria sat down on the sofa and put her feet in their socks up on the table. "Have a break. You might find you feel better for it."

Lo came to sit beside her. "It's just because we had special events. I won't be seeing her for a while." She indicated toward the television with the remote. "It looks like it's either halfway through *Jingle All the Way* or *A Christmas Story* is starting in five."

"Put the one on that hasn't started yet or I'll never figure out what's going on." Gloria returned to the subject of Claudette. "All I'm saying is, don't give her the power to hurt you. I couldn't care less what people say about me."

Lo snorted. "You do a bit."

"People who mean something to me, yes, but the rest, no. All you can do is live your true life, and if people don't like it, then too bad." Gloria hadn't meant to lead the conversation there. She shifted her legs so they were bent in the opposite direction to Lo. "It's a waste of energy." She could hear how pious she sounded.

Lo leaned forward and took a handful of popcorn and threw half of it into her mouth. "Let's not spend any more time on it tonight then." She chewed and swallowed. "If I could stay here every day, just you and me, I would. Unfortunately, there's a world of people out there and as much as you wouldn't like them to have any bearing on our lives, they do. They're my clients, your students, they are the people we interact with on a daily basis. You think you wouldn't care if they shunned you, but you would. Trust me, I've been the object of gossip and judgment. It didn't make me better or stronger, it just hurt me and affected the way I interact with the world around me."

Gloria sighed. "Tell me something then, what happened with Kate? I want the full story."

"Didn't you ever kiss girls in high school or college or whatever?"

"No. That's how I know it's you, I just love *you*."

Lo looked miserably at the television as the movie started. "Do we really want to get into this now?"

Gloria took the remote and muted the television. "Maybe that's our problem, we didn't get into enough before I arrived. It's all fine in letters when we're missing each other."

"There was no other way. We didn't get a dress rehearsal, it was straight to the show."

"There's time now. Tell me, I want to know. What happened with you and Kate? Like I said, it was different for me. I have only been with men."

"Kate and I were college kids. Everything is so extreme at that age. She was my TA in Constitutional Law."

Gloria frowned. "What's a TA?"

"Teacher's assistant, so you can imagine it was against protocol. I was smitten from the beginning. She was smart and seemed to hold the keys to everything I wanted to learn right then." Lo smiled. "She was super-serious and pretty much ignored me. She had a girlfriend anyway, a cool girl that was studying film and wore black all the time and had other gay friends who smoked weed on campus grounds and attended protests. What was her name?" Lo paused and Gloria could tell she was looking back through time. "Nope, I can't remember. Anyway, I don't think Kate knew I existed until the professor read out my paper on the constitutional status of individual rights to the class and said I was mixing personal beliefs into an interpretation of the law or something. I was mortified." She blew on the hot cocoa. "Kate thought she had a new little recruit on her hands to fight the power, which was mainly just protesting about the quality of food in the cafeteria and the lack of diversity among the reading lists and so on."

"And let me guess? You became her minion."

Lo laughed. "No! I was far too scared to pick up a placard and go marching around voicing an opinion. Maybe if I had gone along with it, she would have left me alone, but I found her friends terrifying, especially what's-her-name, the girlfriend, so I said I had too much work to do. She offered to help me and ended up staying on campus to help me over the weekend while her friends marched off in support of some cause. The funny thing was, I was actually up to date with my work and had to redo a paper I was writing just to make it look like I had a reason not to go with them."

"Well, she mustn't have wanted to go herself if she stayed to help you."

Lo took a sip of cocoa. "I didn't know it then, but she was on the outs with what's-her-name. Argh, what was it? Something that reminded me of soup."

"Campbell?"

"No, Adele! That's it."

Gloria screwed her nose up. "What does Adele have to do with soup?"

"Sounds like ladle. She smelled a bit like canned soup too, sort of musty. I think it was from sitting in a dorm with the windows closed surrounded by a fog of marijuana."

"It seems like there was no love lost between the two of you."

"She didn't acknowledge me before I was with Kate and she sure as heck didn't give me a second of her attention once it was obvious Kate was seeing me. It wasn't a long relationship, three, maybe four months, but at that age it felt like everything. Kate was intense, though, and more mature than I was. We would lie around reading aloud to one another and taking walks by the river or sitting in bars over one beer for hours because we were both always broke. She wasn't just my first woman, she was my first love, but I couldn't be what she wanted me to be. She was out, she was an activist, always fighting for what she believed in. I just wanted to get through college and get my degree. She broke up with me because I wouldn't take her home over Thanksgiving break, then I broke up with her, then she broke up with me, and so it went until I dropped out of the class. I was completely brokenhearted and cried for weeks, but I knew I wasn't brave enough. My parents wouldn't have coped."

"Do you stay in touch?"

Lo shook her head quickly. "Gosh, no." She picked up the remote and turned the volume back on. "I met Peter eventually, and that was easy."

Gloria stared at the movie without taking much in. After ten minutes had passed without further conversation, she stood up and threw another log on the fire, then excused herself to go to the bathroom. As she washed her hands, she pondered that not much had changed in Lo's mindset. She was still denying herself freedom and love because she was scared of people's reactions, probably Claudette most of all. Young love was like that though; inexperience and enthusiasm crashing and burning. She wasn't sure if love was a feeling or a project. She smiled. A college group project.

When she got back to the living room, Lo was asleep on the couch, her head on the armrest, one arm hanging toward the ground. It was so rare that Gloria saw Lo asleep but she wasn't surprised. Lo had been working so hard to make the last few days special for everyone that she had exhausted herself. Gloria looked at the cigarette packet on the mantel and debated whether to wake her up or throw a blanket over her. She didn't have the heart to wake her, not when she might not get back to sleep for hours. She gently placed the heavy throw rug over her, making sure she was covered up to her chin, and put the screen around the fireplace. On her way to bed, something drew her to open the closed room that had belonged to Terrence. Sue-Anne went in and dusted it sometimes but always when Lo wasn't around. Lo knew she did it, but it was a mutual nondisclosure. Gloria flicked the light on. The room was still a time capsule, a day in the life of a small boy who would never grow up. The wooden train set and farmyard setup were exactly as she remembered them, and she imagined Sue-Anne carefully vacuuming around the toys on the harlequin-printed rug so as not to disturb them. Gloria had never entered the room before, but she did now. The wooden bed frame was painted white and there was a matching white nightstand. On top of it was a nightlight shaped like a toadstool with a red top with white spots. The bedspread was a pale green that picked up the pastels in the harlequin rug on the floor. There was a wooden toy chest that was closed and on the wall were knee-high scuff marks in one spot above some dents in the floorboards. Gloria went to touch her fingers to the scuff marks, wondering what had caused them, then she remembered the old-fashioned rocking horse in the attic. Ah, yes, a little horse-mad boy would certainly have taken that rocking horse for many imaginary adventures. She smiled, remembering herself at that age, and felt a thread of connection to Terrence. She would have loved to have known him, gone for rides, the three of them. It was obvious that the two things were mutually exclusive. She would never have come if the accident had never occurred. It was a strange feeling. On the wall above the toy chest was a framed print of a unicorn mother and baby under a rainbow. Terrence would never grow up and become too cool for that print or demand that his train set be packed away or given to a younger cousin. The skill of the drawing Blu-Tacked to the white closet door would never develop beyond a sun in the corner and pointy mountains with a flat green earth. She went to look at it. So, Terrence had captured the same view she had; it was a view that inspired. The only view now was her own reflection. She whispered a goodbye and turned out the light, closing the door behind her.

CHAPTER SIXTEEN

As Gloria worked Hamlet the next day, she had to admit the flexibility of her legs was tested by his growing girth. She kept thinking of Lo's unwillingness to let Kate into her life either. Like anyone, Lo was a product of her upbringing, Gloria knew that. Her mother was conservative and concerned with form. Gloria's own parents had been busy and her mother was often at the end of her tether and liable to yell, but they had been distracted by careers and, having realized they hadn't yet broken Gloria's older brother, largely left Gloria to her own devices. Claudette had formed an expectation about what her only child would be, one which had most likely started in utero. It was obvious to Gloria that Lo felt the pressure of perfectionism in every aspect of her life.

"You," said Gloria, giving Hamlet a nudge with her heels, "are worried about no one's expectations right now, are you?" She groaned inwardly as she saw Oliver appear, mounted on his gelding, Leonite.

"Hiya, Gloria. Wow, Hamlet can muster up a trot."

Gloria let Hamlet drop back to a walk. She wanted to say something scathing about Leonite in Hamlet's defense, but Leonite was as handsome and trim as his owner, his black coat rippling with health. "Hi, Oliver. Hamlet will try to get away with the bare minimum if he can, but Caroline has been making me get stuck into him."

Oliver's laugh echoed against the tin roof of the arena. "As soon as Leon sees Caroline, he launches into canter pirouettes."

Hamlet looked at Leon with interest, but Gloria urged him on again. "We are not here to make friends, we are here to work." She sent him into a canter and circled him at the farthest end from Oliver. It would do him good to remember how to work with the distraction of another horse again. Hamlet grunted as he cantered along, his lower lip twitching and foam from his mouth splattering his chest. Gloria caught sight of herself in the mirror; she looked so grim. Oliver paid her no mind and began warming up his horse. Gloria continued with Hamlet, Oliver's comments ringing in her ears, working him longer than she usually would. When she finally dismounted and loosened his girth, Hamlet looked away from her in disgust.

"Wait up, Gloria. I was thinking if the weather holds tomorrow, we could ride out. Leon gets sour if I'm always schooling him. He gets bored like me, don't you, boy?" He slapped Leonite's sweaty shoulder.

Hamlet got his opportunity to sniff Leonite's muzzle. Leonite squealed and stamped a hoof, which made Hamlet roll his eyes and sidle away like he was being persecuted. As they walked from the arena, Hamlet tried to befriend Leonite again, but Gloria moved his head away.

"It's not a bad idea. I have a pretty busy day with lessons, but I could go out at lunchtime?"

Oliver pushed a lock of hair from his eye. "Super. I'm looking forward to the trails here in spring. That river must go crazy."

Gloria glanced over at him as they walked outside toward the stables. "You think you'll be here in spring?"

"Unless I can convince Caroline to come back to Iowa with me, which is pretty much like saying unless Leon grows wings and flies back to his stable."

"What then, though?"

"Caroline is hopeful they can get the medication right then she might be able to function. Even so, eventually she'll have to decide what to do with this place."

Gloria tied Hamlet up outside his loose box and took his bridle off. "Would you take over this place? I mean, if Caroline wanted that?"

Oliver paused on the way to the tack room with his saddle over his arm. "Who knows. She may have to sell and go into care."

Gloria sponged the sweat from Hamlet and put a cooling rug on him. She knew Caroline didn't belong in a home—her mind was way too sharp. She understood that Oliver had his own life, though. She of all people knew what it was like to leave everything that was familiar behind.

Her midmorning lesson had arrived so she went past the top paddock to check that Sonnet wasn't doing anything she shouldn't, but Sonnet was standing by the gate with her back to the wind with Rarity, who she would now tolerate, as long as there was no food around, but would not befriend.

That week, Gloria and Lo moved around the house like Sonnet and Rarity in the field—coexisting, but keeping interaction to mealtimes. Lo had put the watercolors on the wall but Gloria didn't want to look at them. They reminded her of the love she felt for Lo that was ready to burst joyfully from her like the sun over a new day, which she had now pulled a shade sail over. Outside was bleak. Lo departed early to get a swim in before work, but Gloria was often at the barn looking after her little pine cone, Pogo, or leaving for Caroline's. Every day, Lo went for a run along the road toward town and back before dinner. Gloria's body and mind ached from riding and agonizing. She wanted to smooth things over with Lo but she didn't know how. Sometimes Sue-Anne and Kip were around to fill the room with conversation, but when it was just the two of them, they spoke about the markers of their day, the small things, but it was what they didn't say that left a void between them. Gloria watched Lo's hands as she pulled the husks from corn, longed to tuck a stray hair behind her ear, hold her feet on her lap when they watched television, but they had mutually settled on a code of conduct without saying a thing. At bedtime, instead of cozying up together, they each lay on their own side of the bed to read their books in silence. Gloria was all too aware of the age gap, and she felt she had acted like a child but didn't know how to make it right because she did care that Lo spent more time with Peter than her and she did care that Lo wouldn't tell people about their relationship.

In the lead-up to New Year's Eve, Oliver and Gloria found a routine of riding out at lunchtime, either on Leon and Hamlet or Rarity and Sonnet. Oliver was easy to talk to and didn't delve into anything deep. She found out his mother had led a rackety life and his father was an Argentinian polo player who had little to do with him growing up. Gloria didn't ask how that made him feel and he didn't go into it, but it explained why he was such a good rider. He told her he'd spent a few summers in Argentina playing polo with his father's other two sons who were younger than him and much better players, but his father had lost interest when Oliver took up dressage, which he felt was for gays and wimps. Gloria had laughed then and Oliver had joined in, able to see the ridiculousness of the comment. Oliver promised when the weather was better, he would show her the basics of polo.

Gloria was surprised when Lo said she wanted to spend New Year's Eve at home alone with her.

"No Peter?"

"No Peter."

Gloria wanted to feel relieved, but she was racked with the constant worry that Lo was having second thoughts and she wouldn't blame her. She knew she was being awful. She felt crushed; she couldn't live with Lo or without her.

At Caroline's, on the last day of the year, Oliver set up show jumps in the arena and they had a jump-off on two of the horses that boarded at Caroline's. Oliver won by two seconds, which infuriated Gloria so much that she insisted they swap horses and jump again, but he still won.

"You asshole. Give me one more go. This time I'm going to cut that corner and go sideways over the parallel."

Oliver shrugged. "You still won't beat me."

"Watch me." Gloria turned the chestnut gelding toward jump number one and as soon as he landed, spun him on his hocks toward jump two. By the time she got to the last corner, the gelding almost slipped over and she sailed over the jump and yanked the horse back to a trot. "Well?"

Oliver held up his wristwatch which they had been passing back and forth. "Thirty-seven point two seconds. You only had to risk your own life and someone else's horse to beat me."

"I beat you by a second and a half. Don't tell Caroline, she'll kill us."

Oliver grinned. "Your secret's safe with me, I would like to see in the new year too." They began to walk a lap to cool off the horses. "What are you doing tonight anyway? Would you like to ring in the new year with me and Caroline? She'll probably go to bed early, but you and I could hang out?"

"Sounds fun, but I told Lo that I would stay home with her."

"Right." Oliver kicked his feet out of the stirrups and loosened his reins to let the horse stretch its neck out. "You're pretty close with Dolores?"

Gloria shrugged and looked down at the buckle of the reins she was holding. "We're friends, I guess."

"It's cool that you get along with her. I mean, it must be fun living out at the ranch. Maybe another night you can stay and have a glass of wine. I don't cook very well but I know how to order pizza."

Gloria hadn't had pizza in so long. She smiled. "Maybe next year, hey?"

Oliver nodded. "It's a date."

As Gloria drove home in the truck, she thought about how distant she'd been from Lo. It was not who she wanted to be. Lo had been trying hard to make things work and Gloria had put up a wall. She owed Lo more than silence. She drove on past the ranch and headed into town. There was a line at the liquor store but Gloria bought some good French champagne and a box of chocolates.

The cashier opened the register. "The roses are a dollar each. If your man didn't bother, buy one for yourself."

"Sure."

Driving back along the main street, Gloria noticed the little ranch run-around car that Lo used for work now parked outside the office. She pulled in beside it and opened the passenger door, which didn't lock, and left the rose on Lo's seat.

At home she showered and put on a fresh long-sleeved T-shirt and jeans and set the table. She tidied the living room and lit a fire, then took the dirty clothes that were left on the bedroom floor to the laundry. She turned the radio on to listen to music while she chopped salad ingredients to go with the pie she was cooking. As she was mixing up a dressing, she heard the front door shut. She opened the oven to check the pie and listened to the sounds she knew so well: Lo dropping her keys in the bowl on the sideboard, the thunk of her briefcase as she let it fall beside the bowl, the quick flick of Lo's jacket before she hung it by the door, then the kicking off of her shoes and aligning beneath the coatrack.

Lo came into the kitchen. "Something smells great."

"Garlic. I thought I'd make a vegetable pie."

"That was thoughtful of you." Lo came to kiss Gloria's cheek as Gloria sprinkled a pinch of salt over the salad. "I'm going to change out of these clothes. Won't be long."

By the time Lo emerged, barefaced without makeup, Gloria was plating up the food. Lo came to take the plates to the table. Gloria opened the fridge and pulled out the champagne and held it as though presenting an award. "Look what we have."

Lo smiled. "Aren't you a clever girl."

Gloria handed it to Lo to take to the table and turned to get two champagne flutes from the cupboard. "Hey, did you get my rose?"

Lo's brow furrowed and she looked up toward the corner of the room, then her gaze dropped to meet Gloria's. "You put that there?"

"Yeah, who did you think?" As she said it, she realized. Lo must have thought it was Peter.

"I wasn't sure." Lo went to sit at the table. "I didn't realize you had come into town." A sudden blast of wind rattled at the windows. "Kip might be right about that blizzard. I'm just glad you're home."

"I hope Pogo is okay."

"He'll be fine. He has Firecat and Bugsy there and Freddy's down the end. The stables are built tight for this weather. This looks amazing, thank you."

"No problem." Gloria picked up her fork and pulled back some of the flaky pastry. "How was your day?"

"Long! Can I pop this?" Lo began to unwrap the champagne.

"Of course, that's what it's for."

Lo held her face to the side and winced as she eased the cork out with a small bang. She poured them out a glass each and they clinked them together in a salute. "To the new year and to us."

After they finished eating, they went into the living room and sat on the sofa by the fire with the blanket on their legs. There was still a stiffness between them. Gloria hoped the alcohol might relax them enough to say what they had to say. It felt like an auspicious time to clear the air, as they were granted the gift of a fresh start in a new year.

"This time a year ago, I never would have dreamt this up." Gloria raised her brows at the thought and shook her head. "No way. In fact, this time last year I was in the city watching the fireworks with Mike. It was an unnaturally cool evening. I think we got rained on." She laughed. "That feels like a different lifetime ago."

Lo was watching her intently as she spoke. "And now here you are."

"Here I am." Gloria took another sip and met Lo's eyes. "What are we doing?"

Lo sighed and she looked down into the bubbles forming in her glass before looking back up at Gloria. "Are we getting into this now?" Her eyes flicked between each of Gloria's. "I don't know if I can give you what you want."

Gloria thought she was prepared for whatever Lo might say, but it still hurt. "You can't or you won't?"

"Isn't it the same thing?"

"No."

"Isn't this enough for you, what we have here?"

"I don't want to live a double life. It's like you're ashamed of me, or of us."

"I'm not. I care about you." Lo's eyes were sad. "I'm just finding my feet in the world. Can't this be enough for you now?"

"It could be if I knew that it was secret for a short time."

Lo puffed her cheeks and let out a slow breath. "Oh, Gloria. I do love you, but I can't guarantee that right now."

"Is this how you broke up with Kate?" Gloria's tone was bitter.

"Don't. That has nothing to do with this."

"But you'll let things unravel in the same way?"

"I don't want things to unravel! I want you to stay here with me always. I would never have asked you to give your life up and move over here if I didn't want a long-term relationship with you, you know that."

Gloria nodded. She did know that. Lo had integrity and would never intentionally mess anyone around. "How do we make that work, though? Maybe you're used to switching into different modes for work, but I can't. It makes me miserable and brings out the worst in me."

"I don't want to fight, not tonight. I want to have a positive mindset into the new year. Can we just put this on the shelf to revisit tomorrow? Come here." Lo held her arms open. "Come on."

The wind shrieked along the side of the house, bringing a splatter of snow. Gloria reluctantly put her glass on the table and moved into Lo's arms, her head nestled into Lo's neck. She closed her eyes and breathed in Lo's faded perfume and the underlying familiar scent that was just Lo. It felt fleeting and fragile. She felt her way along Lo's neck, her thumb sliding under her jaw, finding the softness between the hard curves of bone, then she ran her fingers up to weave into Lo's hair. She blinked, feeling her eyelashes sweep against Lo's skin. Lo wrapped an arm around her, her fingers caressing up and down the length of Gloria's arm.

They made love there on the couch, sadness adding to the intensity. Gloria was aware of every moment, every kiss, every fingertip pressing into her, every slither of Lo's hair across her skin, the sound of Lo's breath, and that any of it, all of it, could be taken away. Lo brought her into being and for a brief moment she was wiped of all emotion except pleasure. "Lola," she whispered. "My angel."

They lay tangled together, Lo's head resting against Gloria's chest. Gloria felt Lo's quiet tears like beads of boiling water.

"Don't leave me."

Gloria ran her fingers gently across Lo's scalp. "I'm right here." She nudged her with her leg. "Come up near me."

Lo wriggled up slightly so her nose was almost touching Gloria's cheek. She reached forward and kissed it. "My girl."

Gloria let Lo shed the tears for them both. She wondered how Lo had felt when she thought the rose was from Peter. Had she put it in a glass of water on the desk, scared to bring it home in case Gloria asked her about it?

Gloria looked at the clock on the wall and smiled. "Miss Wyoming, it is the new year now. We are officially in the future."

CHAPTER SEVENTEEN

January arrived with a dumping of snow. News breaks brought clips of travelers stranded at airports and cars stuck on the interstate. Kip and Samuel cleared a path from the house to the barn and stables. The snow was too thick for anything other than the Gator to get around on, so they were all housebound for a few days. Gloria was fascinated by the shifting white veil that was cast over everything, making visibility so poor that she could barely see the trees in the garden. The lessons she had booked in were canceled and she had to entrust Hamlet's and Sonnet's care to Oliver, who said he was going to take the opportunity to make Hamlet sweat and Sonnet stop being a madam. Gloria reminded him that pride came before a fall, but she had little choice other than to let him find out for himself. It gave her time to spend with Pogo, getting him used to different noises and sensations like walking on tarpaulin and the feeling of a saddle on his back. He was exactly like a trusting baby, googly-eyed and wary but curious. Kip needed all the help he could get with the cattle, making sure they were close to the house and had access to water and feed. The landscape was so changed, only the fence posts sticking up like black markers among the snowdrifts and the buildings, their colors grayed with frost, gave a sense that the ranch lay somewhere beneath the white.

Lo spent hours in the study, catching up on work that had been missed over the holiday period. Like the snow, it was a deluge that banked up and was hard to shift. When Gloria returned from the stables, she would walk by the open doorway and see her at the desk, her reading glasses on, head bent over papers, her lips moving silently. Other times she would be on the phone, pacing like a caged lion. If she saw Gloria, she would smile and look away.

Gloria found there was less of a searing emotional pain when she stayed out of the house, and on the fourth day when the sun had broken through and there was silence, the roads were cleared and she was able to go to Caroline's. She realized how much she was looking forward to seeing Oliver. She had her paperback copy of *Dressage Masterclass Volume One* to lend him, reread so many times that its yellow cover was creased, the pages soft.

"Gloria!" Oliver came out to the sound of the truck as she pulled into the slushy gravel lot in front of the stables. He waved his arms like he was bringing in a plane.

Gloria was smiling as she climbed down. She held out the book and wiggled it. "I remembered."

"Thanks. Hey, listen, Caroline and I are about to have a coffee. Come inside for a bit."

"All right. Let me see the horses first."

Gloria went to greet Hamlet, who whinnied gratifyingly when he saw her, and Sonnet, who moved away when Gloria tried to pat her, then went up the drive to the house.

Caroline opened the door and she looked so pleased to see Gloria that some of the hollowness she had been feeling was filled with warmth. Oliver came tearing up the path after Gloria, his boots splashing in the newly formed puddles.

"Take those off before you come in," Caroline called. "Gloria, sit down by the fire there before Oliver gets the best seat. I hope you don't mind Cleo, she'll treat you like the furniture."

Gloria took a seat on the velvet armchair that wasn't occupied by a sleeping white cat and looked around at the different art forms covering every available surface. There was such a lot to look at: paintings and tapestries and photographs and art deco lamps and ornate rugs on the floor.

"Oliver, bring a couple of the muffins out with the coffee," Caroline called. She came to sit next to Gloria, easing herself down to one side so as not to disturb the cat who stretched and moved aside to hop on her lap. "It's a lot to take in at once. I just can't let beautiful things go."

"I'm trying to find a common theme."

Caroline ran her hand along the cat's back. "Everything in this room is beautiful to me in some way. Twenty-eight years with an art dealer will amass you quite a collection! Andy and I never had children and I can't bear to throw anything out. Oliver shows no interest in it, but I like being surrounded by lovely things, especially now that I don't get out so often."

Oliver came in with a tray laden with coffees and banana muffins and shortbreads in the shape of stars. He spoke through a mouth of shortbread. "Is any of it worth anything?"

Caroline scoffed. "It's all worth something to me. If you mean, would anything fetch a sum of money, well, some of it, yes, but I'm not telling you which pieces. Just put the tray on the table, Oliver."

Oliver placed the tray on a sculpted teak side table. "Where will I sit?"

"You've got strong legs, come stand by me but don't block the fire."

Gloria bit back a smile. "Oliver, here." She scooched herself over to the side to make room for him.

Caroline raised her eyebrows as Oliver squashed in beside Gloria. "These shortbreads were made by Moira. Don't think I'm not aware that you two were tearing around the jumps on her gelding."

Oliver reached for two muffins and passed one to Gloria. "I swear I didn't tell her!" he hissed. "She's probably got a crystal ball among this clutter."

"There are only two horses here that have been trained to jump fences that size, Luna and Bravo, and judging by the skids and divots in the sand, there wasn't a lot of care taken."

"Sorry, Caroline. It's just that Oliver beat me in a jump-off and I'm very competitive so I couldn't let it go. It won't happen again."

"It was a stupid thing to do. You could have injured the horses or yourselves, and if Moira gets wind of it, there'll be trouble. Oliver, pass me the cup. But Gloria, that's one of the things I like about you, you've got spunk. If you weren't competitive there'd be no point doing competitions."

Gloria mumbled a thanks through a mouthful of buttery banana muffin and pointed toward the plates so Oliver could pass her one.

Caroline watched them tussling over the plate. "Gloria, what happened with you and Keaten? Did he hitch up with that girl who doesn't stop giggling?"

"I'm trying to mend my broken heart. He does seem to prefer Mallory to me."

"Just as well. Every time I'm in town he seems to be with another girl. A bit like some others I know." Caroline shot Oliver a look.

Gloria scrunched up her paper napkin and dropped it into Oliver's lap, then stood up. "I should get to it. Thanks for the muffin, absolutely delicious."

Oliver threw the napkin into the fire and stood up. "I'll see you out."

At the door Gloria paused with her hand on the handle. "You're not coming out?"

"Later. I have to do a few things in here first." His voice dropped to a whisper. "It's hard for her to vacuum or clean the bathroom or anything, so I need to do a bit of tidying."

"I might see you later, then. Hopefully the weather holds."

Oliver put his hand over hers as he opened the door. "Bye, Grant."

As Gloria walked back to the stables, she felt the blood pumping in her cheeks, batting up against the cold air. Sure, Oliver was handsome, but he was more like a brother.

That evening when Gloria came inside from putting Pogo to bed, the house was dark. She kicked off her boots and hung her coat up and opened the back door. She turned the light on and saw that Sue-Anne must have come because the breakfast dishes were gone and there was a cardboard box of groceries on the counter. Next to the box was a folded piece of paper. At first Gloria thought it was a note from Sue-Anne, but when she picked it up, she realized it was written on the back of scrap paper that had been some type of legal agreement. She opened it and saw Lo's old-fashioned penmanship.

Gloria, I am going to stay in town for a few days in case there's another blizzard—there's too much work to do at the office. It might give us time to clear our heads. You can reach me on the office number any time, but I will call you when I'm coming home. Yours, Lo X

Gloria felt devoid of emotion as she stared down at the piece of paper. Yours? It seemed not. She dropped back onto the stool and put her elbows on the counter, letting her chin flop into her cupped palms. She read it again. So, Lo would be staying in the apartment in town with Peter? Was that it then? Lo didn't want to be around her. She was surprised that Lo wanted to be back with Peter. It certainly hadn't been working with him for a long time. Still, the divorce wasn't finalized, they were separated but that could change. Gloria wasn't sure where she fit in with it all. She could just leave. She could go anywhere really, just start again. Obviously Lo wouldn't want to sponsor her as an employee anymore. It felt she was looking at her life from a distance. She left the note where it was and went to pour herself a whiskey in the living room. Her appetite had suddenly left her. She lit the fire and sat, staring at the blank television and sipping her drink. A bubble of laughter rose and escaped. How had it come to be that she was sitting in the ranch house and Lo and Peter had left to stay in town? From above the fireplace, Lo's likeness stared down at her. Gloria remembered being struck by how vibrant Lo had looked in that photograph with Hamlet compared to the Lo she had met. By now she had seen every expression Lo had to offer. Well, she told herself, you take big risks, you have to be prepared to take big losses. She downed the whiskey and went to do the only other soothing thing she could think of, which was to have a hot shower.

The next morning, she lay in the spare bed. She couldn't bear the vastness of Lo's bed without her. Lo hadn't called. Gloria had fallen asleep easily but had woken hours before dawn, her mind whirring in circles until her skull was an echoing chamber. She felt wretched and she knew without looking that she would be late to Caroline's. She pulled the pillow over her head to block out the light and lay there, too full of self-pity to cry. She had imagined the countless things Peter would be saying to Lo and the countless ways that Peter would be touching Lo. The way Lo had left, just like that. Nothing more than a scribbled note. The indifference wounded Gloria more than any hatred might. Outside the window, a stupid bird was caroling away, letting Gloria know that it would be a beautiful, mild day. Gloria didn't care. She didn't call Caroline and tell her she wasn't coming in and she didn't go outside to see Pogo. She pulled the curtains closed and lay in bed and cried. It wasn't until after midday that she dragged herself out of bed and went to make a coffee and mope in the kitchen instead. Outside, she could see Kip taking a roll of hay out to the cattle. She knew he could use her help, but she was sick of being helpful. Lo's note was still on the counter next to the groceries. Gloria scrunched it up and threw it in the trash. Sticking out of the top of the box was a bunch of celery. Gloria didn't want to think about the jokes she and Lo had shared. She felt a sudden elevation of Mallory in her eyes. Who were they to call her Celery when Mallory was successfully conducting a romantic relationship and they were not? Gloria threw the celery in the trash too. Sue-Anne should stop buying it. It only ended up as chicken feed anyway.

By midafternoon, Gloria had taken all of her belongings from the room she had shared with Lo and put them in the spare room. The pine cone sat on Lo's bedside table like a traitorous little bomb. Gloria moved it behind Lo's glass of water so she wouldn't have to keep seeing it. Lo's glass, with the invisible fleshy imprint of Lo's bottom lip. Gloria was tempted to lift it to her own lips. The thought made her begin to cry again. Those lips were no longer hers to kiss.

After the bedrooms were sorted, Gloria began on the fridge, throwing out half-eaten foods and tins in the pantry past their expiry date. The rest of the gingerbread house was still on a shelf waiting to be finished. Gloria lobbed that at the trash too. Every now and then she glanced outside to make sure Kip wasn't around to ask her why she hadn't seen to Pogo. As she was restacking all the dry goods that she had deemed acceptable to stay in the newly wiped down pantry, the doorbell rang. She considered ignoring it, but without anyone else around, she wasn't sure if it was important. She hastily put the last packet of coffee filters away and went to see who it was. She hoped it wasn't a murderer; she should lock the door tonight.

When she opened the door, it wasn't a murderer, just the concerned face of Oliver.

"Oh, you are alive."

Gloria clung to the door sheepishly. "Sorry, I had a headache."

"Your students all showed up expecting the makeup classes they missed during the bad weather."

Gloria sighed. "Awful headache."

"You don't look great."

She knew she looked dreadful: messy hair, her oldest sweatpants which had to be tied up because the elastic was going, her eyes bloodshot from all the crying she had done. "I would invite you in but—"

"Thanks." Oliver pushed past her. "You going to tell me what's really going on?"

Gloria held her palms face up in a gesture of hopelessness. "What do you want, Oliver? I'm sorry, I'll sort it out with them. I just don't feel well."

Oliver squinted at her. "Are you sure there's not something else?"

"It's a migraine. I get them sometimes." She remembered she wasn't wearing a bra and folded her arms across her chest.

"Are you mixing alcohol and prescription meds?"

"What? No! Seriously, I just want to go back to bed."

Oliver looked at the photos that remained on the bureau by the door. "Because my mom used to do that, mix her meds with alcohol. She'd be passed out and I'd get to watch cartoons instead of going to school. I didn't know my multiplication tables but I could quote any episode of *Scooby-Doo*."

Gloria smiled in spite of herself. "Who needs maths anyway?"

There was a silence while they looked at each other. Gloria could tell Oliver wanted her to invite him in but she felt hideous and unsocial.

Oliver scratched the back of his neck and looked at the floorboards. "Well, I guess I'll be going then. I just wanted to check you're okay. The horses are fine. I cleaned the stalls out and gave them their breakfast. They're outside at the moment, but I can work them if you want me to?"

"Thank you. They can have a day off. Hopefully Caroline can get another stable hand in so you're not so flat out. I should be back on deck tomorrow."

"It's quiet without you. No one to hurl snowballs at. Anyway, I hope you're feeling better."

Gloria uncrossed one arm to open the door. Outside the sun bounced off the snow, making her squint. The banks around the house had melted leaving pools of water and mud. "Bye, mate."

Oliver grinned. "Later, Grant."

Gloria shut the door and leaned her forehead against it. She heard the car door slam and the engine come to life. A vast loneliness had settled inside her. She had no one to turn to with her problems. By the time her friend June got home from work in Melbourne, it would be past Gloria's bedtime. Sue-Anne kept the house too neat, there was nothing left to scrub. She had even sewed up the holes in Gloria's socks. The barn had been cleaned before the dance and the stables were always maintained by Kip and Samuel. Gloria thought guiltily of her baby, Pogo. She should take him for a walk.

Gloria and Pogo's walk had turned into an effort as they encountered snowdrifts and hidden obstacles buried underfoot. As Clarence shoveled out the path, he made sure to throw dirty snow on them as they passed. When they got back, Kip had been unnaturally short tempered with Gloria, and she'd had to wait until she was in Pogo's loose box to burst into tears.

The house was so huge without anyone around. Every time she came in from the yard, she checked the phone but none of the recorded messages were from Lo. She tried watching television, then she tried reading a crime novel that Mallory had lent her, then she tried doing both at once. When that failed to hold her attention, she sat on the floor by the fireplace and removed the chipped nail polish from the salon and repainted her finger and toe nails pale pink. There wasn't much use because it just chipped off with all the work she did with her hands, but it was something to do. She thought of ringing her parents but what would she say—she'd broken up with her girlfriend? They hadn't understood why she had ended things with Mike, so they sure as hell wouldn't be able to comprehend that she had a second breakup with a woman they knew nothing about. Gloria wanted to tell them about Lo, but she had been waiting for Lo to be open to meeting them as her partner. Gloria had a feeling they would like Lo. Not now, though. To ease the loneliness, she dried the nails off and went to bed. She was getting the hang of insomnia herself.

The next day she loitered at Caroline's, not wanting to leave the stables and go home to the empty house again. Caroline was off visiting a friend and Oliver went out for a long ride so she could have use of the arena for her students. Gloria hung around, cleaning all the bridles and making up the next day's feeds. Eventually Oliver returned, his sleeves rolled up despite the cold.

"Oh, hey. I didn't know you'd still be here."

Gloria wiped the chaff from her hands on her breeches. "I sandwiched in as many lessons as I could today to make up for yesterday."

"I had to do some serious covering for you with Moira yesterday. I ended up giving her a free one-on-one."

"She would have loved that. Did she even bother bringing the horse?"

Oliver unrolled the support bandages on Leonite's legs. "She wanted to book another lesson but I said I don't usually teach show jumping."

"One day off and you pinch my students from me?"

Oliver hung the bandages over the stall door to dry off. "I'm pretty sure you pinched her from Caroline, but don't worry, I have no intention of spending another minute alone with that woman. Hey, by the way, I have your book for you. If you don't mind waiting for me to put Leon away, I can grab it."

"Sure." Gloria watched him rub Leonite's legs with a towel. "Let me do that. You grab the book if you want."

Gloria finished making sure Leonite was dry and warm and put all his rugs back on. By the time Oliver returned, Leonite was back in his stall.

Oliver handed Gloria the book. "Thanks for doing that."

"No, thank you, for yesterday, and for checking on me, that was really nice of you. Maybe tonight, if you don't have plans, you want to come over and have dinner? I'm not sure if they deliver pizza all the way out there but I can make something?" She hadn't planned on making the offer, but the thought of another night alone was depressing.

A surprised smile lit Oliver's face. "Yeah, I'd like that. Why don't I bring the pizza to you, that way you don't have to cook?"

It was Gloria's turn to smile. She hugged the book to her chest. "That actually sounds wonderful. Just come over whenever you're ready. I'm usually back from checking the horses at home around six."

Gloria wasn't expecting to feel such panic as the time drew near for Oliver to ring the doorbell. It wasn't a date, but it had been so long since she'd had a friend over. She made sure the house was warm, there was something to drink in the fridge, a fresh handtowel in the bathroom. She even lit a scented candle on the dining table. Lo still hadn't called but Gloria pushed the thought from her mind. Like Lo said, they both needed time to think things through. Gloria's hands shook as she put mascara on to distract from the dark circles under her eyes. She felt she had to redeem herself after her haggard appearance yesterday. As a last-minute thought, she repainted the tips of her nails where the polish had chipped. The doorbell rang as she was flapping her hands by the fire, trying to dry the nails off. She took a deep breath. A sudden thought of Lo intruded, Lo's eyes filling with light when she looked across the crowded barn and found Gloria, the secret smile they shared. Gloria swallowed back the lump in her throat.

Oliver had slicked his hair back from his forehead and shaved his stubble. He had on denim jeans and a navy sweater that brought out the blue of his eyes. He was balancing a pizza box and a bottle of red wine. Despite the smell of pizza, Gloria could still make out the tang of Oliver's aftershave.

"Long time no see," he said.

"Hey, stranger. Let me take that from you." She took the pizza box and led the way through to the kitchen, where she put it on the counter. "Thanks for bringing dinner."

Oliver put the wine down and looked around. "The Christmas decorations are gone."

"Yeah, back in the attic. Kip chopped the tree up for kindling. It's dried out now."

Oliver pointed at her watercolors hanging on the wall. "Were those pictures there last time?"

"No. Hey, are you hungry? We should probably eat this before it gets cold."

"Yeah, whatever you like."

Gloria piled plates on top of the pizza box and carried it through to the living room where she got some wineglasses from the dry bar and set them on the coffee table. "I thought we could eat here where it's warmest."

"This is a huge room. Oh, look at Dolores on Hamlet there. I didn't realize she was that good."

Gloria knew without looking what the photo looked like of Lo and Hamlet being presented with a first-place rosette. "Yeah, for the time she competed him, they did well." She opened the pizza box. "A vegetarian pizza."

"How could I forget? It's such a weird thing for someone who lives on a cattle ranch. I hope you like red wine?"

They sat on cushions on the floor and as they ate, they chatted about the horses, moving easily from topic to topic, the conversation and the drinks flowing. She loved that Oliver was so easygoing, laughing off even the heaviest subject. The time slipped by and after an hour she realized she hadn't thought of Lo once. As soon as she did, her happy vibe came crashing down and the heart-sick feeling returned. She took a gulp of wine.

"You okay, Grant? You look like you saw a ghost. Have I brought the migraine back?"

Gloria shook her head. "No, sorry. It's nothing."

"You must miss home. I've only been out here a couple of weeks but I miss watching sports with the guys and the people at work. I even miss my boss, Dina, and we don't often see eye to eye."

"My knees are starting to hurt from sitting like this." Gloria climbed up onto the couch and patted the seat next to her. "How did that all work with you coming here? Did you take time off or quit?"

"My role is equestrian event management. I can still do some from here if I need to, but essentially someone else can handle most of it while I'm not there. We do some of the dressage galas, sales, the eventing, the polo."

"That sounds like a cool job."

"I love it, that's why I don't want to quit. Dina knows that I have a rapport with most of those organizations and suppliers, so she'll cut me some slack for a while. She doesn't want me to walk and take any clients with me. She's a real micromanager and we used to clash, but she's learned I can't work like that and now she leaves me alone for the most part. But, hey, I asked you, though. Are you homesick?"

Gloria watched the flames curling around a blackened log. "Sometimes. I miss Klaus's stables, my friends, my parents. It's the small things too, like my favorite café and the sound of magpies warbling in the gum trees, stuff like that. Even just knowing my way around without directions or a map. This time of year is so hot at home. Christmas barbeques and swimming in the pool."

"It sounds like you had a full life in Australia. Why come here?"

Gloria took a sip of wine and shrugged. "Things weren't going well with Mike and I was feeling suffocated. I needed to do something drastic, so when I heard about the job here I didn't hesitate. Things weren't perfect back home, not by a long shot. Klaus can be difficult at the best of times—big fish, small pond, you know how it goes."

"You're pretty impulsive. Weren't you scared?"

"I was terrified, but it got to the point where things were so bad that it still seemed worse to stay than to go."

"Just like with show jumping. If the fence looks scary, just dig the spurs in, hold on tight, and let fate do the rest."

Gloria laughed. "Yep, pretty much."

Oliver leaned forward and brushed a finger over Gloria's chin. "Sauce."

Gloria swiped at her chin. "Are you kidding me? That must have been there at least half an hour."

"Maybe more. It looked sorta cute."

Gloria shot him a look under her lashes as she took another sip of wine. "Hardly."

"Look, there's sauce on your cheek," Oliver joked, attempting to poke her cheek, but Gloria grabbed his hand, trying to force it away.

She laughed. "Get your fat finger away from me."

"There's more on your nose."

Gloria shrieked as Oliver dipped a finger in some sauce on the pizza box. He held his finger as though he was going to wipe it on her nose and she grabbed his hand again, pushing it away. She fell back and Oliver fell half on top of her, then put a forearm across her and licked the sauce from his finger.

"Get off. You're like a whale. I feel sorry for Leonite."

"I've never had any complaints before," Oliver said, leaning his weight on her.

"Consider this a first. The only reason Leon hasn't bucked you off is because you're too heavy. No wonder he scores so low for his canter."

"Take that back."

"No."

"Take it back!"

"No." Gloria grinned then wriggled an arm out to push at Oliver's face.

Oliver grabbed her wrist and pinned it down. "Say sorry."

Gloria laughed. "No way."

"Then kiss it better." Oliver's face was only inches away from Gloria's, his firm body pressed against hers. He leaned forward and his mouth found hers and she didn't say no. She melted into the kiss and when his hand let go of her wrist and found her neck she didn't pull back. His hands moved over her body, under her shirt, and her hands moved of their own accord, feeling the firmness of his chest, the ropes of muscle in his biceps and shoulders. He moved his mouth to her neck and murmured, "Are you okay, Grant?"

"Yes," she said, her body alive under Oliver's touch. Inside she felt a little less cold, like Lo's distance didn't matter. She was wanted and desired. She took Oliver's face in her hands and kissed him, feeling the rough skin on his jaw, the coiled strength of his body. "Not here," she said.

He looked at her questioningly but didn't object as she took him by the hand and led him to the spare room, almost stumbling on the stairs, banging her hip on the bedpost and laughing. Oliver pulled his sweater and T-shirt over his head and somehow Gloria's pants were on the floor and she knew what she was about to do but she didn't care. It was the happiest she had felt in days.

"Are you sure?" Oliver asked again.

"Have you got anything? Protection, I mean?"

"Yeah, I think so. Wait, shit. I'm pretty sure I have something from ages ago." He picked his jeans up from the floor and rifled through, looking for his wallet. "Yes."

Oliver was accustomed to using his body to subtly manipulate a huge animal, and with Gloria his touch was strong but sensitive. There was no thought involved, he was focused on pleasing her and knew just the right amount of handling and pressure to make her body respond. When they were done, he slumped onto her and laughed softly into her neck. "Shit, Grant. I wasn't expecting that."

Gloria's fingers ran lightly up and down the muscles on his back, like a blind person reading braille. In the semi-light coming through from the landing, Gloria looked up at the ceiling with a feeling like she was floating out of her body. She could feel the heat of Oliver's skin, gravity pulling his form down upon hers, but she felt disconnected from it, like someone feeling the weight of lemons in a bag before putting them on the grocery scale.

"Oliver, hop off."

Oliver rolled off her onto his back. "Sorry." He kissed the side of her jaw. "You're beautiful."

Gloria's mouth smiled but she didn't want it. She didn't want any of it. She sat up and reached for her bra which had landed on the floor beside the bed. She found her underwear and wriggled into it. Oliver pulled the sheet over his waist and legs. She just wanted him to go back to being her friend, not to look at her like she was his to look at.

"Do you want a glass of water?"

Oliver sat up and put a hand on her thigh. "Hey, it's okay."

"I know, I just…"

Oliver leaned forward and grabbed his clothes. Gloria sat on the edge of the bed and looked at the floor, her legs jittering and her head pounding. Oliver got dressed and took her hand. "Grant, it's cool."

They stood up and Oliver held her hand, swinging it between them as they walked to the kitchen. The pipes hummed as Gloria filled two glasses of water. She couldn't meet his eye.

"I can tell you're not all right. Tell me what you want me to do? Do you want me to go now?"

Gloria felt foolish and rude but her desire for company had now switched to wanting to be alone. "Oliver, I'm sorry. I'll see you tomorrow."

"I didn't hurt you, did I?"

Gloria shook her head and chanced a look at his face. "Not at all. It was great, I guess I'm just not in the frame of mind for company."

Oliver shrugged. "I don't regret it, but I'm not going to ask anything from you. I like you, I think you're one cool cat, but I don't need a relationship either, if that's what you're worried about."

"No. I know."

"So, we're good?"

"Yep. We're good."

Oliver cupped the back of her neck in his big hand and kissed her cheek, then squeezed her jaw. "All right, Grant. We'll chalk this one up to digging the spurs in and flying over the fence?"

The corners of Gloria's mouth lifted but she didn't move as he let himself out.

CHAPTER EIGHTEEN

Insomnia was like walking through a dusty city, devoid of inhabitants, the wind blowing through the channels between the buildings. Everything echoed and there was no relief. Gloria's sheets smelled like Oliver's cologne. The clock ticked over to 3:50 and Gloria decided that was close enough to the morning and got up. Her mind clanged like the inside of a giant metal bell, resonating an aftershock over the empty city.

She showered and dressed and stripped her bed and cleaned up the living room. She hadn't realized anything could be worse than Lo walking away from her, but she now realized things could be worse. She went down to the stables in the dark to muck out the loose boxes and give the horses their feeds. She clung to Pogo's neck as he ate his breakfast. He was so good and decent. An impure thought could never and would never enter his head. She supposed she would have to give him up too, but not yet. He felt like her own child, the way he took in everything she did like a little sponge, wonder in his big eyes. He turned and nudged her now, spreading chaff on her parka. She kissed his silky cheek and left him to finish his food.

When she got to Caroline's, the arena lights were on and she could hear the thud of a horse's hooves against the sandy earth. She busied herself cleaning the stalls so Oliver wouldn't have to do anything for her horses. Hamlet was delighted that she was playing around in his room, and every time she bent over, he tickled her back with his whiskery muzzle. When she returned with the last load of fresh sawdust, the sun had risen and Oliver was coming back on a sweating Leonite. He slid to the ground. "Hey, Grant. I've been thinking, and I reckon we should hug it out."

Gloria felt relief wash through her, and she walked over and fell into his arms. He squeezed her, lifting her off her feet, then set her back down. "I like you too much to let such a simple thing as a roll in the hay get in the way of that."

She held on to him, absorbing his innocent goodness just like she had Pogo. Why couldn't she make people feel okay like that? She should have hugged Lo and told her everything would be fine. Instead, she had hurt another person.

That night at home, the wind gusted against the siding, heralding another storm. This time Gloria accepted the lonesome feeling as her due. A snowy purgatory for her sins. She read by the fire until the icy winds of nature won the battle over manmade structures and the power went out.

During the night the wind swirled around the house and down the chimney, branches slapped the walls and scratched against the windows. Gloria lay with her heart racing, convinced that there was someone in the house who would creep up and strangle her in her bed. With the power out and the phone lines down, she would have no way of calling for help. She wondered who would care. Would Lo cry at her funeral? The house creaked and murmured and she was sure someone was on the stairs. She thought of running to Kip's and sleeping on his sofa, but she was too embarrassed to wake him up. Better just to take her chances with the murderer. There was a bang that sounded like the front door. Gloria pulled the covers over her head and huddled, barely able to breathe. Surely those were footsteps. Something touched her leg and she screamed.

"Gloria!"

Gloria peeked out of the covers and saw a person standing over her. For a moment she thought her time really was up, but then she made out the form of Lo wearing several layers of sweaters, her hair in a top knot. Gloria clutched her heart. "Lo! You scared me."

The mattress dipped under Lo's weight as she sat down. "Sorry, I tried to call but the lines are down. I was worried about you with no power out here by yourself."

Gloria sat up. "As you can see, I'm fine."

Lo's features were in shadow, but Gloria could see the glistening whites of her eyes. "I miss you."

Gloria's shoulders hunched. "It was your choice to leave."

"I know. I just thought we both needed time to ourselves to cool down and think about how we move forward."

"So, you left to stay with Peter?"

"You were avoiding me like the plague. It seemed you needed time to yourself. Where else could I go? My mother's?"

"I don't know. Anywhere but to your ex-husband's? Stay here and talk to me, maybe."

"I should have, and you should have spoken to me. I don't think this is one-sided."

"Did you come back to fight with me? It's the middle of the night."

Lo reached a hand out and placed it on the covers over Gloria's legs. "No, I came to tell you that I'm miserable without you." She opened her fingers, waiting for Gloria to take her hand. "But if you want me to go away, just say the words."

Seconds passed as Gloria stared at her hand. Different thoughts and emotions pulled at her. Guilt, fear, relief, apprehension, anger, but she knew the only reason those emotions existed at all was because they bobbed on an ocean of love. Her hand was warm under the covers, but she took it out and let it join Lo's. "I want you to stay. I've always wanted you to stay."

Lo let go of the breath she'd been holding. "That's a relief, because I had to use all my power of persuasion to get Sergeant Barker to drive me out here in the truck."

Just like the first night months ago when Gloria had been set to fly back to Melbourne, Lo climbed into the narrow bed beside her and Gloria folded the blanket over her. Gloria felt a wave of joy and sorrow rising up inside her, crashing through every other feeling, and she took Lo in her arms. They held on, pressed against every part of one another they could. Lo's knee was digging into Gloria's thigh and her nose was squashed but she didn't care. She felt Lo's body, alive and close through the layers of clothing. Lo was home in her arms, but now Gloria had put a secret between them, and even if she agreed to keep their relationship hidden, even if Oliver didn't kiss and tell, she would know what she had done. Whatever they had to say, it could wait until morning. For the first time that week, they both slept.

In the morning, they sat next to each other at the breakfast table, Gloria resting her head against Lo's shoulder.

"Now," said Lo. "I think we need to discuss this like a business meeting."

"Do we?"

"Yes, go and sit over there." Lo indicated to the chair opposite with the pen she was holding. Gloria obeyed even though it seemed stupid. Lo put on her reading glasses and drew a line down the middle of the notepad in front of her. "That's your column, that's mine. First, I'm putting in mine that I don't like the way we create silences instead of saying what we think."

Gloria watched her write down her first dot point. "Well, I don't like the way you go off and do things that are 'surprises.' It just makes me feel excluded."

Lo looked up at her. "Really? Okay, fair point. What else?"

"You prioritize work over everything."

Lo's head tipped to the side. "Now, that's not fair. You're always working too."

Gloria shrugged one shoulder. "You asked."

"I'm going to put it in both our columns. We can discuss that further later."

Gloria chewed the inside of her cheek, wondering whether to say her number one concern. It was the time to do it. "It bothers me how much time you spend with Peter. It's like you're still together. In fact, Oliver thought you were still together."

Lo frowned but she wrote it down. "On that note, you and Oliver seem quite close. Again, we will revisit these subjects more thoroughly when we have time."

Gloria felt the air leave her lungs. All she could do was say, "Okay."

"I know the thing we keep arguing about is when I am going to 'come out,' but I have to tell you, Gloria, that it's something I have to do in my own time."

Gloria was still winded from Lo's observation about Oliver. "Let's revisit that later."

"Definitely." Lo tapped the end of the pen against her lips. "These are discussion points only. We can add to them." She took her glasses off and folded them back into their case. "I want to take you out. No surprises, you pick where, and I would like to start again, properly this time. I can't do this on-again, off-again thing. It's not good for my mental health, or yours, I'm sure. I've had another session with Doctor Linley."

"That's great, I'm proud of you. Did you talk to her about what's been going on?"

Lo stood up and began to slip her suit jacket over her striped shirt. "Not about you and me. We have just picked up from where we left off after Terrence died, but I must say when I think back to that time, I can see a marked difference. I wasn't very receptive to her. Honey, I have to go." She put her glasses case into her bag. "I'm going to make sure I'm home by six tonight."

"Just leave the dishes, I'll clean up." Gloria stood to kiss Lo.

"I missed that. Give me one more, quick."

Gloria pulled her close and kissed her, then let her go. "Bye."

The weather held for her lesson with a woman called Lisa at a small property on the outskirts of town. Despite hugging it out with Oliver, she felt uncomfortable with him because he reminded her that she'd been untrue, not only to Lo, but also to herself. That made her angry more than anything. She was getting sick of winter too, it made everything so hard. She wanted longer days, warmer weather, feed on the ground for the horses, and competition season to begin so she felt all her hard work had a purpose. She was spending so much time outside and her body was fit, if not full of aches and pains, but she felt cooped up, like the world had closed in. Lo had told her that winters were hard, but she hadn't understood the claustrophobia of it. When she mentioned it to Lo, Lo suggested they spend a day skiing so Gloria could see the other side of Wyoming winters. Gloria had never been skiing before.

"You know what," Lo said. "Let's stay at the lodge for a night. I'll take a day off and we'll hang out. I'll teach you to ski."

"I'm booked out for the next few weeks with a backlog of lessons. I can't cancel again. Plus, I've taken on a couple more horses under training. Everyone wants the edge before the season starts."

"I get it, my diary is full too, but I'm trying not to prioritize work, remember? If we plan two or three weeks in advance, can you make that work?"

Gloria nodded. "Of course."

Despite Lo's confidence that she could rearrange her diary and Gloria's assertion that she would sort out her schedule, they then had the challenge of aligning the days with one another. February had begun and there had been record snowfall. Lo had to pull strings with the manager of the Eagle Eye ski lodge to get them a room at short notice.

"How did you convince him?" Gloria asked as they wound along alpine roads in the truck, heading skyward.

Lo grinned. "Fortunately for us, his son is a delinquent and I got him off drug possession charges not once, but twice."

Gloria smirked too. There was a confidence about Lo that surprised and delighted Gloria every day. She felt her own confidence grow alongside hers. Lo's straightforward approach to problem-solving had opened a door for clearer communication, and they had been making an effort to spend at least half an hour each day together, even if it meant getting up extra early. In fact, such a simple thing as talking about their feelings had made Gloria see how many conclusions she jumped to, causing herself mental anguish for no reason and the childish way it made her act. The unpredictability of Klaus's affections had been her founding example of a relationship, but in actual fact, Lo was predictable and what she said, she meant. This had come to Gloria as a revelation and a relief. Lo had been working on herself, attending therapy and swimming or running every day. Gloria was pouring her energy into building relationships with the horse community through Caroline and her clients and getting Hamlet into peak condition. Most of the time she forgot about her indiscretion with Oliver but then something would remind her, like a scene in a movie or the scent of cologne, and she would feel a pit of dread open up and swallow her happiness. For the most part, she and Oliver got along as friends, although they had both taken a step back. They had had one bust-up over Oliver using Hamlet's white bandages and leaving them brown and sodden by the wash bay. It wasn't such a big deal, but it had triggered a fight where Oliver had called her a snob and said she always wanted everything on her terms. Gloria had replied that he was careless and never took anything seriously. Oliver had called her a self-interested bitch and Gloria had slammed the tack room door on him and left a wheelbarrow of soiled sawdust in the aisle for him to figure out, regrettably giving substance to his argument. By the next day their good natures had won out and they were back to imitating Moira when they greeted each other and bickering over who had the arena booked. Gloria still had dreams of having an indoor arena at the ranch where she wouldn't have to defrost the car in the dark to drive to Caroline's every morning and she could have all the horses in the stables together. Pogo hadn't even met Hamlet and Sonnet yet. She had to rely on Oliver again to take care of them while she was skiing, and she was trying to switch off from thoughts about Sonnet's hip and whether upping Hamlet's oats would give him digestive issues. Lo, ever the chameleon of emotion, appeared to have switched off from work and was focused on the drive, enjoying the challenges of the snow-banked roads. These days, she rarely mentioned Peter, which didn't necessarily mean he wasn't featuring in her life, but that that she had the sense not to bring it up.

Every now and then the trees would part like curtains, displaying mountain ranges.

"That mountain looks so steep."

Lo squeezed Gloria's thigh. "We'll start you on the baby slopes. You'll be a natural, I'm certain."

Gloria flipped the visor down and peered at her right eye. "I'm glad you're certain. I think there's something in my eye." Lately she felt like she was falling apart.

"It's just balance and soft knees, right? Sound familiar? If you can ride a horse, you can ski down a slope."

Gloria snapped the visor back up and rubbed her eye. "I'm glad you're so sure."

"I think I have some eye drops in my purse. They are my weapon against insomnia-induced bloodshot eye. Pass me some gum."

Gloria located the gum and rifled around looking for eye drops, eventually finding them in a zippered compartment. "These smell weird, and how strong is that gum?"

Lo held out her hand and Gloria passed her the eye drops. She sniffed them and her mouth turned down at the corners. "That's just what they smell like. I don't think there's anything wrong with them."

"How can you tell over the menthol of that gum?" Gloria grimaced but tilted her head back. "Try not to turn any corners for a minute."

"Sure, honey, I'll plow right through the mountainside."

"Thanks." Gloria blinked rapidly and held the back of her hand under her eye. The taste of the eye drops hit the back of her throat and she coughed. "These are disgusting. I think I prefer an eyelash in my eye."

"Look, here we are." They turned a corner and a city of wooden buildings appeared.

"When you said lodge, I was picturing one house."

"Oh, no. It's a resort. The town is stunning. We'll be looked after, don't worry."

Thick blankets of snow lay on the sloping roofs of buildings nestled into a valley surrounded by mountains. Trees powdered with white stood sentinel between the chalets and people wearing ski suits tramped around in the bright daylight. In the center of the circular drive was a towering fir tree littered with white lights. Lo drove straight up to the main building which was obviously "the lodge." It had towering wooden pillars and long windows to accommodate the view. A poker-faced valet took the keys to the muddy truck. Despite the rustic look from the outside, everything in the lobby was modern, from the charcoal carpet on the ground to the dark gray sofas with burnt orange accents and the sleek glass occasional tables. To Gloria, whose experience of traveling was limited to Klaus's trailer and the ranch, it was mind-boggling. She stood beside Lo as she checked in at reception, but she was staring out of the windows at the vastness surrounding them.

"It's like we're inside a cloud."

"We will be soon."

Gloria stuck close to Lo as they crossed the expanse of lobby where people were sitting on clusters of sofas and chairs, drinking and eating with the benefit of a huge fireplace and the crystal views. A father and young son got into the elevator with them, and they stood back to let the little boy press the buttons.

Lo leaned forward. "Four, please, sir."

The little boy in his pale blue beanie turned around and looked up at his father, who nodded. The boy pushed number four and pressed back against his father's leg. Lo smiled down at him until he left the elevator at level two. Gloria slipped her hand inside Lo's. Being in a new place with people they didn't know was a liberating experience. Lo ran her thumb over Gloria's knuckle and didn't let go when the elevator doors opened.

"Room 401," Lo murmured. "Here we go." She swiped the entry card and they stepped inside.

Gloria stopped in her tracks to gape at the view. "Are you kidding me?"

The room had floorboards peeking around the edges of a large white rug. Windows followed a triangle up to the roof's top, displaying the mountain's jagged peak. A glass chandelier hung from the ceiling and one side was devoted to a white king-size bed and the other to a white corner sofa that was positioned to gain benefit of the view. The furnishings were white and pale gray with textures of fur juxtaposed against sleek glass and blond wood. Their bags had already been set in the corner by the concierge.

"Like I said, Randy owes me a favor but he could only find us one night."

Gloria went to the window and looked out at the lifts creating a production line of tiny skiers populating the mountainside. "This is incredible, thank you. I have never been so glad that a teenager got caught with pot."

Lo came and wrapped her arms around Gloria's waist and dropped her chin onto her shoulder. "Cocaine."

"Ah, snow. Makes sense."

Lo kissed her beneath the ear. "I can't decide what I want to do more. Slopes or you."

A rush of intoxication hit Gloria and she closed her eyes. Lo-La, autumn faery queen, ruler of realms inner and outer, as above, so below. Her lungs quaked as she took a sharp breath of air. She turned in Lo's arms and kissed her, her lips parting. She made a soft sound in her throat, melting into the soft feeling, then she pulled away.

"Slopes. If we come all this way and I don't prove you wrong about my skiing ability, I'll be very upset."

Lo squeezed her waist. "Aargh, okay, I know you're right. Let's get dressed."

* * *

"Come on, my little snowplow," Lo encouraged as Gloria attempted to stop on the beginner run. "Just go."

Gloria gave a yelp as her skis slid out from under her and she almost fell, only saving herself by digging a pole in. Lo was barely recognizable in a white ski suit with teal and black stripes down the side and a black headband above big glasses. If it wasn't for her jaw and mouth, which was familiar terrain to Gloria, and the copper ponytail, she would look as unfamiliar as any of the strangers doing the same thing. Gloria was dressed in Lo's spare suit which was purple and white, and she felt like a clumsy polar bear. She was also annoyed that a twenty-something ski instructor called Christian kept putting hands on Lo even though Lo was perfectly competent. When he offered to show Lo where the best bar was after his shift, it was all the motivation Gloria needed to get her act together and attempt a more difficult run.

Gloria had never ridden a chairlift before. She loved swinging her legs as they were transported up the mountain, taking in the views with Lo's gloved hand in hers. At the top, the chair stopped with an unexpected jolt and they scrambled off and Lo glided across to the start point while Gloria tramped her way after her. There was a line of people waiting. Gloria looked at the small children, already proficient on the slopes, and felt incompetent, a humbling reminder to her of the way her students must feel when faced with her experience.

"Let's go, honey!" Lo yelled.

Gloria wobbled as she took off then found her balance. Behind her Lo yelled, "Don't look down at your tips!" and Gloria wobbled again. As she picked up speed, her sensitivity to balancing on a horse told her how to absorb a bump and where to distribute her weight over her hips. She got to the bottom with a big grin on her face. Lo was right there alongside her.

"You did it!"

"I don't think I can turn properly, though."

"Doesn't matter, you'll learn. Let's go again."

Gloria was having so much fun that she didn't realize they'd missed lunch. "I love skiing!" she said as they made their way back indoors that afternoon.

Lo looked at her own reflection in the elevator and touched her nose. "We should have reapplied sunscreen."

Gloria looked at her own pink nose. "Sue-Anne will be vindicated. She told me to protect my face and she also said that she knew I wouldn't listen."

Lo pulled her headband off as they walked back to their room. "I'm starving. I want steak. Make that two steaks. Sorry."

Gloria was struggling out of the cuffs of her pants. "Have your cow. I am desperate for a hot drink and a hot shower. It'll have to be the other way around, though." She draped her clothes over the back of a metal-framed chair and threw her socks underneath. She went through to the bathroom which was white and pearly gray with a double vanity in white granite. "The shower is gigantic!" She turned the water on and tested it with one hand, adjusting the heat. "I'll be lost in here. Come on." She stepped into the water, feeling her extremities tingle with the change of temperature. Seconds later, Lo appeared through the steam with her hair in a bun on top of her head.

"I am not wetting my hair and I am not fooling around with you in here. I am far too hungry."

"All right, all right. Just let me hug you once. You looked disturbingly sexy in your ski suit."

"No!" Lo squealed as Gloria drew her under the water.

They emerged from the shower, Gloria pleased with herself and Lo trying to be angry but her smile giving her away. They toweled off in the bathroom and went to find something to wear.

"We are sunburnt," Gloria commented as she zipped up her jeans.

"I can't talk, my stomach is taking all my attention. I don't know why I let you seduce me in the shower."

"You're an easy touch."

Lo raked a brush through her wet hair. "Shut up."

"And you look cute when you're angry."

Lo gritted her teeth. "Throw me your purple sweater. It's mine tonight."

Gloria bit back her grin as she tossed it to Lo. She would wear her blue one instead. She went to pull it from her bag and was suddenly reminded of the last time she wore it—when Oliver came over. She froze, one hand on the top, guilt exploding like a powder bomb inside her. Her head jerked as she realized Lo was saying something. "Hmm?" She turned her head to catch Lo's words.

"I said, I like your new jeans."

"You going to steal them too?"

Lo came to hug Gloria from behind and murmured into her ear, "No, you look way too good in them, but I will take them off you later."

Gloria grabbed her black jacket from the bag and ducked her head away from Lo's embrace. "Let's go before your rumbling stomach creates an avalanche."

Lo frowned but she picked up the room swipe card from the table without saying anything. Gloria breathed deep, trying to rid herself of the chalky feeling that had settled inside of her. "Lolly!" Lo stopped in the doorway and shook her head at Gloria's use of her childhood nickname. Gloria smoothed a clump of Lo's damp hair behind her ear. "I love you."

"I know."

Gloria swatted at her shoulder and Lo wrapped an arm around her waist. As they walked through the corridor and into the lift, Lo left her arm where it was and Gloria could see their reflection in the elevator looking like a couple, love and affection written all over them. An elderly man and woman got in on level three and smiled a greeting. Gloria smiled back and dropped her head onto Lo's shoulder. It filled her with happiness. Thoughts of her infidelity lurked at the corners, jeopardizing her happiness in a way that she had never experienced with Mike. With him she had felt secure, but not this wild undulating love which filled her and spilled out of her like a glow. The elderly couple exited the elevator before them and Lo said in a quiet voice to Gloria, "Love you, too."

The sun was climbing down into the mountains as they sat by the window in the restaurant, watching the snow blaze orange and pink.

"This is so nice," Lo said, taking Gloria's hand across the table. "I never want to leave."

"Thanks for making it happen."

Lo looked down at their hands. "I'm not very good at navigating a relationship, but I do want to make you happy. You know, when I was staying in town at Peter's, it was awful. I cried every night."

"So, you and Peter never—"

Lo looked up sharply. "Slept together? How could you think that?"

"Sorry, you're right. I have too much imagination." Gloria gave her head a shake. "Forget I said that."

"Gloria, done is done for me. Once I call quits on something, I don't go back. I slept on the foldout sofa. If I had known how uncomfortable it was, I never would have bought it when we were furnishing the apartment. It has this metal bar right across your back."

"What did you say to Peter? Didn't he ask you why you were upset?"

"Peter works very late. I tried to keep my tears to myself. He's used to it, anyway. If anything, it probably reminded him that I may seem cool and collected most of the time now, but underneath it all I'm still a mess."

"I think you're figuring things out."

A waiter came with a basket of bread and Lo ordered a steak with pepper sauce and vegetables and Gloria ordered a miso-stuffed eggplant. Lo asked the waiter to pair a red wine for them and as soon as he left, she took a piece of bread and slathered it in butter. Gloria wrinkled her nose and bit into a plain piece.

Lo sighed contentedly. "That's better." She squinted out into the sunset. "I'm still brainstorming ways we can have an indoor arena by next winter."

Gloria shrugged. "It's something to dream about anyway."

"Yeah, I know, but in the next year or two you'll be starting Pogo under saddle and I think if Caroline's stepping down a bit it's a good opportunity to get your business up and running. Those guest houses are longing for someone to stay in them. They pain me when I see them like blots on the countryside. I've been thinking if you do keep Pogo intact you could breed him with Sonnet. I think it would be a complementary bloodline. She wasn't always so temperamental, remember."

Gloria squeezed her eyes shut. "I can't think of my baby that way yet."

"Ah, trust me, if he gets out in the paddock with a mare soon, you'll have to think that way."

The wine arrived and they thanked the waiter. After he'd left, a secretive smile played across Lo's lips. "You look booby in that top."

Gloria glanced down and laughed. "You're just saying that to make up for the fact that you stole my purple one."

Lo's eyes were laughing as she took a sip of her wine.

The aroma of food hung in the air, and every time a waiter emerged from the kitchen with meals they watched longingly, hoping it was theirs. Lo pushed the basket of bread away. "Don't let me eat any more."

The food was worth the wait, or else they were just so hungry that anything tasted delicious. Despite Lo's enthusiasm, she couldn't squeeze in dessert, but they sat finishing their wine and watching as the light faded from the sky, bringing their own reflections into being.

"This is surreal," Gloria said, tripping over her words from the alcohol. At least it had numbed the growing ache in muscles she didn't know she had. "I wonder if we'll see a shooting star?"

Lo's chin was in her hand, her expression serene. "We'll turn the lights off in the room later and see if we can spot one."

"Should we go? I feel like I'm about to pop the button off my jeans."

"Come on, you're my shooting star."

Gloria realized she was tipsy and she sucked herself together, hoping she was walking like someone who wasn't inebriated. "I need to pee," she whispered to Lo.

"We'll be at the room in thirty seconds."

Gloria linked her arm through Lo's. When she felt her close, all was right in the world. In the room, she went to the bathroom and when she emerged Lo had turned all the lights off except the lamp in the corner, and was lying back on the white sofa with her head on a cushion.

"I am going to be stiff tomorrow."

Gloria tugged her jeans off and found her sweatpants and hoodie. "I can't deal with tight clothes right now." She changed and turned the lamp off, then went to lie on the other end of the sofa with her legs beside Lo's so they could both look out at the night sky.

Without the light from inside, there was still a mist from the hotel lights but they could see the stars dotted across the sky in their various sizes and intensities. They silently watched but they didn't see a shooting star.

Lo tapped Gloria's foot with her own. "Are you falling asleep? I'm going to get ready for bed."

Gloria had to admit, now that she was horizontal, she was feeling the effects not only of the day, but of the past couple of months. They brushed their teeth and stripped down to their T-shirts and got into the huge bed.

"This is fun," Gloria whispered.

"Why are you whispering?" Lo whispered back.

"So I don't scare off the shooting stars."

"Right. Come here, the sheets are cold."

They giggled like schoolgirls as they hugged each other. "Oh, Lola," Gloria said, squeezing her tight. "My love."

CHAPTER NINETEEN

In the morning, Gloria awoke to a gray dawn. Lo was on her side, and Gloria wasn't sure if she'd just woken or if she'd been watching her. She'd given up worrying about how she looked when she was asleep. She stretched her arms and legs, feeling her muscles resist. A huff of laughter escaped her throat at the tight feeling.

"Morning, Miss Wyoming. Did you sleep?"

Lo tucked her hands under the side of her face. "Mostly. We should have drawn the curtains."

"It's worth it to see the sunrise. It looks like it'll be cloudy today. I hope the horses can still go out for a run."

"Don't think about them. Let Kip and Oliver worry about it."

"I know, you're right. Why are you all the way over there?" She wiggled forward to bridge the gap. "Hmm." She ran a hand up Lo's side beneath her T-shirt.

Lo squirmed. "That tickles." She pulled Gloria on top of her, their legs twining around each other.

Gloria looked down at her and smiled. Lo smiled back and their smiles split wider. No words were necessary. The look in Lo's eye mirrored her own; she could tell that without seeing her own face. Lo's fingertips flowed up the nodes of Gloria's ribs and she brushed lightly over her breasts with her palms. Gloria lowered herself down on top of Lo and kissed her. She felt the might of crashing arctic icebergs in her veins as Lo's hands traveled the map of her body. As day broke over the mountain, she was above the clouds. Lo's every twitch and utterance was her own pleasure. Afterward, Lo lay on top of her, unable to move, and Gloria's arms held her close. She had never known these heights existed.

"Ow!" She laughed as Lo rolled off her chest.

Lo blinked up at the ceiling. "I don't even know what to say."

"Coffee?"

"Oh, god, yes. Just give me a second, I don't think I can move yet."

Gloria idly ran a hand up and down the smooth skin of Lo's stomach. "I'm going to shower." She sat up and climbed out of the bed. "Which of my clothes are you going to pinch today?"

Lo was watching her, her hands behind her head on the pillow. Her expression grew serious. "No, your breasts are bigger."

Gloria cocked her head to the side. "Huh?"

"Did you have your period this month?"

Gloria began to smile, but the smile froze on her lips and she looked down at the white rug on the floor. "I don't...I can't remember."

Lo sat up too. "You haven't."

Gloria shrugged, her back to Lo. She stood a second longer, then walked off to the shower. It felt like time was standing still as she leaned against the vanity, staring at herself in the bathroom mirror, her mind careening along through the passages of time back to her night with Oliver. She had been drunk but they had used protection, she was sure of it. Her reflection told a different story. Lo was right, her breasts looked fuller and there was a feeling inside her being that suddenly spoke a truth she hadn't been aware of. The water gushed behind her, but she was unable to move. All she could do was move the air in and out of her lungs, a conscious effort that made her wonder how she had ever breathed unconsciously before. After a while, Lo appeared behind her and their eyes met, Gloria's stricken and Lo's wise in their resignation. Lo stepped around her and got into the shower. She was only in there for one minute and emerged with red skin, then wrapped a towel around herself and left again. Gloria could hear the tap dripping behind her. She took a deep breath and turned the shower back on, not caring if it was hot or cold. She washed herself and she thought she was quick, but it felt like even one blink of her eyes took a long time. Her mouth was dry and she gagged as she brushed her teeth. When she emerged, Lo had packed her things and was standing by the window with her arms wrapped around herself, watching the eager skiers beginning their day below. Gloria felt raw, like the sunlight struggling from behind the clouds.

"Lo, I'm sorry, I didn't mean it to happen. I thought we were over and I—"

"Stop." Lo moved away from the window without looking at her. "I'll be out front." She picked up her bag and walked past Gloria and out the door.

Gloria sat down on the edge of the bed and stared at the floor. She had to prompt herself to pack her things, like she was operating the body of someone else. She wanted to fly out into the day and disappear like vapor in the wind. She scanned the room, but Lo had tidied everything. She closed the door behind her, too devastated to cry.

CHAPTER TWENTY

The drive back from the lodge had been quiet, with only the most basic of communication. Lo had one arm on the window ledge, almost leaning out of the car to distance herself from Gloria. Any words Gloria had tried to speak, Lo had silenced or ignored until they got home, then Lo's fury had begun to surface.

"Oliver?" she asked when they stood in the ranch kitchen.

"Yes, but it was a mistake."

"Did you know you were pregnant?"

"No! I swear. It wasn't until before when you asked. We…" And that's when her eyes had filmed with tears because she knew it was little consolation to anyone. "We used protection."

Lo held up a hand. "I don't want any details." Gloria went to Lo and tried to take her hand, but Lo stepped back. "Don't. Don't touch me."

"I'm sorry. If I could turn back the clock, I would. As soon as it happened, I wished I'd never done it. I was drunk."

Lo let out a hollow laugh that turned into a sob. "There's nothing anyone can do to change it."

"Can't we just talk about it? I'm not ready to be a mother."

"Fuck! Just stop." Lo spun around and swiped her hand across the table, sending the fruit bowl crashing to the ground. Neither of them moved as the bananas dropped with a dull thud and the apples bounced across the floor, coming to a wobbly stop against the edge of the cabinets. She dropped her face into her hands and began to cry. Gloria's own tears came properly then too. Knowing how she had hurt Lo was the most painful part. Lo, who had lost a child, would now lose Gloria because she had been so careless. There was no child yet, but either way Gloria looked at the pregnancy would involve a death for Lo. She tried to hug Lo, but Lo pushed her roughly away and walked from the kitchen. Gloria heard her heavy footfalls and the bedroom door slam. She looked around at the kitchen she would never enjoy again, then bent to pick up the broken pieces of the fruit bowl.

Caroline's house was much smaller than the ranch. Oliver was sleeping in the spare room, but he set up the foldout bed in the study for Gloria. She was used to sleeping in the tiny room above Klaus's stables but not to the close proximity of people other than Lo. She had been at Caroline's for two weeks, and every night she curled in a ball and cried into her pillow so no one would hear her. She wondered if Lo was doing the same.

She hadn't had the guts to tell Oliver or Caroline yet, and it hung over her like the threat of rain at a picnic. Oliver was perplexed and tried to cheer her up, but Caroline just let her be. Gloria didn't know what to do. She knew she had to tell Oliver. Different scenarios played in her mind but none were what she wanted other than to go back in time and erase the night with Oliver. It was a stubborn loop that played over the top of any activity she was doing. It was nothing compared to what Lo must feel about Terrence's accident, but she now understood the guilt and constant revisiting of a day, an hour, a minute. She couldn't eat and she felt sick all the time, and she wasn't sure if it was the pregnancy or emotion. She got through each day by focusing on the task she was doing and enduring it, but no longer for the love of it. There seemed no point. She was exhausted, and eventually broke down while she was unsaddling

Rarity and couldn't stop crying. Oliver, who was about to lunge one of Moira's horses, pulled her into the tack room and shut the door.

"Grant, what is going on?"

She tried to speak but she was sobbing too hard.

"Are you dying?"

She shook her head and tried again but just made a high-pitched sound.

"Come here." Oliver pulled her into a hug. "If you're not dying, then whatever it is can be solved." He rubbed her back vigorously.

"I'm pregnant."

Oliver's hand slowed and she could almost hear him thinking. "Okay. That's not so bad, is it?"

"It's yours!" Gloria pulled back and wiped at her face with her sleeve.

"Are you sure?"

"Oh, I'm sure!"

"But we..."

"It must have broken. I don't know."

Oliver had one hand on Gloria's arm but his unfocused gaze was on a pile of folded rugs behind her. He looked back at her. "Are you sure?"

"Yes!"

"Fuck, Grant." He turned and paced the few steps to the saddle racks, rubbed his palm over his chin, blinked a few times, then paced back. He looked at her, then paced another lap. "What do you want to do?"

"I don't know."

"This is...wow. Look, I'm sorry. We should have...wow." His eyes bugged. "Whatever you want to do, I'll help you. Will you be okay for one moment?" He shook his hands vigorously. "I think I need to take five to process."

Gloria nodded and Oliver let himself out of the tack room. She heard a crash which sounded like he'd walked into the wheelbarrow. She was conscious of Rarity waiting in the cold so she made her way back out, hoping not to bump into anyone coming to see their horses.

After their conversation, Oliver was solicitous and kept trying to make sure Gloria was comfortable. He even offered to work Sonnet and wouldn't let her push the wheelbarrow. It only made Gloria feel helpless and irritated. In the end, she went inside the house to make a ginger tea and pick at a piece of dry toast by the fire.

Caroline returned from a meeting with the dressage association and found Gloria slumped with Cleo the cat on her lap, staring at the embers, her eyes and nose red from crying. Caroline threw another log on the fire and shuffled the coals with a poker, then sat down beside Gloria.

"Well, the board want to raise fees again. As if folk don't spend every last dollar on their horses in the first place. The good news is, though, Nancy Blatt has a girl who wants to get some dressage experience so there'll be some help around here. I think she'll come in next week and have a look. I'm not sure how she rides, but I suppose she'll soon pick up."

Gloria nodded. "That's good."

"You going to tell me what's eating you?" When Gloria didn't respond, she used the armrests to push herself up out of the chair and went to a cluttered sideboard and opened the drawer. Gloria could hear her pushing things around but didn't bother to turn her head. Caroline returned with a hardback book and passed it to Gloria. "Page ninety-four."

The book was heavy and the dust jacket was black with a print of painted green leaves with red berries across the front. It said, *Women in Art* in gold type. Gloria opened it up and flicked past glossy pictures of paintings and photographs to find page ninety-four. On the page was a painting of the heads and shoulders of two women facing each other. One had her head turned, looking straight at the artist, her eyes daring and direct, the other was in profile, looking at the woman in front of her. The background was dark blues and greens, possibly a blurry room or view from a window. Gloria glanced up at the wall to her right. "It's the painting over there."

Caroline smiled. "Yes."

Gloria looked back down at the book and read the caption aloud. "*One*, by Ida Almasi, 1976." There was so much power in that direct gaze, Gloria could feel it like a force coming from the page. Gloria had often looked at the picture on the wall and felt like the woman was looking directly at her. She had paid less attention to the one in profile, but now she looked from the page to the wall to Caroline, who was watching the flames. She was older, but the nose and the brow were the same.

"That's you."

Caroline nodded. "Yes, and Andy."

"Your Andy?"

"Yes, Love Fool. If I have any advice, it's this: let a horse find his own balance without interfering, and don't let love pass you by or you will spend your life in regret." She smiled at Gloria and her eyes were misty. "Go get your redhead and tell her how you feel."

Gloria sniffed. "There's no point. I stuffed everything up." She closed the book and put it beside her leg so she wouldn't squash Cleo. "I'm pregnant." She took a deep breath. "To Oliver."

"That does complicate things, I'll admit. Does Oliver know?"

"Yes, but only just."

"And?"

"He's being supportive, but it doesn't change anything." She passed Caroline the book, and Caroline held it on her lap and placed a protective hand over it.

"Do you want a child?"

"Yes, I think so, but not yet. I have so many aspirations with the horses."

"So? You have the kid and you keep going. You wouldn't be the first."

Gloria ran her fingers through Cleo's white fur. "Not on my own, not like this. I have no support, nothing. I'd have to go home and move in with my parents. I don't know what job I could do."

"Gloria, life gets in the way of despair. No matter how bad you think it'll be, the world goes on and takes you with it. If you want me to help you set up any appointments, I will."

"Thank you. There's just one."

CHAPTER TWENTY-ONE

It was a long ride to the clinic. Oliver insisted on being a support person even though Gloria didn't care if he came in or not. She had made up her mind and she wanted to hold on to her resolve, but his questions cast doubts over her decision. Caroline had made sure she had spoken to a therapist first so she was informed and felt okay about it, whatever okay meant.

"Do you need some water?" Oliver asked, breaking the silence again.

"I'm not meant to drink anything else now."

"Right, right. Do you want music on? I think there's a CD in there somewhere." He indicated the glove compartment of his Tahoe.

"I don't care."

"Grant, if you change your mind at any point, just say so and we'll turn around."

Gloria's nostrils flared and she rolled her teeth from front to back in an effort to maintain her composure.

"We could get married?"

"Oliver, shut up!" She felt bad enough that he was paying for half the medical costs and driving her there. "Sorry," she said in a quieter tone. "I appreciate the sentiment, but we would make each other miserable, and that wouldn't be good for a child either. What would we do? Cart a kid around in a horse trailer with us?"

"It would be kind of cute."

"I'm sorry, I see nothing cute about a screaming baby and dirty diapers everywhere. It's not possible. Plus, surely there's a point where I wouldn't be able to ride. It's stupid, Oliver, and you're not helping."

"I think I do have some say."

Gloria shook her head and looked out at the low brick homes of suburbia.

"Well, we wouldn't have to stay together."

Gloria tipped her head against the cool glass and shut her eyes. She should have gone alone. She knew Oliver was just having a last-minute panic, but she was trying to suppress her own. After a moment she reached into the glove compartment and plucked out the first CD she found: *Top Hits 1998*. The sounds of a boy band that Gloria couldn't name blared out and she turned the volume down slightly but left it on in the hope Oliver would channel his feelings into the music. Gloria watched the people going about their business, oblivious to her situation, no doubt preoccupied with whatever their own problems were. A woman walking along the street with a bag of groceries reminded her of Lo, the length of limb, the way she held her herself and was observing everything going on around her. As they passed her by, Gloria saw that actually she wasn't that similar after all. She would never see Lo or another like her again. Her breath had fogged up the glass, blanking out the view. She turned back to Oliver.

"Was Sonnet all right getting on the truck?"

Oliver braked at a school crossing. "I gave Kip a hand because I could see he has a firm approach that would clash with Sonnet. We put Hamlet on first and she was okay. I forgot to mention that he asked after you. He said you should stop being a stranger and come annoy him again."

"Did he say anything else?"

A group of teenagers finished crossing the road and Oliver eased the car back into drive. "Ahh…oh, yeah, he asked if you have Pogo's papers."

Gloria nodded. She knew it was bound to happen. She had been the one to arrange for the horses to go back to Lo's. Her life was running through her hands like bathwater but she felt a certain relief. There was nothing left to hold on to, nothing left to fight for. She was just tired and didn't care about anything anymore. She felt detached as she marveled at how close she had come to having the life she wanted.

"If it's any consolation, Caroline would love you to ride Rarity. She's no longer in her prime but she still knows her stuff."

Gloria tried to smile. "Yeah, maybe. I'll be going home soon anyway. It'll be nice to feel my toes again and ride outdoors."

"Back to Klaus's?"

"If he'll have me." Gloria huffed a half laugh. "Who am I kidding? He'll play a game, making me feel uncertain if I can go back, but I know he'll have me. He will be so happy that he can gloat and boss me around. He didn't want me to move over here. He offered me a damn good horse but that offer will have been retracted."

"You won't have trouble getting offers of a good horse, surely. I will miss you, though."

"I'll miss you too. Thanks for everything, it's been fun hanging out."

Oliver reached a hand to cover her mouth without taking his eyes from the road. "Shh, I'm not ready for goodbyes yet."

Gloria pushed his arm away. She remembered Lo's words from months ago. *Life is just a series of departures.* Lo was right.

"I think that's it." Oliver ducked his head to see a gray stucco building with a sign beside the door. "Parking at rear. At least there are no crazy picketers or anything."

Gloria relaxed a fraction—she had been worried about that too. Behind the clinic was a small concrete car lot with some sad-looking shrubs. Oliver reversed into a spot and turned the engine off. "At any point, you just say the word and we will leave."

Gloria turned to him and took his hand. "Oliver, I need you to stop asking me now or you'll have to wait in the car."

Oliver chewed his lower lip and clasped her hand. He pumped it once and let out a breath. "Okay, Grant. It's your call."

They stepped out of the car and walked across the lot to the back entrance, Oliver remaining a couple of feet behind, which suited Gloria just fine. Inside it looked like a house that had been converted into a clinic and there was a reception window cut into the wall of what was once a living room. Oliver hung back and Gloria spoke to a friendly woman who confirmed her details in a computer and asked her to take a seat. Gloria sat beside Oliver, her hands folded between her knees. There were two women sitting to her right, perhaps a mother and daughter. They all took care not to look at one another. Oliver had the good sense to be quiet. He remained silent until a nurse came to call Gloria, and then he only said, "I'll be right here, Grant."

On the drive home, Gloria turned her head to the window so Oliver wouldn't be able to tell if she was asleep or awake. She was empty; there was nothing left of her to give. Oliver asked her if she wanted a hot drink at the drive-through. She didn't comment but he bought her a hot chocolate and put it in the cupholder anyway. It sat there for the rest of the trip. He was trying his best to be kind and stay out of her way. She would thank him one day. She was so caught up in her own thoughts that the trip seemed to go by much quicker, or perhaps there was nothing to dread now.

Oliver drove her right to Caroline's door and helped her down even though she tried to wave him away. They had barely exited the car when the house door was flung open.

"Oliver! Don't you answer your cell phone? I've been trying to reach you."

Oliver frowned and patted his pocket. "It must be on silent. What's wrong?"

Caroline looked at Gloria. "It's Dolores, she's in the hospital."

Gloria felt the blood drain from her face. "What? What do you mean?"

"I don't know. Kip called to tell you. All he said was she's at Diamond Rock." Caroline's eyes were heavy. "I'm sorry, Gloria. I spoke to her."

But Gloria had stopped listening. "Oliver, give me the keys."

"No. What? You need to go inside and rest."

Gloria held her hand out, tears already filming her eyes. "Give me the goddamn keys."

"No. I'll take you, just get back in." Oliver shot Caroline a baffled look but Caroline shooed him toward the car with her hands.

Gloria climbed back in and slammed the door, watching Oliver impatiently as he sat down and buckled his seat belt. He hesitated with the key in the ignition and looked at her, then seemed to think better of it and started the car. Gloria clutched the seat, trying to imagine what was wrong with Lo. She remembered when she used to worry that Lo's depression would get the better of her and she would jump out of a window or slit her wrists. She thought those days were behind her, but things had fallen apart and it was Gloria's fault.

Oliver didn't look impressed as he turned back onto the main road. "Are you feeling okay?"

"I will be when I know Lo is."

Oliver pursed his lips and moved slightly to the left to see if there was traffic in front of a cattle truck that was slowing them down. The first flakes of snow for the day began to flutter down and Oliver turned the wipers on and overtook the truck.

Gloria had never been inside the hospital before, but it was a smaller local hospital that had one visitor entry point. She told Oliver to drop her off.

"How will you get back?"

She was already opening the door before he'd even stopped. "Don't worry." She paused quickly and looked at him. "Thank you for everything today." She shut the door before he could respond and ran to the sliding doors. On the left was a small gift shop with flowers and soft toys and on the right was a café. Up ahead was an information desk and a map. She hurried over to the two women behind the desk and said, "I'm looking for someone who was admitted today via emergency. Dolores Ballantyne."

The woman closest to her with dopey eyes and a jutting lower lip said, "Do you know which ward she's in?"

"No, I just heard she'd been admitted."

"Are you family?"

The other woman, a pert-looking gray-haired woman who was chewing gum, said, "Visiting hours are about to end. Come back at seven when the patients have had a chance to eat."

"No, can you tell me where she is?"

The gray-haired woman opened her mouth, ready to repeat herself, but the other woman pointed a finger diagonally toward the right. "Your friend is in room 104 but you only have five minutes."

"Thank you!" Gloria took off toward the corridor, reading the signs with various room numbers. She almost collided with a man holding a bunch of flowers and apologized. She found room 104 and looked through the glass panel of the door but all she could see was the end of a bed with the white sheets tucked in and an empty plastic chair. She pushed the door open and could smell antiseptic products. There was the rhythmical beeping of a machine. Gloria's heart was hammering in her chest and she looked along the bed at the shape of Lo lying on her back. Her face was pale and there was a plaster across her forehead. Her hair looked darker against the white pillow and there was crusted blood around her hairline. Her eyes were closed and there was a drip in her left hand which was resting across her abdomen. Gloria looked down at her, watching her chest rise and fall. Lo's eyes fluttered open and Gloria felt weak with relief. Her eyes were bloodshot, dimming the amber of her irises. Gloria took the plastic chair from the corner and dragged it beside the bed. "Oh, my love." She gently held her fingers with one hand and pushed a strand of hair away that was caught across her eyelashes. Peeking from the top of Lo's hospital gown was another wound dressing. Lo blinked slowly.

"Gloria!" she rasped, her eyes opening wide.

"Shh." Gloria leaned forward and kissed her forehead. "I'm sorry."

"I tried to tell you." She blinked slowly again.

"What happened?"

"I wanted to tell you."

A man came in wheeling a meal on a tray. "Oh, hello there, you still have a visitor. Do you want me to help you to sit up?"

"No, just leave it, please."

Gloria turned to him. "I'll help her."

The man looked uncertain. "I think visiting hours are over." He must have seen the desperation in Gloria's eyes because he said, "I'll be back to collect the tray after."

He wheeled the trolley back out and Gloria turned back to Lo. "Do you want to sit up?" Lo nodded. Gloria found the remote attached to the side of the bed and raised the backrest then adjusted the pillows behind Lo. She pulled the table the tray was on so it sat over the bed, but Lo pushed it away.

Lo swallowed with difficulty. "I wanted to tell you that you don't have to do it."

"Do what?"

"I spoke to Caroline and she said you were going to the clinic. I wanted to tell you that I want you and I want the baby. I guess I was speeding, I don't know. Apparently, a truck hit me at the intersection. They said the car looks like a crushed can."

Gloria's grip tightened on her fingers. "A car accident? Where are you hurt?"

Lo shook her head. "All I remember was the truck coming at me then the sound of the collision. I bumped my head and glass from the window sliced me here." She touched the dressing across her collarbone. "The doctor said whiplash, but they must have given me something strong because I can't feel anything."

Gloria's heart was racing. Lo had almost departed the world. She hadn't been around to watch over her. If she hadn't fucked up again, Lo wouldn't have been in the car at all. She folded forward and rested her forehead softly on Lo's lap. "Thank god. Thank god. Thank god." She felt Lo's fingers winding up through her hair at the back of her head. "I'm sorry. This is all my fault."

"No, I'm sorry. I don't care about any of it. I just want you."

Gloria rested her head even as Lo's hands grew still. She was so tired too, in the warmth of Lo's lap.

She jerked awake at the loud exclamation of a nurse who had come to check on Lo. "Ma'am, it's in between visiting hours. You'll need to go and wait out there until seven."

Gloria twisted her body, trying to stretch out the stiffness from being folded forward.

"No!" Lo croaked. "She's my partner."

The nurse raised one eyebrow. "I don't care if she's the goddamn Queen of England, she can wait outside until seven o'clock."

Gloria squeezed Lo's hand. "I'll go and get a coffee and come back."

Lo's eyes were sad but she didn't object. The nurse was standing looking at Lo's chart but she didn't move out of Gloria's way, so Gloria brushed past her back and made a face at Lo. The corners of Lo's lips lifted and Gloria felt her heart lift too. She had no idea what the time was until she saw it on her receipt at the coffee shop. She sat down on another plastic chair with a watery coffee and a limp pastry, knowing that there were sixty minutes until she could go back in and talk to Lo. She realized she was starving and ate the pastry even though it was sugary and doughy, a far cry from the Italian pastry shop where she used to buy almond croissants in Melbourne. The coffee she sipped slowly, grateful for something hot. Lo had said she wanted her, but things were different now. She watched hospital staff and patients getting in and out of the lift. The man she had almost collided with came and sat down nearby, holding a polystyrene cup instead of flowers now. He looked her way and nodded so she asked him for the time. Without checking his watch, he said, "Twenty more minutes." Gloria smiled a thank-you and stood up to go and browse in the gift shop. Visitors had begun to gather in the foyer, and some had the same idea as Gloria. She looked at the pale pink and blue bears and pushed away thoughts of the clinic. There were cellophaned roses and balloons and magazines. There were bottles of scented lotions and plush toys and books. Lo wasn't really a magazine reader but there was a self-help book called *Every Day Magic* that she thought Lo would be into. At the register she grabbed a box of chocolates and a small gray bear holding a red love heart even though it was corny. As the woman at the register was ringing up the purchases, Gloria said, "And a red rose too." She wanted to make up for the rose that she had left anonymously in Lo's car. This time there would be no mistaking who it was from.

The woman laughed. "I thought Valentine's Day was done for the year."

Gloria blushed. She had spent Valentine's Day contemplating scooping her heart out with a spoon. "Call it delirious fatigue shopping."

The woman nodded. "We see a lot of that."

Gloria declined her offer of a carry bag and stacked things onto the book.

This time no one questioned her as she went back to Lo's room. Lo was sitting up and it looked like she'd eaten most of the food. Color had returned to her cheeks but there were the purple beginnings of a bruise on her forehead. Gloria placed the things she was holding on the small table beside the bed and went to sit next to Lo.

"You came back." Lo's tone had changed, and Gloria wondered if she had been out of it earlier when she had said she wanted her. She had told the nurse she was her partner too. Gloria had no feeling for that term, but she did have feeling for the sentiment behind it.

"Of course I did. I brought you a book but I don't know if reading is something you feel like doing."

"I want to go home, with you. Don't leave me in here, I'm fine."

"I think you have to stay here so they can keep an eye on your head. Maybe you need a scan."

"I'm fine, just tired. I hate hospitals. This is where they took Terrence."

Gloria felt even more ashamed for her actions. "We can ask, but it seems like you'll be here tonight at least."

"Will you come back home?"

Gloria looked down at the impersonal hospital blanket. "I should go home."

"To Caroline's?"

Gloria shook her head. "No, back home to Australia."

Lo sat up straight and winced. "No! I want you to stay. I spoke to Caroline this morning and she told me that you were on the way to the clinic. I wanted to tell you that you don't have to go through with it, I'll look after you."

Gloria felt unworthy of Lo's charity. "You really did bump your head."

"Maybe if I wasn't speeding the truck wouldn't have hit me and I could have made it."

Gloria realized she was serious. "Lo, I know my own mind. Oliver was in my ear, trying to convince me not to do it, but it's not his life and it's not yours."

Lo nodded. "I know that, I just wanted to tell you. I know what it's like to live with regret and I didn't want you to make decisions you might regret because you felt unsupported." She touched a hand to her chest where the dressing was.

Gloria sighed. "I've been regretting plenty, don't worry about that, but I've also been thinking about all the things I'm thankful for. This experience here in Wyoming, the ups and the downs, the people I've met, and, of course, you. I'm grateful for every moment I've had with you, and I'm truly sorry for all the ways I hurt you."

"Then stay, I want more moments with you. I want to build a life with you. I don't care who knows it, in fact I want everyone to know it."

"Really?"

"Yes, I love you, Gloria Grant."

Gloria took Lo's hand. Her voice trembled. "I didn't do it, I couldn't. It's my responsibility and I'm going to figure it out."

Lo's fingers tightened on Gloria's hand. "The baby?"

Gloria smiled sadly. "Yes. Well, the jellybean or whatever it is."

Lo's eyes welled. "Oh, my god, you're going to be a mother." The tears spilled over and she started to gently sob. "I want to be there with you. I want you to be with me always."

"That's a big statement. I've made up my mind, but this is real and I can't have someone wandering in and out of my life and the child's. This is a commitment."

"I've been doing nothing but thinking for the past two weeks. You broke my trust but that was partly my fault too—I walked out on you with barely a word. But I want you and I already love the jellybean."

"But, Terrence...are you sure you want another child around?"

"It's a blessing, Gloria. One I never thought I'd have. I didn't think I would have any love for a child, but I've realized love is always there, enough for everyone. Would you consider it?"

"I will. Tonight I will go back to Caroline's and think it over, not just what's best for me, but best for you and the jellybean too, and I want you to think about it as well and give me your answer when you're not concussed and delirious. Not a rash answer, but a considered answer when you're not feeling emotional."

"My answer won't change. Come here." Lo held out one arm and Gloria could tell that the gash on her chest was limiting her movement on that side.

Gloria touched her forehead to Lo's then softly kissed her lips. "You scared me."

Lo held her there. "You scared me."

The door opened and there were voices and Lo let go. Gloria turned to see Kip and Sue-Anne standing there. Sue-Anne's eyes were round but Kip was grinning.

Kip's eyes strayed to the rose on the table. "Well, Dolly, we came because we thought you were in a bad way but it looks like you're doing all right."

Gloria tried to move away but Lo held her hand. Sue-Anne placed a bag of grapes and a Tupperware container on the table beside the book. "Homemade corn fritters." She went to touch the back of her fingers lightly to Lo's cheek. "Oh, Dolores. You look a fright."

Lo murmured, "I'm fine."

Sue-Anne turned to Gloria. "Gloria, how are you, honey?"

Gloria stood to hug Sue-Anne. "Better now that I know Lo is okay."

Sue-Anne shook her head brusquely. "Kip had a cry on the way here, but I reminded him that it takes more than a truck to slow Dolores down. Still, it does pay to mind yourself when the roads are icy."

Kip had gone to kiss Lo on the cheek but he rolled his eyes and snatched Gloria into a hug. "Don't listen to her lies, Gloria. I had some dust in my eye."

"It's lovely to see you too. I've missed you both."

Lo cleared her throat. "I've asked Gloria to come back and live at the ranch, for good this time."

Sue-Anne sat down in the chair Gloria had vacated. "We never wanted her to leave. It was you two who had a falling out."

"No more," Lo said, then winced again.

Sue-Anne placed a hand on Lo's leg. "Just calm down and lie back. You're injured. Have they given you the scan yet?"

"But, Sue-Anne, I'm trying to tell you I love Gloria."

Gloria turned pink at Lo's attempts to profess her love, but Sue-Anne laughed. "Do you think we were born yesterday?" She looked at Kip and Kip raised his eyebrows with a bemused expression on his face.

"But…" Lo looked from one to the other.

Kip slung an arm around Gloria. "We just wish you two would stop arguing so Gloria won't keep running off. Gloria, if Dolores don't want to make an honest woman of you, I will."

Sue-Anne scowled at him. "Now, it's one thing to be gay but marriage is reserved between a man and a woman."

Lo tried to speak and coughed. "If Gloria wants to marry me, then I'll push to change that legislation."

The look on Lo's face was so serious that Gloria laughed. "Lo, I'm going to let you have some time with Kip and Sue-Anne. Kip, can I get a lift to Caroline's with you after?"

"Caroline's?" Lo asked.

"Just rest up. I'll speak to you tomorrow." With Kip and Sue-Anne there to bear witness, she said, "I love you."

Lo smiled shyly. "You too."

Kip bumped Gloria affectionately with his elbow as she walked out. Gloria waited back at the café, her hands stuffed in the pockets of her jacket, watching the various people passing through. Some wore expressions of hope and joy, others sadness or fear. She realized the fine line everyone walked each day between experiencing those emotions. She was so very tired, and it was making her nausea more insistent. She put a hand on her stomach. There was a gravity to her decisions now.

CHAPTER TWENTY-TWO

Gloria barely slept, there were so many thoughts whirring around her mind. The risk-taker in Gloria sat on one end of the seesaw and her sensible side sat on the other. Up-down, bump-bump. Normally she would have gone to pour her heart out to Hamlet, who was by far the best listener of anyone she knew. Say she did stay…what then? What of the horses she had spent so long bringing to peak condition, could she keep riding? And Lo, how would she cope hearing the pitter-patter of tiny feet through the ranch corridors? There was every chance she had changed her mind, but Gloria needed to give her that time. It had to be something that was given thought.

Gloria had promised Caroline that she and Oliver would mend the broken fencing in the yards. There was a cruel wind and the ground was frozen solid but Gloria and Oliver toiled away. Oliver was careful not to mention their trip yesterday but she was able to tell him what she knew of the accident. Finally, unable to contain the words, Oliver asked, "Are you feeling okay today?"

Gloria held the rail steady for him as he hammered a nail in. "Oliver, I didn't go through with it."

Oliver looked up at her. "You didn't do it?"

"No. I'm sorry. I don't expect you to be a father to the baby, but I just feel it's the right thing to do."

Oliver wrapped his arms around her, still holding the hammer. "That is the best news. I am going to be a dad to this kid, if you'll let me. My own dad was never there and I won't do that to this kid. I mean, as much as you want me."

"That's something we can discuss, but I don't know what I'm doing yet. I need some more time to figure things out, but I would like this kid to know you too. I think you'll be a good dad."

"What are you doing out here fixing fences? Go inside."

"No. Haven't you learnt yet? I can't be bossed around."

Oliver let out a long breath. "Whoo-wee. This is big, Grant. This is really big. My mom is going to be so excited. I never had much family growing up, but I can't wait. You realize this kid is going to be an Olympic rider?"

Gloria laughed and picked up another nail from the box on the ground. "Come on, let's get this done. This kid may not be into horses. They might play tennis or something."

Oliver gave her a withering look. "Tennis, get real. I'm going to start looking for ponies now."

"Oliver," Gloria said gently. "I might go back to Australia."

"Pass me that nail. You can do what you want, but there is a future dressage star in there so I'm going to be paying close attention." He looked off into the distance. "A son or a daughter. Could it be twins?"

"I frigging hope not. Pass me the hammer if you're not going to finish it."

Gloria waited until Lo was home before going over to the ranch. Sue-Anne had set Lo up on the sofa under a blanket with an array of snacks, the television remote, and a jug of water. When Gloria found her, she had the book she'd given her open on her lap but she shut it and put it on the table. The dressing was off her head but there was a row of stitches at her hairline and clumps of dried blood in her hair. There was bruising under her eyes and her movements were slow and stiff.

"I look awful."

"You look sore."

"I am a bit."

"How's your head?"

"The scans were clear, thank goodness. Come sit here." She patted the sofa next to her.

Gloria sat down. She could see the needle mark where the IV had been in Lo's hand. It made her own stomach tighten. Things felt different now that she was thinking about a child. Pain frightened her, as did loss.

"I'm glad you're okay."

"I feel ridiculous. Sue-Anne won't let me do anything. She took the phone off the hook because Peter kept calling with work questions. How are you feeling?"

"A bit nauseous, but sitting still only makes it worse."

Lo smiled. "I remember that feeling. You look well."

Gloria chewed the inside of her cheek. Once small talk was started it was hard to steer to bigger topics. "How is Pogo going?"

"He's good. Kip has been working with him." Lo fretted with the edge of the woolen blanket. "Have you given it any thought? Moving back here, I mean."

"I have. What would we do with the horses? In a few months I may not be able to work them."

"I will."

"Really? You don't have time."

"There'll be more daylight and the days will be mild."

"But how would we look after the baby if we are both working?"

"I've done it before. Between you, me, Sue-Anne, and day care we can swing it."

Gloria raised her eyebrows. "That is a lot of people for one child."

"They say it takes a village. Children are born to working parents the world over. I have no intention of abandoning our child to others anyway. I want to do all the things I missed out on."

Gloria looked at her thoughtfully. "This isn't about you reliving missed opportunities, is it?"

"I have to confess that there's a part of me that feels I have unfinished business as a mother and I was happy to leave it that way. But this is about my life with you, and I truly believe together we can give this baby a better chance in the world with two parents who love it and love each other."

Gloria smiled in spite of herself. Lo was right about that—Gloria had no idea how to be a parent. "Oliver is champing at the bit. He has already made a Father of the Year plaque with his name on it."

Lo looked down. "Are you considering moving in together?"

Gloria took Lo's hand. "No. I'm considering moving in with you."

"And?"

Gloria sighed. "I don't know. My senses say yes but I'm nervous. We have been so up and down. How do we know things will work out?"

"We don't, but no one ever does. All I can tell you is that I will always try for you and no matter what happens, once I'm in this child's life I will always be there. I know it's a responsibility. Think about it anyway. I have to ask you, though...you and Oliver, can I trust that it won't happen again?"

"I promise I will never cheat on you or try to hurt you. I honestly thought we were finished and I only did it to distract myself from my misery at being without you. I want to say it was the mistake of my life, but now that there's a baby involved, I have to view it differently, so all I can say is it was incredibly selfish and I hope I've grown since then. Is there anything I can do to reassure you?"

Lo looked at her for a long moment. "I believe you, and I know I played my part. I won't say it didn't hurt. It did, a lot! But there has been a lot of hurt these past two years and I don't want any more of that. I will be careful with your heart if you promise to be careful with mine?"

Gloria brought Lo's hand to her lips. "I promise."

"There is one other thing." Lo grew still. "If I am going to accept having Oliver around, well, regardless, you need to be more accepting of Peter. It's not easy for him either. You need to trust me, like I trust you, that I am here with you fully and intentionally."

Gloria felt her cheeks burning. She had expected a lot of Lo. "Uncle Peter is welcome anytime." She smiled. "This is going to be a unique family."

Lo squeezed Gloria's hand. "It will be. Now, do you want to see my cut?"

"I'm not sure."

Lo pulled down the neckline of her T-shirt and moved her chin aside. She pointed to the lump of bone by her throat and drew a line above the stitched cut. "Any more that way and it would have been my throat or that way and it would have been my breast. Can you deal with the scar?"

The sight of Lo's physical wounds made Gloria feel tender and ashamed anew of the pain she'd caused. "It's not the scar that scares me, it's the idea that you could have been taken from me. I want to be here with you."

"You do?"

"I do."

EPILOGUE

Gloria picked up a fluffy giraffe toy. "Have you ever seen so many presents in your life?"

Lo smiled. "You only turn one once." She had Charli on her hip and spun a little circle. "She can't help it if she's popular."

Gloria bent down to pick up some cardboard packaging from the floor and threw it into the trash bag she was holding. "She's getting spoilt."

Lo hugged Charli to her and kissed her sandy blond head. "She's a baby. She can't be spoilt."

"Oliver bought her a pony for her birthday and she can't even walk yet."

"That's the idea. She'll be riding before she can walk. I think she needs to go to bed, though."

Gloria held out her arms. "I'll take her and I'm going to put up this lovely new print of a rainbow and get rid of that hideous gun dog picture from her room." She looked over at Caroline, who was ignoring Sue-Anne's efforts to shoo her away from tidying up the leftover food. "Why don't you go see if Caroline wants a coffee?"

Lo gave Charli's hand one last squeeze. "But she hasn't had a bath."

"She'll survive."

"All right."

Gloria went upstairs to the spare room that had been her room. The house looked different now. Sue-Anne and Lo had joined forces to baby-proof everything, and Gloria grumbled that it was like breaking into a vault just trying to get a plate from a cupboard. Charli was an easygoing baby, with Oliver's fairer hair and blue eyes and Gloria's unruly curls and facial expressions. The result was not unlike Lo either. Lo had branched out with her own consulting business that she ran from home as much as possible. Gloria had found that she'd made even more friends through having a baby, and between Lo and Oliver she had time to both ride and teach. Much to everyone's delight, Charli was endlessly fascinated with the horses, particularly Sonnet, who was gentle with her but would still kick the vet or farrier if given the opportunity. Hamlet accepted the grueling competition schedule that Caroline and Gloria had set him with as much vigor as he did anything else, and he refused to come alive until he heard the dressage bell signal the beginning of his test. Pogo was filling out and garnering interest from breeders. They had been doing well with their savings for an indoor arena but had tipped the money into Charli's college fund instead.

Gloria could feel Charli growing heavy against her shoulder as she climbed the stairs to the bedroom, which had been refurnished as Charli's room with pastel rainbow colors. Terrence's room had been left as it was; Lo wasn't quite ready to change that, but she was thinking about it. Gloria laid Charli down in her bed and placed the blanket over her. Fortunately for all of them, Charli slept like her father. Gloria went to the wall and unhooked the gun dog painting. Lo had been sentimental about it, but Gloria couldn't stand the violent image in the baby's room. She tiptoed out and shut the door partway. As she walked into the kitchen, she exhaled, feeling suddenly taller and more adult. She loved being a mother but she loved adult conversation too. Caroline and Lo were sitting down with a hot drink and Sue-Anne was putting birthday cake onto paper plates for Oliver and Caroline to take home. On the walls were Gloria's watercolors, and beside them hung the photo of Gloria, Lo, and Pogo on Christmas Day and a photo of Terrence from his last year at school. Charli had to know of her older brother.

"What's that?" Oliver asked.

Gloria turned the painting so he could see. "An ugly painting. I'm going to give it to Goodwill."

Lo frowned. "That painting was in the nursery when I was a kid. Gloria thinks it's disgusting."

Caroline patted the pocket of her pink shirt, looking for her glasses. She slipped them on and held out a hand. "Bring that here, Gloria."

Gloria brought the painting closer and balanced it against her knee to show Caroline.

Caroline peered at it then looked up at Gloria. "That is an Elliot Dawson. That's worth more than the horses."

Gloria laughed. "This ugly thing?"

Caroline glanced at the painting then back up at Gloria again. "Yes, that ugly thing."

Lo's face was pink with surprise. "Are you sure?"

"Quite."

Oliver laughed. "Well, girls, there's your indoor arena."

"You're absolutely sure?" Lo said.

"I'll find the number of George who does valuations tomorrow, but there's a lot of interest in Dawson's paintings of dogs and farm life. I have a book of his paintings at home that I can show you."

Gloria and Lo turned to each other with shock on their faces. Gloria spoke first. "I think I need some fresh air."

"Me too."

Lo opened the back door and they slid it shut behind them and stood on the back porch in the cold night air. "I don't even know what to say!" Lo's eyes were like saucers.

"Wait until we tell Kip."

"Don't tell him, we'll just give him and Celery a really nice wedding gift."

"A painting? That would be universal synergy."

"Yes. You always make magic happen." No sooner had the words slipped from Lo's mouth than a shooting star coursed across the sky. They turned to each other, then they both laughed and said, "I love you," the words tumbling out at the same time, and they started to laugh again. As they fell into one another's arms, their shadows joined into a pool of blue in the porch light.

Bella Books, Inc.

Women. Books. Even Better Together.

P.O. Box 10543
Tallahassee, FL 32302

Phone: 800-729-4992
www.bellabooks.com